THE
BAD BOY'S
WIFE

ALSO BY KAREN SHEPARD

An Empire of Women

THE
BAD BOY'S
⟳WIFE⟳

KAREN SHEPARD

ST. MARTIN'S GRIFFIN ⧪ NEW YORK

Excerpt from "Little Gidding" in *Four Quartets*, p. vii, copyright © 1942 by T. S.
Eliot and renewed 1970 by Esme Valerie Eliot, reprinted by permission of
Harcourt, Inc.

www.stmartins.com

Library of Congress Cataloging-in-Publication Data

Shepard, Karen.
    The bad boy's wife / Karen Shepard.
        p. cm.
    ISBN 0-312-31896-0 (hc)
    ISBN 0-312-31897-9 (pbk)
    EAN 978-0312-31897-0
    1. Married women—Fiction. 2. Triangles (interpersonal relations)—
Fiction. 3. Mate selection—Fiction. 4. Horse trainers—Fiction. 5. Ranch
life—Fiction. 6. Adultery—Fiction. 7. Kentucky—Fiction. I. Title.

PS3569.H39388B24 2004
813'.6—dc22   2003069722

First St. Martin's Griffin Edition: June 2005

10 9 8 7 6 5 4 3 2 1

For Aidan,
Emmett, and Lucy

And the end of all our exploring
Will be to arrive where we started
And know the place for the first time.

—T. S. Eliot, *Four Quartets*

THE
BAD BOY'S
WIFE

⬿ ONE ⬾

July 2000

THE EVENING THE STATE TROOPER CAME WITH THE NEWS OF Georgia's accident, Hannah was sitting on a stool in the open doorway of her ex-husband's barn. The early evening cicadas had just started up. It was July, and it was Kentucky, so it was hot and humid. She could taste the heat.

She was crossing items off her list. Her therapist said that lists would help her feel more in control. (He was teaching her how to take care of herself.) She had just checked off *Ride Blue* and circled *Make paper butterflies.* She liked to circle the next item. When she went home, she was going to make paper butterflies with Mattie, their ten-year-old. She'd been promising for weeks.

The state trooper pulled up to the front door of her old house and rang the bell. Her ex-husband came to the screen, his new baby on his hip. It was hard to make them out in the seven o'clock light. The trooper chucked the baby under the chin as he talked. Cole listened, and cupped the back of his son's head the way he used to cup Mattie's. He looked towards the barn. He called Hannah. Her name in his voice was still intoxicating. There he was, gorgeous and worried and calling her name.

There'd been an accident. The new wife was in the hospital. Could Hannah stay with the baby?

She took Sam from him. Their fingers touched, his hands a parody of a horseman's. Knuckles like knots in rope. Skin the texture of rawhide. His hair was a flurry of blond. It always looked like he'd spent time styling it with mousse and texturizer. He used neither. Of course she could stay. As long as he needed.

Cole tucked a piece of her dark brown hair behind her ear and thanked her. Her hair was layered, chin length; she'd been trying to grow it out for months. It never stayed behind her ears.

She watched the two cars pull out of the driveway, and then went inside, closing the door with her foot the way she had when hefting baby Mattie around.

When she was ten, she had gone snorkeling with her best friend, Ellie. Hannah had never even been to the beach before, and here she was in Florida with her best friend and her best friend's family.

The two girls and Ellie's dad stood in the calm thigh-high water, and he helped them wrestle their flippers on over wet feet, and stretch and pull their masks into place.

Hannah's mask was black and smelled of the shower curtain back home. It felt like nothing she could think of. It was tight and stiff. The mouthpiece felt too big. She gripped hard with her teeth and tried not to taste the rubber.

"Okay?" he asked the girls.

They nodded.

The surf picked her up and set her back down. She was standing on the back of a rocking horse. She was a circus rider in a sparkling leotard. The sand under her feet felt completely dry. It puffed around her in slow-moving clouds. She reached her hand under and watched it disappear in the swirls.

Ellie tapped her on the shoulder. Her mask was in place too. She went cross-eyed at Hannah. Hannah smiled.

Ellie's dad leaned down. He looked silly in his mask without his glasses.

"Remember my instructions," he said.

The girls nodded. Stay within sight of him. Don't touch anything. Don't stand on the reef.

With her hands by her thighs, she quietly practiced their emergency signal.

"Okay, then," he said, and the three of them pushed forward into the blue, blue water.

Years later, she would bring that twenty minutes out like a favorite sweatshirt: its scary safety like riding a roller coaster in slow motion. The slightly blurry view through her mask. The sound of below water. The way the reef seemed to shift and surge beneath her. The way she could be staring at a rock or a crevice or the sand for minutes before seeing something. She brought her head above water, oriented herself in terms of shore, light, sound, only so that she could enjoy dropping into that other world over and over.

She'd lived in this house for fifteen of the twenty years she'd been with Cole. She'd been moved out of it for two. When Cole had left her for Georgia, he'd offered to move out, but she'd told him that *he* could live with the memories, and anyway what could she do with two barns, three pastures, and forty head of horses? She'd rented a small place for herself, Mattie, and the dogs: Potpie, the Jack Russell, and Pete, the Lab mix, five miles away. A cottage on the grounds of the thoroughbred farm whose books she kept.

She'd left almost all their stuff. A lot of it was still here. Since the divorce, she'd stood in the doorway a couple of times—picking up or dropping off Mattie—and after the baby was born, she'd been in the nursery, but other than that, she'd stuck to the barn. She checked herself out in the entryway mirror, which was hung too high for her. She came up to Cole's chest. Once, she'd stood back-to-back with Georgia, and the top of Hannah's head hadn't even reached the nape of Georgia's neck.

Even so, standing in this house made her feel like she'd been dropped into the middle of her kindergarten classroom, everything about it too small, everything about herself the wrong size.

Blue was Georgia's horse. She'd bought him about six months ago and had asked if Hannah would be interested in training him. Hannah hadn't had much to do with training in years, and wondered why they weren't doing it, but had agreed without asking any questions because she needed the money. The weirdness of the situation hadn't fully occurred to her right away; she assumed it hadn't to Georgia, either. She wondered if Cole had noticed this as a significant similarity between the two women. She looked in the mirror again. She wished she could see similarities between her and Georgia.

Sam yanked on her earring. He was eight months old and looked like his mother. Red hair, blue eyes, round face. A painting out of an art history book. When Georgia wasn't training horses with Cole, she was a painter. Hannah didn't know what to make of the baby. Mattie adored him.

She sniffed him. "You smell like you've had a bath," she said. "Have you eaten?"

He stared.

She carried him into the kitchen. There was her pot hanger. There were her copper pots. The high chair tray was streaked with blueberry yogurt and something orange.

She held Sam out in front of her. "Well," she said. "Well."

She put him on the floor and began cleaning up.

Cole had wanted kids. She hadn't. She hadn't trusted herself with them. They were just like horses, he had told her. No, they weren't, she'd answered.

Here's what we'll do, he'd proposed. We'll have sex every day for two months, and if we get pregnant, we get pregnant, and if we don't, we don't.

He had a way of saying things like this that made her feel surges of good feeling for him. At the time, she'd found it an endearing proposition.

She'd been standing at this kitchen sink when he told her he was ready to leave. That's how he put it: as if he'd been preparing for twenty years, and now the packing was done, the travel arrangements settled, and all that was left was to say good-bye to the wife.

Her hands had been wet, and she'd stood there letting them drip. He'd handed her a dishtowel and left the room.

Later, she'd wished she'd told him that if anyone was doing the leaving, it was going to be her. Think back, she wished she had suggested. Think back to when he'd wanted her and she hadn't been so sure about him. But she hadn't said any of that, because that woman had been gone for a long time.

When he'd told her, she'd been wearing her red clogs. He liked when she wore clogs. They made her taller.

Sam was on his back. He reached for a piece of crud and put it in his mouth. She watched.

She had to call Mattie. In the old days, the phone nook at the far side of the kitchen had been covered with a mess of thorough-bred and polo magazines, gardening catalogues, and pencils with chewed tops. Now it was bare. A mug to hold pens, a message pad, two phone books, and a phone. She decided it was a sign of sterility in the marriage.

Once she laid out the situation to Mattie, Mattie was disconcertingly skeptical about her mother taking care of Sam. She kept proposing possible disaster scenarios. Since the divorce, disaster scenarios were Mattie's thing.

Hannah imagined Mattie in the cottage on the phone. The receiver looking giant next to her small face, like she was a baby with a prop.

Sam shimmied across the floor on his belly. "All right," Hannah said. "I'll see you soon."

"Maybe not," Mattie said matter-of-factly. "Georgia could be in bad shape. Georgia could be finished."

Mattie was frank about her jealousy. Before Georgia, her father had always referred to her as his slow-dance partner.

"I think she's going to be fine," Hannah said.

"Nobody knows who's going to be fine," Mattie said.

It was moments like that that made Hannah know, with a fierceness that surprised her, that despite everything, going back to Cole would be the right thing to do. If he asked.

After she hung up she realized she hadn't apologized about the paper butterflies.

Sam had his hand under the stove. It came out gray with dust. She took him to the sink to wash his hands. He started to cry. She tried to talk him out of it. His cries escalated. She carried him up to his room and put him in his crib. He made his whole body stiff and screamed some more.

The phone rang in the middle of this.

She answered the extension in the master bedroom. It was Cole. She told him to hang on, put the receiver under a pillow, and went to close the doors to the nursery and the bedroom.

"Okay," she said. "I'm back." She stretched out on her side of the bed. Mattie's drawings were taped to the opposite wall.

"What were you doing?" he asked.

"The kettle was boiling," she said.

"How's Sam?" he said.

"Fine," she said. She was pretty sure he couldn't hear the crying. She asked about the accident. One of Mattie's drawings featured a square-headed man with an expansive chest and a tiny waist. It was captioned *Daddy*.

They were still running tests. It was pretty bad. She was unconscious.

She asked how it had happened.

Georgia had been coming back from a gallery in town, asleep in the back seat. Her friend was driving. On that stretch of 29, right before Crestwood, that patch with no shoulder that could get hairy.

Hannah knew what Georgia looked like asleep in a car. Georgia could sleep anywhere. She'd tuck her long, thick hair under her head, and in minutes, she'd be gone, her freckled skin smooth across her face.

Hannah nodded, saying nothing, but he went on anyway.

The friend had dozed long enough to run into the concrete retaining wall. How the friend had remained unhurt, he had no idea.

Hannah was light-headed. Her skin was tingling. She had her eyes closed. It was like one of Mattie's disaster scenarios. It was like being a horse in a starting box waiting for the bell.

So when he told her that Georgia had been thrown over the

front seat and through the windshield it was pay-off. The electric-
ity on her skin broke. She thought of the morning after Mattie's
birth when Cole had wanted to have sex, and she had let him. At
some point, years ago, she had stopped asking herself why she felt
the things she felt, and did the things she did.

By the time she got off the phone, Sam had stopped crying. She
checked on him. He was asleep; his face was splotchy and wet,
and she found herself blowing on it, like a human hair dryer. If
someone had asked, she wouldn't have been able to explain herself. Other people never seemed as baffled by her as she was by
herself.

Downstairs, she fixed herself a drink. One of Mattie's unitards hung over a baby's rocking chair near the liquor cabinet.
The juxtaposition annoyed her. Georgia had told Mattie that
black was her color because it set off her white blond hair. Since
then, Mattie had insisted on black unitards to replace the pink
and purple ones she'd wanted before.

Cole wasn't going to be back until late, if at all. The bottle of
Maker's Mark in the cabinet was her old one. Her Magic Marker
lines were still on its side. After his announcement that they were
splitting, they hadn't for months. The marker lines had been her
way of tracking her downward spiral. She should've marked the
NyQuil bottle. One night, waiting for him to get home, she had
downed the NyQuil and what was left of the Tylenol PMs and
flopped onto the couch. She'd wanted him to find her, one arm
flung over her head, her face to the ceiling, the skin of her
throat white and cold. The room had spun, her head had
fogged, and she'd thrown up. Cole had stayed out the whole

night and she'd never told him about it. She'd felt stupid. The eighteen-year-old boy who kills himself imagining the eulogies at his memorial service.

The ice in her glass rearranged itself with small cracking noises. The unitard still bothered her. She went to the phone and called the cottage. Lois, their baby-sitter, answered.

Hannah told her to bring Mattie over.

"She's asleep," Lois said. She waited. "It's after ten," she added.

Hannah told her to bring her anyway. "Wrap her in a blanket," she suggested. "She'll sleep in the car."

"Why?" Lois said.

Hannah had no response.

Lois got her testy maternal voice on. "Why should I wake up a happily sleeping little girl and take her out in the middle of the night?"

Hannah pushed at an ice cube with her finger. "Because I can't afford to pay you for all this time, and because I need some company over here."

She could hear Lois softening. Lois was near sixty and had sympathy for the kind of damage men inflicted.

"All right," she said after a minute. "We'll be there in a bit."

Hannah hung up, took a sip of her whiskey, and threw the rest of it into the sink.

Ten minutes later Lois called back to remind her that her car was in the shop. "I'll stay," Lois said. "Free of charge."

Hannah glanced around the kitchen. "No," she said. "I'll come get you. I'll drop you off on the way back here."

"What about Sam?" Lois asked.

Hannah told her Sam would be fine.

She grabbed her keys and went upstairs. He was still asleep. She watched him breathe. She imagined the scene in a movie. What would she think of a woman doing what she was doing? She knew what she used to think. Now, it was like how she felt when she had a cold, staring out at a world full of the healthy. It was like she'd had a cold for years.

She went back downstairs, closed the front door, eased the screen door shut, and got in her car. She pulled down the driveway slowly, wincing at the crunch of the gravel beneath her tires, and didn't turn on her lights until she had pulled onto the road.

The cottage looked small in the moonless night, and the air had cooled considerably, and she didn't want to go inside. She honked, and Lois came out carrying Mattie bundled in a cotton throw. Mattie had gotten long and lanky in the last year. Her arms and legs hung out of the blanket like a baby giraffe's. Potpie stood on his hind legs, watching from the front window. Hannah reached over and opened the passenger door. Lois settled Mattie carefully and strapped her in. "I'll just go lock up," she said.

Mattie opened her eyes. She stared blankly at her mother, then peered into the backseat. "You *left* him?"

Hannah said, "I knew you would say that." She put the car into gear. "It's ten minutes."

Mattie kept staring at the backseat, as if she could make her brother appear.

The porch light went off, and Lois came back to the car.

"Fingers and toes," she reminded Mattie as she swung the door shut. She climbed into the backseat.

Mattie said, "She left Sam in the house by himself."

Lois looked around her.

Hannah backed down the short driveway.

"You left him?" Lois finally said.

"That's what *I* said," Mattie said.

Lois ran her hand over the empty seat next to her.

"He's a baby," Mattie said.

Hannah accelerated. "Ten minutes," she said again. "He's asleep; he'll be fine." Part of her believed it. Part of her didn't.

They were quiet until they pulled into Lois's driveway. Her husband had left the kitchen light on. Hannah could see a sandwich and a beer waiting on the table.

Mattie rolled her window down. "I want to stay here," she said.

No one answered.

Lois got out and leaned through Mattie's window. Mattie reached a hand up, and Lois kissed her knuckles.

"I like you, Hannah," Lois said. "You're not the kind of woman who leaves babies in houses by themselves."

She hadn't asked for an explanation, but Hannah knew she was waiting for one. "The longer you keep me, the longer he's on his own," she said. She couldn't explain herself. The fact crept through her like a thrilling surprise.

Lois backed away from the car. She said, "You call if you need anything," and when Hannah didn't say anything, Mattie answered for them.

It was almost eleven by the time they got back to the house. Mattie ran upstairs. Hannah stayed where she was, standing in the entry.

When Mattie was two, Hannah had been maneuvering around her in the kitchen with a pot of steaming water. Some of it had landed on Mattie's hand and foot, and there'd been screaming and blistering and a trip to the emergency room. She still had small scars on her heel and palm.

Cole hadn't said a word. When they got home, he put Mattie to bed, and Hannah followed him to their bedroom, apologizing, and he'd told her she'd been right not to want kids, and it was his fault for thinking she could handle it. He'd pointed at her, and said, "Stupid."

She'd retreated downstairs and had found herself standing in the entry, taking her clothes off piece by piece. Naked, she returned to the bedroom, stood in the doorway, and said, "I know I'm stupid," and while she spread her legs for him and he made himself hard, they'd traded synonyms for the word.

She heard the nursery door close. She looked down at her riding clothes. Her hands still smelled of leather and sweat and horse.

Mattie appeared at the top of the stairs.

"Let's take a bath," Hannah said.

"He's all right," Mattie said.

"I'll run the water," Hannah said.

Her daughter held on to both banisters. "Why should I do anything with you?" she asked.

"Because," Hannah said.

Mattie stared.

Hannah felt tears starting. "Because sometimes you make me feel better about myself," she said.

Mattie looked worried, then she said, "Lois says that's not my job."

Hannah didn't say anything. Mattie looked even more worried. Her dark brown eyes made slow sweeps, tracking like a radar.

Hannah loved her eyes. They were dark, dark. "She doesn't miss a trick," she used to marvel about Baby Mattie.

The girl didn't move. "Are you mad?" she asked.

Hannah stared at her feet. The urge to cry was gone; she tried to will the tears back. Then she said, "I'm not mad. Go to bed; I'll see you in the morning."

"I want to call the hospital," Mattie announced.

"It's too late," Hannah said.

"I want to talk to Daddy," Mattie said. Her expression was unpleasant.

"He'll be back any minute," Hannah said. Her daughter waited. "They don't have phones in the operating room," Hannah pointed out.

Mattie looked skeptical, but finally went back down the hall.

Hannah stayed at the bottom of the stairs, listening to her daughter's noises. After a silence, the water ran in the bathroom. The toilet flushed. The water ran again.

She went back to the liquor cabinet and grabbed Mattie's unitard. On the way up to the master bedroom she found herself holding it to her nose. It smelled like Cole's aftershave.

When she reached the master bedroom, the door to Mattie's room clicked shut. She dropped the unitard in the hall and took off her shirt and bra, adding them to the pile.

In the bedroom, she sat at Georgia's dressing table and took off her paddock boots and britches. In the mirror, her features seemed drawn tight like the cord on a backpack. She'd become someone pinched and parched, she thought. Her socks were still damp. Sawdust and hay came off with them. She swept them into the cracks between the floorboards with her foot.

She stood up, naked. She went into the bathroom. Cole's side of the double-sink counter was unchanged: a cheap razor, and

Edge shaving cream for extra-heavy beards. A toothbrush, bristles worn and splayed like a tiny, sad bouquet.

Georgia's side was filled. Lotions, bath salts, hair gels, aromatherapy candles, Q-tips and cotton balls in glass jars. Ribbons and scarves poured out of the drawers. A lipstick case like the ones on cosmetic counters in department stores held twenty or thirty different shades. An old juice jar for makeup brushes. Perfumes lined up behind them, snaking over onto Cole's side.

She wiped one of the larger brushes across her cheek. She closed her eyes and dusted them. She picked up a tiny comb whose use escaped her and after a moment tested it on her pubic hair.

Perfume was something Cole had complained about. Her lack of it. She hadn't known it was a problem until they'd talked about his decision to leave. She'd said, I can wear perfume. He'd looked at the floor.

A drawer in the lipstick case held labeled circles of eyeshadow— Pink Chocolate, Gold Apple, Perfect Amber. Some were more used than others. The Gothic Eggplant was almost completely worn away. The white plastic revealed in the center made it look like a peculiar eye.

Mattie came home from weekends here with her nails polished. She'd also taken to colored lip glosses. Hannah hunted around in the cupboards. She found the polish lined up in one of the drawers, in a display case that allowed them to be tipped back.

She chose a lime green and sat on the bathmat cross-legged to apply it. The smell gave her an immediate headache. She breathed deeper.

Sam was crying again. She had one more finger to go on her right hand. She finished and reached up to the counter for a Q-tip to fix the edges.

The crying was louder. Mattie appeared in the doorway, Sam

balanced on her tiny hip. "What are you doing?" she said.

Hannah screwed the top back on the polish and stood, flexing her wet hand away from her body like someone imitating a penguin. "Here," she said, reaching with her other arm. "Give him to me."

Mattie hesitated. Sam continued to scream, arching his back, and stiffening his arms and legs.

"Mattie," Hannah said.

The girl passed the baby over, struggling under his weight.

"I'll take care of it," Hannah said. "Go to bed."

"He sounds sick," Mattie said.

He was overheated and his pajamas were soaked. He wiped tears and snot on Hannah's shoulder. His hand found her breast, which seemed to calm him a little.

She turned to block Mattie's view.

"Where are your clothes?" Mattie asked.

Hannah concentrated on the baby. "I'm taking a bath."

Mattie looked over at the dry tub.

"Go back to bed," Hannah said. "I've got it." She cupped Sam's head with the back of her hand, and rocked it back and forth.

"You're getting nail polish in his hair," Mattie said.

Hannah kept her hand where it was.

"You're *painting* your *nails*," Mattie said. She shook her head. "Maybe we should call Lois," she said.

"Bed," Hannah said.

She led her out of the room and down the hallway, then watched her get into bed and closed the door behind her.

Sam was still crying.

She took him back to the bathroom and set him on the counter while she searched the cupboards for medicine. There was a bottle of children's Benadryl at the back. It was half-full. She picked him up and sat back down on the floor, leaning against the bathtub. The porcelain was cold.

She read the box for dosage directions. *Under age two: consult your doctor.*

She tried to remember how much she'd given Mattie. She couldn't remember Mattie ever needing this kind of medicine.

Sam's head tipped back towards the floor.

She filled the dropper and lifted him up. He seemed to like the taste of it. He opened his mouth for it. She thought of fish. She thought of Georgia and that concrete wall. The crying was winding down. She thought of Cole's way of asking Mattie for a kiss. She thought of the way she'd copied that, had made it her way of telling him she was ready to perform oral sex.

Sam's thumb was in his mouth. He was calming himself.

She could put him in the crib now. He would drop off to sleep. She pulled his hand away, and held it down by his side. He protested.

"Shh," she said. "Shh." With her free hand, she lifted her breast to him. He took her into his mouth as if he had always known her this way. She stretched her legs out in a vee in front of her. His foot dropped between them. His mouth worked around her. His eyes were closed. His saliva ran slowly down the outside curve of her breast. Her skin was alive with goosebumps and heat. She could smell baby and horse. She could smell herself.

She imagined herself as a twenty-year-old witnessing this scene. She imagined her confusion. She imagined her shame. How had she become someone who did something like this? If someone had shown her this, she wouldn't have believed it.

The phone rang. Sam jumped, but his eyes stayed closed. His mouth continued to suck. She got up carefully, and went to the bed. She lay down in her spot and resettled him across her.

Cole was suspicious. "What took you so long?" he said.

"I was taking a bath," she said.

"Here's the thing," he said. He sounded suddenly worn out. "She's not doing so well. Something about a bleed in her head. They're talking about surgery to release it."

She slid her pinky into Sam's mouth. He frowned. She could feel his tongue and her nipple.

Even after everything she and Georgia had been through, she still cared about her. "I'm sorry," she said.

Cole took a breath. "Well," he said. "What can we do, right?"

It sounded like he was rubbing his cheek with the receiver.

"You've been great," he said. "Thanks."

She took her finger out of Sam's mouth and held her hand out in front of her. The polish had dried all scratched and ruined. "When are you coming home?" she asked.

He exhaled. "I don't know. They say I should, that we're not going to know anything for a while. But, I don't know." He hesitated. "I don't know. What if she wakes up and I'm not here? What if she needs me?"

A tightness worked its way up her throat. What did she want? she thought. What had she ever wanted, and what had she been willing to do to get it?

She took Sam from her breast and laid him on the bed next to her. She swallowed. The tightness wouldn't go away. "You should come back," she said.

"You're probably right," he said. "It's just I want to be here, you know?"

She heard the hospital intercom behind him.

She waited.

"I don't know," he said. "We'll see."

He told her he'd call in a little while, and then he hung up.

She was cold. She got under the covers, turned on her side, and tucked a pillow between her legs. "We'll see," she said. She watched Sam's eyes move from side to side under almost translucent lids.

She got out of bed and put on one of Georgia's robes. She went and got the Benadryl. She gave him some more, and then slid the empty dropper between his lips. In his sleep, he sucked and swallowed.

She left him in the bed and went to take a shower. The dirt from riding ran off in streams. She washed her hair with a shampoo that had things like papaya and coconut in it. The water was hot and made her dizzy.

She dried off, put the robe back on, and stood in front of Georgia's lipsticks. Minutes went by. Her reflection registered neither pleasure nor displeasure. She chose a perfume by the shape of the bottle and dotted her wrists and her inner thighs.

She headed down the hall to Mattie's bedroom.

Mattie was asleep, wheezing a little with each breath. She'd been officially diagnosed with asthma when she was four, but Hannah had known she had it well before then. She'd recognized the signs from her own childhood. She'd talked Mattie through her first nebulizing visit to the emergency room. She'd taught her to use her inhalers. They'd walked around the house together, placing inhalers in strategic spots that they called "breathing stations." She'd explained in language Mattie would understand what was happening inside her straining little lungs. Watching Mattie under attack, a miniature version of herself, made her feel closer to her daughter than at any other time.

She pulled Mattie's hands out from under the covers and

arranged them across the bedspread. The nails were tiny and bitten. She bent over them, moved.

A car was coming up the road. She went to the window, but it passed their driveway.

Cole, she thought. She wanted Cole. Even in the early going, when she'd seemed tough on him. Whatever else there'd been, she'd always wanted Cole.

She returned to stand over Mattie for a minute, and then she went to the window seat to wait.

She waited until the sky was predawn blue. The first night she'd been with Cole, the sky had gotten this color before he'd even tried to kiss her. He'd turned out the light, and said, "But the bad thing is now I won't be able to see you." And she'd answered, amazed at herself, "But you can still feel." And he'd found her mouth with his, and her nose against his lip, the smell of him, had gone right to the center of her like a sip of whiskey when you're still too young to drink.

Her hand against the windowpane felt the beginnings of morning heat. The tightness returned. She imagined all of them in Georgia's car the day before, Cole at the wheel. Those few months before Hannah had finally moved out, he'd had sex on a regular basis with both women. Hannah had known, Georgia hadn't. *Look what an asshole he is,* Hannah had told her friends. *Your father can't keep away from me,* she'd told Mattie. Had that been the beginning of doing things she'd never imagined being capable of? No, she thought sadly, for that, she'd have to go back much further.

Mattie was asleep on her side, her knees tucked up.

Hannah was crying. She went to the bed and tightened the sash of her robe. She knelt, lifted one of Mattie's hands and pulled it to her. She pressed it to her forehead and then to her cheek. It was damp and smelled of dirt.

Maybe she knew things now that could've helped her then. But what did she know? What?

She buried her face in her daughter's hair and inhaled until she stopped crying. Mattie rolled onto her back. Mattie was so great.

Hannah stood up and backed out of the room.

She was crying again. What kind of man did the things he had done? What kind of woman let him?

She knew the answers. The other question was, when had she become one of those women?

"Mommy?" Mattie murmured in her sleep.

Her heart shied at the sound. "Shh," Hannah said. "I"m right here."

Mattie quieted.

I'm a mother, Hannah thought over and over, as if thinking it enough would make her feel it as real.

The first time Mattie as a baby had slept through the night, Hannah had snuck into her room to nurse her. All that quiet had been a rejection she couldn't stand.

Mattie's breathing was regular and louder now. Hannah crept down the stairs, remembering which creaking ones to skip. She stopped at the front door. She was listening so hard it felt like her head was underwater.

She was about to leave two children in the house alone because she felt like it.

Her thoughts moved from *What could happen?* to *What about me?* and she found herself somehow calmed.

She was barefoot and naked beneath her robe, and made her way gingerly down the gravel driveway to the barn. Her skin glowed an unearthly shade in the moonlight. The dirt of the center aisle was like a balm on the soles of her feet.

Blue's head appeared in his stall door. His ears twitched at her. His eye regarded her.

She ignored the ladder and shimmied up a post into the hayloft. It made her feel young and able to do things. Her eyes weren't yet used to the dark.

The hay pricked her hands and knees as she found her way to the corner where Cole kept old tack and blankets. Bridles hung like the empty armor of sentinels on the back wall. She recognized the smell of his first working saddle before she felt its shape. It was on its back against a pile of hay bales. She sat inside the wide reach of its flaps. She closed her eyes and apologized to everyone for things she never would've imagined herself being responsible for.

Tonight had been a train wreck. Her life had been a train wreck. How had she gotten here? What would happen now?

Old mistakes, new mistakes, she thought sadly. And then she opened her eyes, sweeping the darkness in front of her, searching for whatever other familiar objects she could find in the time she had left.

∽ TWO ∽

April 1999

ONE OF THEIR DOGS HAD A TUMOR THE SIZE OF A KICKBALL
in his abdomen, and Hannah did what she'd always done when
faced with a problem, large or small. She called Cole.

The divorce had gone through eight months earlier. Hannah
had forgotten how to mark time any other way. The appearance of
irises and jewelweeds, jack-in-the-pulpits and redbuds went unno-
ticed. For the rest of the world it was April.

Since August, she'd called him dozens of times: the tub was
leaking, Mattie had a rash, squirrels bounced around through her
walls. For a while, he'd done things without being asked. He'd
stacked a half cord of firewood when she was gone. He'd left
turquoise earrings for her birthday on her doormat.

Hannah had pointed out these kindnesses to Mattie and had
assured her that you didn't do those kinds of things when you
didn't love someone anymore, but in fact she didn't really know
what all the gestures meant, and she worried she was telling Mattie
these things more to reassure herself. She wished she could ask

Cole to write a letter, put all that he was feeling and thinking down on paper. She thought back and knew that it would've helped. Something for her to go over and over at her leisure. Something she didn't have to respond to right away. Maybe not a letter. A letter wasn't really Cole's thing. Maybe a tape. He was good at talk.

Recently, he'd begun to suggest that she call someone else. There *is* no one else, she told him, leaving the *you left me all alone* unspoken.

She hated the way she sounded—a victim, a whiner.

But when she called about Pete, and asked Cole if he'd come with her to drop the dog off for the surgery, he said right away that he would. Cole had brought him home the week after they'd found out Hannah was pregnant. He'd thought it was good for kids and dogs to grow up together.

Pete was a beagle/Lab mix. Black, with a square Lab head and nose, and those beagle ears. Cole had found him in the paper. A barely adult couple was giving him away. They lived by the river in a hollow that must've gotten sun thirty minutes a day. They had three other dogs and six cats in a two-room house. The girl had the grimy look of ten-year-old girls who've been playing outside all day. The boy was shirtless. Burn scars climbed one side of his neck. Their landlord was getting after them; they needed to get rid of the pets.

The other dogs barked and tumbled. Pete peered from behind a chair. Cole and Hannah got down on their knees and held out cupped hands, and Pete came to them. Cole and animals had always been a good mix. Once he'd gotten a cardinal to land on Hannah's hand.

Over the last ten years, dogs had come and gone the way they do on a horse farm, but Pete had stuck. Hannah thought of him as the best kind of frat boy: thick-necked and sweet. Not the date rapist but the football player whose best friend was his mother.

He wouldn't go with the technician at the vet. They had to walk behind him, and even then, he strained at the leash, craning his head around to keep them in sight. His eyes registered a combination of resignation and dismay.

He was headed for exploratory surgery. Either it was nothing but a giant benign tumor that they could take out no problem and he'd be good as new, or it was cancerous and had infiltrated all the organs and they'd put him to sleep right there. There were other options in between. They'd know more by late evening.

She told the vet that even if it was cancer, she wanted him woken up. He hadn't seemed to be in pain, and it was too hard to think about him just never coming back from exploratory surgery.

Cole said that what she wanted might not be the thing to put first right now.

Hannah snorted, and said, "I don't think I'll be listening to you about that."

The vet cleared her throat and said that waking Pete up would be fine, and she'd call when the surgery was done.

Outside, they lingered by their cars. Hannah had gotten the Buick. Cole his AMC Eagle. Over the driver's side wheel well, the silver gave way to a dull gray. He liked to lean against cars. He was leaning there now, chewing on one of the coffee stirrers he'd plucked from the stash he kept in his shirt pocket.

"Have you told Mattie yet?" she asked.

He shook his head. "I'll tell her when she gets home from school," he said.

It was Thursday, a Daddy Day, in Mattie-speak. Hannah stopped herself from chiding him about the delay.

When Mattie was five, her favorite barn cat had gotten hit by a car.

"I've got some sad news," he told her. "Miss Kitty got hit by a car last night and she died." Mattie had stared back at him for a minute, smiling. "Daddy," she'd finally said, "are you teasing?"

Cole told the story to friends with an odd pride, made jokes about how only a daughter of his would think he was teasing about something like that. The more he told the story the more Hannah realized how much he'd been bothered by Mattie's response. He'd talked to Hannah about it more than once. Did Mattie really think he was the kind of father who'd tease about something like that? *Was* he that kind of father?

Since the divorce, she'd found herself wishing that they could sit down together across a wide table and track it all out. She would tell her version of the past twenty years, he would tell his, and together they'd mark the spots where they'd gone wrong. Together, they'd fix what they could.

She was crying.

Cole was trying to console her without actually touching her. "Listen," he said. "It's gonna be fine. It'll probably turn out he's eaten a kickball."

The dog had once swallowed half a bag of Nestlé Tollhouse chips, twist tie and all. A few hours later he'd thrown the whole thing back up, intact. Before one of Mattie's birthdays, he'd eaten a multilayered cake, leaving the box on the kitchen floor. When they'd started entertaining he'd once, in the time it took them to greet dinner guests at the door, downed two pounds of shrimp.

The bowl had been so clean it had taken them several minutes to realize anything was missing. They'd served their guests potato chips and saltines.

Two cocker spaniels were being walked around the small patch of orchard grass in front of the building. Their noses stayed low, ignoring the butterflies. They can smell fear, she thought. They can smell upset.

She reviewed Cole, looking for signs of change. There were practically none. He still had that impossibly thin waist, those basketball player shoulders. He had the face of a carpenter, someone good with his hands.

She'd spent eight months waiting for him to call and tell her he'd made a mistake. Then they'd be a family again and she'd have back that invisible place where she belonged. Every time she'd seen him since the divorce—every Wednesday and Sunday exchange of Mattie—she'd looked for a sign that would tell her what to do to get him back.

That kind of optimism hadn't been easy. After they'd separated, people had started telling her things. He'd hit on her best friend, Donna. He'd been in a car crash with Mattie that he'd never told her about. He'd slept with just about every one of his polo grooms.

She'd still wanted him back. Because as she tried to figure things out, she formulated ways in which it was probably her fault. She'd taken him for granted. She'd brushed his hand away when all he'd wanted was to touch her cheek. She'd resisted more kids. She'd kept secrets that could've helped explain some of their problems. Why would he have left unless she'd done something to make him leave?

Despite what it sometimes seemed like, she wasn't just a victim. She'd played the game with him. So why couldn't she keep playing?

It didn't have to be that the game was over and she'd lost. What she'd ruined, she could fix.

She'd told him about a book she'd read that cited studies to prove that children of divorce had it tough. They ended up being the bullies, the anorexics, and underachievers. The book said it was possible to be good parents without being good spouses.

It was something they could aim for, she'd said. Mattie had always been their chance to be better people. She could still be that.

He'd assumed that squint he got when something saddened him and had held her hands and said that he was already aiming for that. And he couldn't do it without her help, he said. C'mon, he'd coaxed, thinking he was being charming. For Mattie's sake.

It was clear he thought he had Mattie's best interests at heart, and she didn't. Hearing the phrase "for Mattie's sake" made her feel sorry for herself. It was not an ideal mother's reaction. She knew that. So maybe he was right about her. It was sometimes hard to separate his feelings about her from her feelings about herself. Her stomach had tightened, and she'd had to fight the urge to shout, "What about *my* sake? What about me?"

It was the one thing she'd *known* pretty much her entire adult life: no one had ever taken good enough care of her.

The cocker spaniels disappeared into the clinic.

In the eight months since the divorce, Cole had maybe lost a little weight, but was still in those old ropers, those Wranglers with the back pocket worn from his canister of Skoal. He wore his clothes so often, for so long, that they were filled with familiar little worn spots. His shirtsleeves were creased and darkened from being rolled and left that way. Where he grabbed his hat to lift and lower it, there were two marks where the felt had lost its nap, where the oil from his fingers had darkened the gray. He smelled of sun-heated hay. She didn't recognize his shirt. It was a green oxford thing he wouldn't have bought for himself.

"Georgia get you this?" she asked, reaching for it, but stopping short.

He looked down at himself and nodded.

"It's nice," she said. It made his eyes greener and his hair blonder, but she didn't tell him that.

"Hey," he said.

It still sent a shiver through her. "Hey," like there was nothing simpler or better than being here talking to her.

Twenty years ago, it had been the first word he'd ever spoken to her. "Hey," he'd said, coming up alongside her on the horse he'd been working. She'd been on the two-year-old filly she'd just finished galloping, walking her in slow cooling circles around the field behind the practice track. It was Alabama. It was June. Just coming up on six in the morning. "Hey," he'd said, smiling. "I saw you grab mane."

She'd blushed and leaned forward to stroke the filly's wet neck.

"It's okay," he said. "I won't tell." He waited till she looked over, and then he winked.

Of course she knew who he was. Every girl working the farm that summer knew who he was. A laugh you could hear clear across the racetrack. Rumors that everyone believed. Looks that even the other guys mentioned.

He'd reached across and pressed a flat hand against the back of her saddle seat. The edge of his hand rocked against her rear. She resisted her instinct to flee. "Your saddle doesn't fit right," he said. "Come to the barn and I'll fix you up."

"Okay," she said. The beginning of twenty years of saying okay to whatever Cole Thompson had to offer.

Here he was now, still standing next to her, still offering something. "Why don't you come to the rodeo with us this afternoon?"

Things churned in her belly. "Oh, I don't know," she said.

"Come on," he said. "It'd be good. Mattie'd love it."

She dawdled with her answer, enjoying the sound of his persuasion.

He touched her shoulder. It was what she'd been waiting for. She hoped his touch would never stop going right to her core. She closed her eyes. "Okay," she said.

He smiled as if congratulating her on a smart bet. "Pick you up at four," he said. "You can ride with us."

He opened the Eagle's door and ducked his head to keep his gray Resistol hat from hitting, and then was gone.

She snuggled in her car a minute before starting it. An elm and willow made competing shadows across the hood. Her heart was alive. She tried to get herself to calm down. She went over what he'd said. It was just a rodeo. *Don't get all in a fit about this,* she told herself.

Her friend Donna's husband had walked out, and then they'd gone to a horse sale and gotten back together. Something casual could mean that much.

She started the car and headed to the mall. *Don't blow it,* she thought, her mind going over the last eight months, the last twenty years, her whole life. *Don't blow it like you blow everything.*

The woman in the white coat at the Clinique counter stood over her, studying her face. Hannah was on a high black pleather stool. Her feet didn't reach the floor. She straightened her back.

The woman's name tag said Oralynn. Her nail polish matched her lip color. She smelled clean.

She brushed Hannah's short dark hair away from her face, and said, as if to herself, "What do we want to start with here?"

Hannah had nothing to answer. She never knew what to make of her face. Her eyes were blue. Her hair was brown. Her nose was a little too big. She had good teeth and small ears. She tanned well, never burned. She had the kind of looks that made people want to put their arm around her and rub her upper arm. She was like the child of a favorite relative.

As Oralynn worked, she explained the intricacies of her project: the rule for foundation was one shade lighter than you thought. Always line the eyes completely, top and bottom lid. Make sure to powder your ears as well as under your chin.

Hannah had nice skin, she said. What did she do to take care of it?

Hannah shrugged.

As she was putting the finishing touches on Hannah's lips she asked the occasion.

"No occasion," Hannah said. She allowed herself a small smile. "A date with my ex-husband."

Oralynn stepped back and put her palm up, as if you couldn't tell her a thing about ex-husbands and ex-wives and the dates they went on.

She swiveled Hannah around and positioned the mirror.

She leaned over Hannah's shoulder. "There isn't a man in the world could resist you now," she said, with genuine kindness. It made Hannah think that Pete would make it, and Cole would be on time, and she would be lucky for the first time in months.

At home, she picked up around the house trying not to move her face. Cole thought the mess of her house was a sign of the state of her life. Sometimes, when he came to the door, he registered the dishes, the unfolded laundry, the heaping trash cans with what looked to her like some sadness, a little guilt, and a lot of judgment.

Potpie snuffled around behind her, investigating her scents. He lifted his ears as if to ask what she'd done with Pete.

Mattie's My Little Ponies and Fashion Fillies were scattered like war victims across intricate Lego dioramas that they'd designed and built together: barns and paddocks and jumping courses. Flat green building boards simulated grass.

Hannah had loved horses too at that age. The first book she'd read by herself had been *A Treasury of Horse Stories*. At odd times she still remembered section titles like "Fantasy & Folklore," "Three Famous Rides," "Races & Runaways," and "Horses—Old & Young, Grave & Gay."

She put her hand on her hip and stilled herself for a minute. As a calming exercise, she tried to pinpoint the moment she'd lost real interest in riding and training. She couldn't. Sometime somewhere back she'd decided all of that was Cole's world. She'd do the books for the business, and the rest was his.

There'd been a time after that when she'd wondered if her decision had been painful for him. But by then, she'd given up on reading other people as being something she wanted to do, something she wanted to be better at. Now she imagined herself as two versions of the same body on either side of a glass door.

Her mother had been excited when Hannah had first told her that she was seeing a polo trainer and player. Oh, she'd said, holding her hand to the pearl necklace she always wore. Is he very, very wealthy?

She'd felt the teasing undercurrent in her mother's question, and the quiet insult implied.

Even so, her mother had never really been able to get over her disappointment. Cole's had turned out to be more a fly-by-the-seat-of-your-pants operation. He was the borrow-money-from-everyone-you-knew-then-borrow-more kind of trainer. He was the charm-the-feed-store-owner's-wife-into-letting-their-tab-go-just-six-more-months kind of horseman. In the twenty years she had been with him, he'd gone bankrupt, sold his stock, and started from scratch four times. Each time, he'd kissed her head as she'd stared at the books in despair. Each time, he'd told her not to worry. Starting over was his thing. He'd said things like "thang." He'd stood her up and pressed her to him with his hands on her rear. Starting over, he'd said each time, made him want her even more. And what could be better than him wanting her?

During a fight, he'd torn her *Treasury of Horse Stories* in half.

The two halves of the book were in a box under the shoes in her closet. She took them out sometimes to try and touch his rage. Some kinds of anger were a form of care.

She pushed Mattie's constructions to the side of the room near the fireplace and scooped the toys into the basket under the window. Mattie had braided and decorated the manes and tails. Some were tied with the tiny rubber bands designed for the braces on her back molars. One had a barrette clipped to its rear end.

Lois would play anything with Mattie. Hannah *said* she'd play anything, but couldn't sustain the interest. Mattie didn't like doing mind-benders and puzzles. She liked gardening even less. She read on her own, anyway. She did pretend play with friends or Lois. She did barn stuff with Cole. She did craft projects with her mother. Though since Georgia the Artist had arrived, Mattie also did those kinds of things with her.

When Cole had still been there, they'd gone on Monday afternoon drives. The horse world took Mondays off, the horses getting

a day of rest after Sunday's game. The grooms spent the day wash-
ing saddle blankets and wraps at the Laundromats, changing the
oil in the dualies, cleaning out the trailers, and going to a movie.
Cole would spend the morning on the phone setting up his week,
and then he'd grab his hat, lead Hannah out the door, and they'd
get Mattie from school and head out anywhere. Adventure Drives,
he called them. A nearby state park and a different hike every week
and while they walked, Mattie recited facts she'd memorized from
library books. They built stick forts across small creeks using logs
left over from beaver dams. They drove into Louisville, had ice
cream and iced tea at the Seelback Hotel and talked about the best
and worst names for dogs. They walked across the George Rogers
Clark Memorial bridge and back, stopping in the middle to see
how long they could stand the wind before their eyes started to
tear. They followed fire trucks to fires. They drove home, happy
and quiet, with the radio turned down.

Now Hannah and Mattie watched movies, or Nickelodeon, or
played Disney channel games on the Web site. Hannah had two
TVs in her bedroom. One stacked on top of the other. One got
sound, the other a picture.

She still had some serious picking up to do. He'd be here
sooner than she thought. She rewound the video of *Dirty Dancing*.
Cole hadn't wanted Mattie to see it, so Hannah had made it their
little secret.

Every so often she offered her outstretched hand and said in
her Bad Boy voice, "Nobody puts Baby in a corner." If Mattie felt
like playing, she'd allow herself to be swung up and into a few
minutes of dancing. If she didn't, she'd make herself deadweight
and give her mother the same look she gave her when Hannah
climbed into her bed late at night ready to talk, to make the ten-
year-old her confidante, her late-night confessor, her friend.

That had started after they'd moved out. Sometimes she told Mattie what Cole had said or done.

On a muggy, restless night a few weeks earlier, Hannah had told her a joke she'd heard from one of the divorced mothers about a couple in their eighties who'd filed for divorce. The couple said they'd been miserable for decades. The judge asked what had taken them so long. The couple said, "We were waiting for the children to die."

Mattie hadn't thought it was funny.

The divorced mothers had laughed and laughed. Hannah laughed just remembering. "I don't think you get it," she'd said to Mattie.

"I get it," Mattie had said.

Hannah told her more than she wanted to know. Mattie's expressions usually said as much, however proud she was about keeping certain things to herself. So she heard about the time, years ago, that her father had explained that he was just the kind of guy who needed to have sex every day. She heard about the hearing where the judge had ruled that $293.75 a month was all her father had to pay, and had told her mother that she was the one with the college degree, so that theoretically, she should be earning more than he did.

Hannah would try to shut up, but the feel of Mattie's body under the comforter, the glow of her crescent moon nightlight, the sounds of the dogs sleeping on the floor all made it impossible to stop. Trying to rein herself in, she'd ask questions about Cole and Georgia. Mattie had been happy to complain.

Georgia had eaten cookies that Mattie had made for her teacher. Georgia had made Cole skip the weekly riding lesson he gave Mattie to shop for house paint.

Complaints gave way to reportage. Georgia had painted the

back of the kitchen door and the inside of the bathroom sink with "splatter art." She'd pulled up the wall-to-wall carpeting and laid down wide-plank floors. The wood they use on basketball courts. She was getting the house painted light gray with blue trim.

Hannah had wanted hardwood floors. Hannah had hated the old green of their house, but Cole hadn't been able to afford the changes, and he'd forbidden her to ask her parents for help.

She'd curl herself around her daughter and say it sounded horrible. And she'd feel better when her daughter answered, "*I'll say.*" And she'd know that it wasn't the way Mattie really felt, or at least the only way she felt. And she'd hate herself a little more for reasons she wasn't able to articulate and didn't have the courage to explore.

She washed dishes, filled the dogs' water bowl, and swept off the front stoop. She tried not to work up a sweat. She made the bed. She peed.

It was 3:19.

She stood in front of her dresser and stared at the photo of Cole from the year they'd met. He thought she'd changed too much. When he'd told her about being in love with Georgia, he'd returned again and again to how much she'd changed as a way of explaining how he felt. She knew she'd changed. She knew that more now than she used to. But she thought she'd changed in ways that made him love her more, not less.

There were more framed photos in the hallway. A whole wallful. She told friends she'd put them up for Mattie.

Hannah had always been the girl who brought the camera to parties. The girl who everybody teased, but was secretly grateful to. It was less expensive to buy film than to develop it, so she kept a cardboard file box under her desk of undeveloped film. Every now and then, when she had a little extra money, she'd pick one out, get it done, and delight and surprise herself with the images she'd forgotten.

When she'd gotten Cole's first support check, she'd taken out all the rolls it would cover and gotten them developed. She'd filed through them in her new bathroom, throwing all the preseparation ones into the tub. She'd stared at the pile, taking in those images of herself before she knew. She hated that face of the idiot who had no idea of anything. When he'd told her he was leaving, of course he'd taken away her future, but her past wasn't hers anymore either. Looking at images of herself before she knew was like viewing a corpse.

She lifted the jewelry box on her dresser and pulled out her marriage certificate. No one knew it was there, so she didn't have to explain it.

Standing there, the thick paper in her hands, she asked herself the question she'd been asking since he'd told her about Georgia. Why did she still want to be with the man who'd taken all that away from her?

And she answered herself like she always had. Because before he was like a lighthouse beacon, and she was a ship that hadn't known shore was so close. That hadn't even known it was lost.

She'd spent most of her marriage wondering how she'd landed someone like him in the first place. It seemed only natural to wonder now about how to get him back.

She stripped to her bra and panties and perused herself in the stand-up oak mirror her grandmother had left her. For the past few days, she'd been working in the garden in a bikini top, and her shoulders were tanned.

Her arms were good. Muscular since she'd started tennis with the women at her parents' club. They'd been the women in her mother's group. Every single one of them was divorced now. Two of them had left their husbands for each other. They all had good arms.

Divorce had been the best diet she'd ever been on.

She'd taken to dancing by herself at night to things she'd never listened to before: the Violent Femmes and Alanis Morissette. She wore sleeveless shirts when she could.

She turned to her side. There was her butt.

She took off her bra and panties and gave herself a sponge bath with cold water. She dried off with a hand towel and baby powder. She got between her thighs and under her breasts.

She lay in the center of her bed and could feel the air from the ceiling fan on her lipstick.

She touched herself. She closed her eyes and saw Cole and Georgia, naked in the house that used to be hers, her daughter down the hall in her room. She'd seen Georgia's naked body more than once. She'd touched it. She'd kissed it.

When Cole had told Hannah what was going on, Hannah had said, "Oh, well, Georgia. Georgia's beautiful."

Georgia had dark red hair and freckles. Georgia had been her friend. For—what? An hour? Less?—Georgia had been her lover. Hannah had never told anyone. She wondered what Georgia had told Cole.

She stopped touching herself. She was going to cry. *Don't,* she told herself. *You'll ruin your face.*

She was ashamed of herself. She knew that whatever had been done to her, there were also things she'd done to herself. Decisions she'd made. And she knew how good she was at running away from any kind of useful examination of those decisions.

She smelled her fingertips. Once, when the Divorced Mothers

Group had gotten together, a few of them had initiated a Girl Pride session. They'd talked about which part of their bodies they liked the most. They'd squatted and examined themselves with hand mirrors, chanting, "Our vaginas are beautiful." They'd touched themselves, brought their fingers to their noses and inhaled.

Then she'd felt just a kind of awkward silliness. "It's 1998," she'd said to herself on the way home. "The seventies are *over*." But these women had grown up together in affluent southern suburbs; had married guys they'd known forever; had raised children who went to the same private school they'd gone to. Garden clubs, fund-raisers, field trips. During the sexual revolution or the feminist whatever, they'd been pressing their husbands' jeans and throwing their Derby parties. Hannah had stayed at the Girl Pride session because she'd been too embarrassed to leave. All those women, herself included, doing all those ridiculous things to keep their sadness at bay.

Now even those women had moved on, but here she was, alone in a barn cottage, giving the dogs sips of her beer.

She closed her eyes. She wanted to lie here and feel cool and clean and sexy. Cole used to sniff her all over, especially behind her ear and under her chin. What *is* that? he'd say. What *is* that smell?

She began touching herself again, and tried to keep remembering. *I don't know,* she always told him. *It's just me.*

She felt sordid. Shamed about who she'd become, what she wanted, and how she tried to get it. There'd been a time when she could've taken or left him. She felt like she was looking at that time through a window with a partial view.

Cole, Cole, Cole, she thought. Even when she tried to think about something else, her thoughts were still about him. It could be a definition of healthy love, she thought a little defensively. When had it become something else?

Cole wasn't late. She couldn't believe it. At four, the Eagle pulled too fast down her driveway. "American Pie" was blaring on the stereo.

She gave herself a once-over in the mirror, and gave her shirt a quick tug.

Cole was driving. Mattie was in the back staring straight ahead. Georgia was in the passenger seat.

Hannah's ankle gave way and she fell to the ground. Perfect, she thought.

Cole turned off the engine and came out to help. Georgia followed. Mattie said to no one in particular, "I told you this wasn't a good idea."

Hannah got up before they could reach her. "I'm fine," she said, dusting her hands off, checking her palms for scrapes from the gravel.

Cole took her hands and peered at them. Hannah wanted to snatch them away. *This has to stop,* she wanted to yell, to both of them. *You can't just keep offering people what you can't give.*

He found himself swimming around in lies because he'd been trying to tell people what they wanted to hear. For a long time, she'd defended the lying by citing its good intentions.

But even in that situation she didn't have the words for how the backs of her hands against his callused palms made her feel. The image of a bird settling into a nest came to mind. And the way Mattie's tiny body used to roll and roll inside her own.

So she didn't say anything—walking to the car, or sitting in the back with her daughter, her ex-husband and his new girlfriend in front of them, on their way to the rodeo.

The fairgrounds were hot. They were in the middle of a two-day heat wave. It was late afternoon and over ninety. Cole and Georgia walked a little ahead. They were holding hands. Dust made small clouds beneath their feet.

Mattie waited until they were through the gates before saying, "So, what's with your face?"

Hannah mentioned wanting a change.

Cole and Georgia glanced back.

Mattie said, "It looks good. You look fancy."

"Yes," Georgia said. "It looks really nice, Hannah."

Hannah wanted to spit on her. She hated that Georgia had used her name. Like it was nothing to toss off the name of the wife and mother, the friend, you'd stolen from. But even Hannah understood that the anger and resentment were, in part, a way to keep other feelings at bay. It was not so different from the way Hannah operated with Cole. Georgia was, Hannah had known for a long time, much more like Cole than Hannah had ever been or would ever be.

The carnies were listless. The passed four of them before someone said, "Play a game; win a prize. Everyone's a winner."

She glanced at her watch. Pete had been under at this point for twenty minutes. The surgery was supposed to take at least two hours.

Some of the rides weren't open yet. Mattie wanted to go on the teacups. They were spinning and rattling madly with no one on them. Hannah hated rides like this. They made her nauseous.

Georgia said she'd go. Cole looked from Georgia to Hannah for a minute, then said he'd wait this one out too.

Georgia and Mattie tried two or three cups before settling on the perfect one. Mattie giggled as the ride operator lowered the worn metal guardrail and hooked the inadequate chain. She straightened her skinny legs and flexed her sandaled feet in anticipation. She released her tight grip on the guardrail with one hand to wave. Hannah waved back and tried to be happy for her daughter's happiness no matter its source. It didn't matter that her happiness cost Hannah something. It mattered that she was happy. When Mattie was born, Hannah had been thrilled and daunted by her role as the place of Mattie's happiness. "Sometimes, it's just nothing but her mother. Only her mother will do," Cole would say, passing her the baby, and Hannah's heart would leap and shy.

Mattie was saying something they couldn't hear. Hannah nodded at her.

No, Hannah corrected herself. *Her happiness shouldn't cost me anything. Her happiness should be my happiness. There,* she thought, warily pleased with herself. *I can do this. One step at a time, I can teach myself. I can change. Get back some version of myself I haven't seen in a while.*

Georgia blew a kiss at Cole. He smiled.

Hannah smelled horses and pellets and water. She imagined Cole doing the afternoon feeding before coming to get her.

"You're a dick, you know that?" she said, watching Georgia and Mattie spin in and out of sight. The noise from the ride was loud and metallic.

Cole looked at the ground, and said, "You're probably right."

"You know I'm right," she said, noting Mattie's wide smile as she spun by.

He was drawing in the dirt with the toe of his cowboy boot. "I don't know," he began. "I just thought—" He broke off, rubbing his hands on his jeans. "I don't know," he said again, a conclusion this time, not an opening line.

He'd spelled out "Sorry" in the dirt. He looked at her and shrugged.

"You're *shrugging?*" she said. "You're writing 'Sorry' in the dirt with your boot and *shrugging?*"

He shrugged.

"Don't even *talk* to me," she said, turning to watch Georgia. Her wild hair flew around with each turn. Mattie's hands gripped the guardrail.

Every time Georgia's face came into view, Hannah imagined a name for her. Homewrecker. *Girl*friend.

Once, a couple of months after the divorce, at the tennis club, there'd been a tournament and a new woman had signed up. She'd been a second wife. Everyone had known the first. The club pro was making the pairings; all the women were standing around him on the hard court. Hannah had worked up her nerve and had stridden over. She'd said, "I will not play tennis with that—" She'd hesitated a minute and then glanced at the second wife. "That adulterer."

She'd been thrilled with her assertiveness. She'd described it to her therapist as a watershed moment.

Her therapist's response had been to ask Hannah to talk more about Jackson, the man she'd known years and years ago and described as a soul mate.

Hannah had reminded him that she hadn't actually slept with Jackson, and had avoided his eyes.

The ride ended, and Georgia and Mattie came weak-kneed and dizzy down the rickety stairs. They were laughing.

Mattie saw the message in the dirt. She pointed. "You told her?" she asked her father.

Cole shook his head. Georgia's hand went to her forehead, and she held her bangs back from her face.

"Told me what?" Hannah asked.

"Oops," Mattie said.

"Way to go, Mattie," Cole said.

Mattie reddened. "Well, you shoulda told her already," she said. "It's not my fault," she said. "None of this stupid life is my fault."

Georgia put her arm around Mattie, and Mattie shrugged it off.

The PA speaker announced barrel racing in the arena in five minutes. "Get your good seats now," the voice said without any enthusiasm.

Hannah looked from Mattie to Georgia to Cole. "Anyone?" she said.

Cole still wasn't talking. He palmed Mattie's head with his hand and rocked her back and forth gently.

Georgia took a breath. "We're going to have a baby," she said, looking at Cole.

"Oh, boy," Mattie said, eyeing her mother.

Hannah looked at them as if weighing her options. Whatever she had done in her life, this was worse. Cole had moved behind Mattie and had his hands on both her shoulders.

"What?" Hannah said. "Are you afraid I'm going to hit you?"

Cole tried to laugh. "Well, you've done it before," he said.

She had. The week before she'd moved out. She'd taken to waking him up in the middle of the night to yell at him, and one time he'd lost it, leaning so close to her that she'd backed up, almost off the bed. She bored him, he'd yelled. "I can't stand you," he said. "How can you stand yourself?" And she'd hit him, hard, against the jaw with an upward movement like she'd seen in the movies. She'd remembered while she was doing it that it was called an uppercut. Her hand had swollen up. Both of them had been black and blue.

"Look," he said, making eye contact with other fairgoers like they might back him up. "I was gonna tell you. You know, we haven't really seen that much of each other." He reached out a hand.

Hannah put a finger up. "Don't," she said. She repeated herself.

His hand went back to Mattie's shoulder and he rubbed her arms.

Georgia put her hand on his back, and said, "Listen, Hannah. We know this is hard for you to hear. But it's going to be okay. I know it is."

Hannah closed her eyes and told her ex-friend that if she'd stop to think for one minute she'd realize that she shouldn't be talking at all.

She understood that in some ways, the affair, the divorce, had made her more assertive than she'd been in years.

Mattie said, "I'm gonna be a bridesmaid. Maybe you could make my dress."

Hannah noted that her daughter was trying to help, but all she could think about was Cole telling her that the great thing about Georgia was that she wasn't one of those marriage-obsessed women. She didn't care about things like that. There were other things about Georgia that she didn't want to think about.

"Maybe I could," she said.

She could feel people walking by them on their way to the arena. She kept her eyes closed. She could feel the three of them waiting.

The summer she was six, there'd been a plague of caterpillars. She'd found the matches her mother used to light the gas stove and had gone outside to squat under the oak that was the most full of caterpillars. They'd dropped regularly to the ground around her, sometimes on her. She'd let them stay where they landed, enjoying the feel of their movements through her T-shirt and on her skin.

It had been a dry summer. She'd drawn a line in the dust with the end of a matchstick and placed caterpillar after caterpillar a good distance from the far side of the line. The caterpillars that crawled away were spared. The ones who crawled toward her were burned when they crossed the line. Her mother had come out to check on her and had put an end to her experiment.

It bothered her that she couldn't figure out why she would think of that right then.

She opened her eyes. Why had she come here? Why had she stayed? To see this: her daughter, her husband, and his pregnant next wife standing in a group in front of her. And herself: the ex-wife, standing on the other side of a pathetic little message in the dirt.

∽ THREE ∽

September 1997

THE FIRST THREE PEOPLE COLE TOLD ABOUT THE SEPARATION
didn't believe him. His mother, his sister, his best friend. It took
him ten minutes to convince them that he wasn't joking, ten minutes before they even got to the whys and hows, the are-you-crazys
and the what-are-you-thinkings.

He made the calls in a single day. He'd wanted to get them over
with, and he and Hannah were supposed to be going out to Massachusetts to visit his family the next week. He'd needed to explain
why she wouldn't be coming. A few days before, he'd mentioned
to Hannah that she needed to let his family know it would just be
him and Mattie for the trip, and she'd looked at him like you look
at a horse who has surprised you one more time than you thought
possible.

"What?" he'd said.

"Hey," she'd said. "I told *my* parents." Then she'd added,
"And I'm not packing for Mattie either."

So he'd made the calls, and in the midst of them had suddenly felt like he was closer to understanding what she'd gone through when she'd lost their first baby. She'd wanted to tell friends and family right away; he'd advised waiting until she felt stronger, but hadn't advised it very adamantly since the whole thing left him feeling way out of his league. She'd written out a list—names on the left, numbers on the right—and had worked her way down it the afternoon after the procedure. It was the longest he'd seen her on the phone. Afterwards, she'd felt better. Like losing the baby had been one thing, but getting through those phone calls another.

He told Hannah that he'd heard about one woman who'd gone with her husband who was leaving her to tell all their friends and family. They'd spent two weeks going around town and making joint phone calls. Hannah'd told him she'd rather die.

He made his calls on Labor Day. Monday was the barn day off. He'd be less likely to be interrupted by calls from the two Aussies he had working for him. He lay on the bed, his feet crossed at the ankles and a hand behind his head, the other holding the phone. Through the bedroom doors that opened onto stairs down to the back deck, he could hear Mattie, her best friend, Celia, and Hannah in the aboveground pool that had come with the house.

He started to dial Tommy's number, then speed-dialed Georgia instead. While he waited for her to pick up, he leafed through the stack of magazines on Hannah's bedside table that had been accumulating since he'd told her he was in love with Georgia. *Make Him Want to Stay: Five Easy Steps. Got Three Weeks? Turn Yourself into the Woman He'll Never Leave.* Parts of the articles were highlighted: "Seventy percent of those who divorce have a lover when the breakup occurs, only 15 percent wind up marrying him or her." "The ex-wife's spectacular and ongoing ineptitude makes the ex-husband feel needed."

Cole grabbed the highlighter and circled his own sentences:

"Eighty percent of divorced people get married again." "The only way to have a good relationship with your ex is to take no money. Ever. No alimony, no child support."

Georgia picked up. She was down at the barn, taking care of the few horses who'd needed to be kept in.

"You know," Cole said, "the money thing is really bugging me again. Her family's loaded; why don't they take care of her?"

Georgia sighed and asked if this was what he'd called to talk about. Georgia came from Virginia money. Her father did something financial Cole didn't understand. Her mother's family had owned Georgia Pacific or something like that. She could afford to sigh at conversations about money.

Cole took a breath and fought the notion that he was moving from one rich woman to another, that to both families, he was the kind of guy more likely to be hired than invited to dinner.

He and Georgia talked horse for a while, and then she said she needed to finish feeding before it got too late.

"What do you see in me anyway?" he asked, half joking.

"What do you see in me?" she answered.

"No fair," he said.

"No rules," she said. "That's something you love about us. I know what you love; I know what you hate. I know what jokes you're gonna laugh at, and which ones you're not gonna get. You're me," she concluded, as she always did, "at a slower speed."

"You wish," he said, and told her he loved her way more than she could ever love him. She said they loved each other exactly the same.

He listened to her hang up and then stared at the barn out the bedroom window, imagining he could see her lips moving. When they'd fallen in love, he'd made a habit out of getting up at three or four in the morning, walking down to the barn, and standing outside the windows to her barn apartment. He strained to hear her breathing or moving in her sleep and heard nothing but barn owls and bats. He couldn't believe that she was in love with him. She seemed to have his number and still chose to stick around. He didn't understand it. He'd stay there outside her apartment hidden by the low limbs of the blue pine until he saw her light come on and watched her walk into the bathroom. On his way back to his own house, he'd count funnel webs visible under a layer of dew.

Now, on his bed, he closed his eyes and tried to smell her through the phone. Sometimes he felt like he was still watching her through a window. It was like she was standing there, still and naked, just for his eyes. She had legs longer than his. Her knees were knocked. Her toes were long. She had a blue birth-mark the size of a dime in the small of her back. She got little scaly spots in the winter between her shoulder blades and on her elbows. The sleeves on her shirts were never long enough for her arms, so she preferred shirts with short sleeves or, even better, none at all. Her neck tended to get sore, so she held her head as if she were thinking about it, as if she were tucking her chin just a little farther than what was natural. Her hair, out of its braid, covered her back. It looked like the kind of hair that you wouldn't be able to comb your fingers through. But that, he knew, was an illusion.

When he tried to know her better than that, when he tried to add up all the parts and see how they worked, it was like she suddenly came to, leaving the window to slip on a robe and disappear into a back room.

He wished Georgia would make the calls for him. He debated the order of the telling. He could start with the separation or with Georgia. He could open or close with reassurances about Mattie.

The order of telling could be determined by his audience. His life had become a sick parody of the salesman's life he'd always led. He used to brag that a man who could sell horses could sell anything.

It was as if God was telling him to shit or get off the pot. He called Tommy first. He was the easiest. Then his mother, then his sister. Kate was two years older than he was, and scared him.

When their father had died last winter, Kate was the one who wouldn't let their mother get away with all her he-was-a-saint revisionism. Finally his mother had said something like, "There wasn't a man who could hold a candle to your father," and Kate had wheeled from the counter, grabbed her by the shoulders, and said, "Please. He wasn't even a particularly good man. Your life'll be better without him." Their mother had stood frozen for a minute and then had left the room, her face in her hands.

Cole hadn't been able to fight the feeling that his sister had done the wrong thing.

His father had been an old New Englander, a Boston Catholic whose hands were ruddy and chapped though he'd worked in an insurance office his whole life. He used pencils until they were nothing but eraser, and chewed out anyone else who didn't. At the dinner table, they all paused before eating, as their father closed his eyes and listened. He could hear if a light was on that was supposed to be off. He drank Johnny Walker in a tumbler with a Red Sox logo on the side. His name was Eddie Thompson, and he considered it a failure that he had only had two children, and even more of a failure that only one of them was a son. But there'd been complications at Cole's birth, and Annie Thompson had been told not to have more children. "So that's it," Eddie had said, standing at her hospital bed, regarding the doctor suspiciously. His wife had reached a hand to his arm and reminded him that they now had two beautiful, healthy children. They should thank God for that, she said. He had glanced down at day-old Cole and said that she was right, that this one was going to have to do.

This one hadn't, right from the beginning, done well enough at all. His father was a hunting man, and seemed to get more pleasure out of woods devoid of people than anything else. As if in response, Cole became obsessed with animals, and in particular, horses. He lugged any kind of horse book he could find out of the library. He pretended his bike was a famous mustang or cutting horse. The famous pacing white mustang that no one could catch until he moved two hundred miles from his territory at Onion Creek and was waterlogged with a deep drink, the first he'd had in miles. Then he was caught, tied so he couldn't choke himself, and staked. A sawed-off barrel of water was left within reach. For ten days and ten nights he remained with grass all around him, water at his nostril's tip, without taking one bite or one swallow. Then he lay down and died.

Or the famous black stallion that was caught by two cowboys out on a peninsula. He snorted and plunged into the soggy-bottomed lake. He floundered in the mud. The cowboys backed off, giving him a chance to get back on land. He paused, and then plunged farther out, pushing and pushing forward until he drowned.

Even as a boy he realized his games had an oddly martyrish air about them.

There was only one other rider that he knew of in his extended family: a distant cousin on his mother's side who'd joined the mounted police because it was the only way he could afford a horse. For a stretch when he was ten Cole considered his cousin's method but rejected it as a kind of riding that was too sissy. He was looking for something cowboy. That was what he wanted to be—anything cowboy.

He'd read about the kind of life he wanted. In the 1860s, a guy from Hamilton County, Texas, went up the trail with a herd of cattle. One night he was on guard, but fell asleep. The shaking of the whole earth brought him to life. The cattle had stampeded. And there his horse stood, two feet on one side of the guy's body, two on the other.

He annoyed his parents with his here-today, gone-tomorrow plans. He tried to set up rinky-dink corrals in any spare yard space—little pickets made of pointed saplings and scrap wood stuck into the ground side by side and fastened with wires. Once the yard was a mess, he wrote an elaborate story on several yellow pads about an orphaned foal that a boy's mother would feed through a crack in the fence by the kitchen door. "There's that foal, hungry again," the mother would say, wiping her hands on the apron she had sewn herself. Because of the way the foal eyed them through the fence they called her Witness.

In Cole's story, the foal could open every gate on the place. With her mouth she could pull out the pin that held the latch to the feed-room door. The family had to buy a Yale lock on which she almost broke her teeth.

The life Cole wished he had when he got older wasn't much different. A bunch of children with a bunch of horses all bred from the same mare.

None of that brought him much closer to his father. His father never got mad, but was baffled by his son's interests. Cole found himself surprised at how much his father's bafflement had surprised him, and it felt like a betrayal. He realized only later on that he'd always been hoping that caring about horses would've been seen by his father as something they could share.

One night when Cole was ten and working at his desk on the latest installment of the Witness series, he heard his father on the stairs and then in his doorway. He felt him watching. He pretended not to notice. His father stood for a minute, and Cole could hear his breathing. The ice cubes in his father's glass clinked like marbles. Cole kept writing, imagining each word as a brick in a small, tight tower. And then his father crossed the small hallway to his own bedroom where Cole heard him say to the empty room, "What the hell. What're you gonna do, right?" before lowering himself onto the bed.

Cole's mother put an end to the Witness series when he was twelve. He came home from school and found his mother turning the last pages of the latest yellow pad. She'd told him she was proud of his writing.

She smiled and asked how school had been. He said it had been fine. She'd brushed his bangs back from his forehead and had left her hand there, as if checking for a fever. She said, "I think it's probably time to move on from this story, don't you?"

Maybe it had been because he couldn't stand to disappoint both his parents. Maybe it had been the odd sense of shame he'd felt because of the way she'd asked it. For whatever reasons, he let his mother put all thirty-two of the yellow pads in an old blue suitcase, and never asked to see them again.

The last entry he'd written—the one she'd been reading—had been this:

> Billy put a feed bag on the head of one of Witness's children. Witness was confused. She nickered in alarm. In place of her child, a monster now stood. The colt high-stepped towards his mother's nicker. Witness panicked, fell backwards, squealed and ran. The other children

*joined the rush. They circled the colt at a wild gallop, neighing and
nickering.*

*The boy stood to the side crying from laughter until his mother came
out and wanted to know what he was up to. Even after he'd explained,
even after he'd been scolded, he couldn't stop laughing. His mother had
had to take the feed bag off the animal; Billy had been laughing too
hard to help.*

Now here it was, thirty years later, and he was making calls
about leaving his wife.

His best friend, Tommy, said, "Well, I hope Georgia's rich,
'cause you're sure gonna be poor."

His mother started weeping, and then said, "I *like* Hannah,
and I don't know anything about this Georgia person."

His sister told him he was a jackass who'd better start thinking
about the family he was supposed to be responsible for.

He got off the phone and lay there like a manikin. He remembered calling home after he'd run away for the last time—to work
for a cowman in Texas. He'd tried to explain his work to his
father. Breaking broncs, grubbing prickly pear, chopping firewood, holding the cut when a big herd was being worked. It wasn't
a glamorous job, he'd said, but a lot could be learned. There'd
been a pause, and his father had said, "But what do I tell people
who ask me what you do?" Hannah's mother had said almost the
same thing when Hannah had announced she and Cole were getting married: are there one or two words, dear, that sum up what
it is he does?

A few minutes later Mattie and Celia ambled into the bedroom,
water running down their backs from their slicked-back hair. He'd
wanted children almost more than he'd wanted anything. Mattie

was perfect, but there was still only one of her. She handed him a damp fax. "Here," she said. "Whatever this means."

It was a Levi's ad: *Button Your Fly.* It was from his sister.

"Beats me," he said, trying to keep his voice even.

They hadn't told Mattie yet. Cole figured she was so used to him being away that she probably wouldn't notice anything for a while. He'd been sleeping in the living room practically the whole summer. The time Mattie had asked about it, he'd said, "I don't want to catch Mommy's cold." He didn't think she was going to be that bothered by all this anyway. She liked Georgia.

She eyed him now. She dripped on the floor. Celia came up next to her.

He stood up, took Celia's hand and spun her around. She let him. He sank to his knees and sang, "'*Cecilia, I'm down on my knees. I'm begging you please to come home.'*" It was a thing he did with her. He did it at least twice a visit, sometimes more. Mattie rolled her eyes and traded looks with her friend. She said, "Her name is *Celia.* You're so—" She searched the walls for the right word. "Inappropriate."

He said to Celia, "So when're you gonna run away with me?" He couldn't tell what she thought of him; he was pretty sure she found him charming, unlike other dads. She was part-Indian or something and her eyes were hard to read.

"Hey," he said, snapping the shoulder straps on his daughter's bathing suit. "Go tell your mom to come in here a minute."

"Hah," Mattie said. "Tell her yourself." She took Celia's hand and they hopped their way out the sliding glass door back down to the pool.

They made him think of young horses who'd been inside for a while let loose. The explosion of movement was as close to poetry as he got. He remembered that that kind of explosiveness always led to collisions that the horses in their euphoria always seemed stunned by. They'd buck apart, stand a few feet from each other, giving each other cautious, wary looks.

Watching his daughter and her friend in the pool made him think of the first time he and Georgia had had sex. By the river, poked by roots and pine needles, bitten by gnats. Afterwards, they'd both peed on the same patch of grass. He'd told her that wild dogs scent-marked one after the other on the same grass so the other dogs would know they were a pair. She'd told him he was crazy and had come at him even before he was finished and they'd had sex a second time.

Wednesdays were Therapy Days that summer. Cole had told Hannah right from the start that he wasn't interested in staying. She'd said the therapy wasn't for that. The therapy was to do the leaving in the rightest way possible. When he hadn't reacted, she'd added, "For Mattie," like he was an idiot. He'd said, okay, fine, and had reiterated that he was leaving; nothing any therapist could do was going to make him stay. She'd reddened and told him she'd heard him the first time.

So she'd gotten the name of some therapist guy from one of her in-touch-with-yourself woman friends, and they'd started weekly sessions. They'd gone about six times, and Cole was sure that no matter what she said, she was counting on him changing his mind, and he was beginning to think the therapist guy—"Call me Bruce," he'd instructed them on their first day—was in on it with her. They got homework from the guy. "Try to find an activity you can share," Bruce had said. Cole had pointed out that if they'd wanted to share activities, they wouldn't be splitting up. Hannah had said if Cole had kept some of his activities to himself they might not be here in the first place. Bruce had held up his hands and asked them to take a minute, to breathe. He told them that finding an activity to share helped all couples—the ones who stayed together and the ones who decided it was best to separate. He reminded them that they'd have to be parents together for the rest of their lives.

So they'd gone home and tried to find an activity. It wasn't supposed to involve Mattie. Hannah suggested a new flower bed, and Cole had rolled his eyes. Cole suggested rebuilding the old MG he'd had in the barn for years. Hannah had just looked at him. Cole suggested more sex, but she didn't think that was funny. So they decided on dinner out once a week. They lined up Lois for sitting, and they were going to take turns picking the restaurant.

Georgia hadn't been too happy about any of this, but he'd tried to explain the way Bruce had. He stressed the expert-advice part of the process. Georgia hadn't bought a word of it. If you're leaving, you're leaving, she'd said. It was cruel, she'd said, to make Hannah think otherwise.

So he kept rescheduling the dinner night. They'd picked Sunday nights—after polo, before Mondays off—but the first couple of weeks, he'd had to go out with the other players. Then the next couple of weeks they'd had a couple of friends up from Texas, and he'd needed to entertain. He'd taken Georgia with him, trying to make up to her. So he and Hannah hadn't gotten to their dinner until this Tuesday. They were supposed to report on it this week in therapy.

They left Mattie with Lois, who gave Cole a withering look as he walked out the door, and drove in the AMC. Hannah was quiet. He asked her if she wanted to know how his calls had gone yesterday. She didn't. He told her his mom was rooting for her.

Hannah told him he was a piece of work and, satisfied that he'd done his bit, he rode the rest of the way in silence.

He wondered, sometimes, whether Hannah and Bruce called each other up and planned the traps to lay for him. Questions like the one the Wednesday session started with: What was the greatest compliment anyone had ever paid Cole? The best thing someone had said about him? As if his answers would make him think in ways he'd never thought before, and all would become clear, and he'd throw himself around Hannah's legs begging for forgiveness, ready to work on making himself into the man she wanted him to be.

Cole had once seen a Barbara Walters interview on TV. She'd asked Katharine Hepburn what kind of tree she'd be if she were a tree. Apparently, it was a signature question. He thought about making a joke about Barbara Walters and trees. Hannah was looking at the floor. Bruce was smiling encouragingly.

Bruce's office was in a small shopping center just outside of town. He shared it with a chiropractor and a personal trainer. During their sessions they could hear bits and pieces from the other offices. "Just five more. Pull your hips to the wall. Make it count." The chiropractor was quieter. Occasional grunts and groans. It made Cole feel like he was in a motel. Sometimes he liked it.

Hannah and Bruce were waiting.

He asked Bruce if he'd told him the story about hauling horses up from Oklahoma one winter. Bruce glanced at Hannah and shook his head.

Cole stretched his legs out in front of him and crossed them at

the ankles. "I wasn't driving," he said. "One of the Aussies was."
He turned to Hannah. "It was Angus. The one you had the hots
for." Hannah looked embarrassed, and said, "Why are you telling
this story? This is a horrible story."

"Anyway," Cole went on, "he made it down, no problem. With
an empty trailer, who wouldn't have? He picks up the horses from
a guy down there I know." He gestured at Hannah. "Carlos."
Hannah nodded. "He puts oil in the truck, fills up the tank, fills
the tires, loads twelve horses, and gets on the road.

"Goes back the same route he came. Comes to the first over-
pass; the air in the tires makes a difference, and he can't make it.
Shears the top of the Featherlite right off, runs into the concrete
divider. There are horses all over the highway."

Bruce said Hannah had a good question. "What is it that you
want Hannah to take away from this story?"

It was reactions like this that made him feel like it was two
against one. And it was reactions like this that guaranteed he
wasn't going to tell them that stories like these had been running through his head for weeks. This one, and the one Tommy
had told him about working out West, and the wild horse they'd
caught that had rammed his way through the seven-foot fence,
and after he got out, killed seven stallions and mares. He'd
never heard anything like it—a horse turning against his own
kind.

"I don't want to talk about this," Hannah said, suddenly all
business. "I want to talk about our date."

Bruce asked if switching gears was all right with Cole. Cole
shrugged. Therapy didn't seem any less pathetic than leaving
highlighted magazines around. When had they stopped being able
to talk to each other? Had it been a choice, or had that bone just
been broken from the start?

Bruce gestured with his palm extended towards Hannah, indicating the floor was hers.

She closed her eyes. She always did that before starting a story. God, he had loved listening to her talk. "Tell me a story," he used to say to her, lying in her single bed at the farm where they'd met. "Talk me to sleep." And she would.

He put his hand up before she could begin. "I know what she's going to say. She got all bent out of shape about something I said on the way to the restaurant, so we might as well just get to my explanation."

Bruce reminded him that you should never assume what your partner was going to say. "Remember," he said, touching his ears, "the first rule of good partnering is good listening."

Hannah began. "It takes six weeks for him to go on one date. Six weeks of 'I have to do this. I have to go there with so-and-so. Not tonight. Next week. For sure, next week.' And this whole time, he's seeing her every night he can." She looked at Bruce. "I know you said it didn't serve any purpose to forbid him from seeing her, but—I don't know—" She turned in her chair to face Cole. "I hear you, you know. I can hear you going down to the barn every night."

"Not every night," Cole said. There'd been more than a few nights this summer when he'd stayed in the house, sleeping in their bed, doing other things in their bed. She'd asked him not to tell anyone. She was ashamed or something. Thought it made her seem desperate. The way he looked at it, what they did in bed was an easier way of showing her he was trying than therapy was. He'd always been more a do guy than an explain guy. She used to like that about him.

"I lie there," Hannah went on, "listening to your footsteps on the gravel."

Everyone was quiet for a minute. He hated how she could do that—turn herself into a poster child in a matter of seconds.

She went on, "So it's yesterday. Lois comes; we kiss Mattie good-bye; we get in the car and head out. Cole's driving. I'm talking. I'm talking about the garden and my book club, and last week's polo game, and the latest on Mattie's summer camp adventures, and everything I've been waiting six weeks to talk about. I don't even have to pretend. It feels like a real date." She grabbed a tissue from the low glass table between their chairs, but she wasn't crying.

"And we're not a mile down the road when he says, 'Hey, listen, you better stop talking now. You better save something for the restaurant, or we're not going to have anything to talk about.'" Now she was crying.

"What is she all over me about?" he asked Bruce. "I was saying what I was thinking. I was thinking out loud. That's what you told us to do."

Hannah pressed the tissue to one eye and then the other. "I just sat there. I should've told him to turn around and go back home. But I didn't. I went to dinner, and ordered three courses and coffee, and made like nothing had happened." She looked up at Bruce. "What's wrong with me? Why didn't I leave?"

"Exactly," Cole said. "Why don't we ask that question instead of going on and on about me?"

"What do you want to say about that?" Bruce asked.

What Cole would've liked to have said is that you learn about yourself through working with horses. And that's what Hannah gave up on when she gave up on horses, and it'd been hard to forgive her for that.

What he would've liked to have said is that all you needed to do with a horse was reach an understanding that there was a job to be done. You didn't need to crack him over the head, or lick his ear either. If he heard another thing about horse whisperers, he was going to break someone's leg. You just figured out how to knock a horse, how to say in small ways, "C'mon, you know what I'm talking about here; you were gonna do it anyway."

He sat there, watching his wife get points for crying, and tried to think of how to say that since he'd known the marriage wasn't going to work, since he'd taken up with Georgia, he'd given Hannah about a million knocks. The Hannah he'd fallen in love with would've gotten the picture right away; the Hannah she'd turned out to be never had. He understood that when he'd said his vows, he'd signed on for change. But he hadn't taken vows with this woman.

He should've known that with her it would be like with flight animals, prey animals. Push the flight animal away, and her instinct is to return. Most horses would rather be at the bottom of the pecking order than be left by themselves. When horses wanted to make a point with a misbehaving member of the herd, they'd turn their backs on the truant, keep her from reentering the group, snap or paw at her if she tried. The more the herd pushed her away, the more she wanted to be back in the group. The Cherokees exploited this for years. Push a horse away, then turn around; the horse would follow, get into rope range, and be captured.

"Listen," he said. "Ground-tying is a nice thing to believe in, but a ground-tied horse is a loose horse. Hannah just thought I would stay, and never bothered to ask herself why she thought that, or why I should."

Bruce observed that Cole used horse metaphors a lot when talking about Hannah. "Why do you think that is?" he asked.

Cole slid down in his chair and thought of those guys he'd met when he'd first worked on a ranch, horsemen so strong they could catch a horse by the tail, take hold of a post, and instruct the other hands to let the rest of the horses out of the corral.

Hannah had her face in her hands. Her sobs moved across her back. Cole put his hand between her shoulder blades. She was so much smaller than he was. It used to make him feel doltish and clumsy. Now he felt like he could palm her, like a basketball.

"Here's how it is," he said. "It's like if I said to you, you have to be married to Tommy. You like Tommy and all, and you'd think, okay. I have to make a life with Tommy. Okay, I can do that. And you might even learn to be real fond of him. But you wouldn't ever feel like this was the one."

Her back moved under his hand. He rubbed her in circles, like he was currying a horse. He didn't know how it felt to her, but it made him feel better. Yesterday on the phone, his sister had accused him of taking the easy way out. She'd said he'd never been the kind of man who could go the distance. He'd been amazed. He'd told her that he may have wished he'd worked harder on the marriage, but he didn't think what he was doing was the easy way out. Easy would be to stay.

He had the sense that now was the time to keep talking, that he might never find it in himself to do it again.

So he reminded her of the time they'd taken an hour-long tour of a time-share condo. They'd gotten sucked in by the promise of a free TV. At the end of the tour, they'd sat in a sad little room, drinking bad coffee out of Styrofoam cups, listening to a guy who couldn't have sold a raft to a drowning man try to talk them into buying a condo. He'd listened for as long as he could stand it, and then he'd said, "There is nothing, nothing you could do or say to make us buy a condo. We're not buying a condo." The guy had tried again. Cole had repeated himself, and the guy had stopped.

He pushed gently on Hannah's shoulder. She looked up at him sideways, her head on her knees.

He turned to Bruce. "C'mon," he said. "By the time two people come to you, it's too late, right?"

Bruce nodded. He said, "For most couples, that's right. But most couples I see don't have anywhere near the respect I see between you guys. And I'm not sure either of you has ever really tried to change." He said "change" like he could make them understand what he meant through enunciation alone.

On the way home, she wept, wiping her tears with the hem of her T-shirt. It offered him an image of her as a ten-year-old. Mattie did the same thing. It made him forget all that he was angry about. It made him wonder if there wasn't some other way. Didn't people sometimes stay married and work something out? For an irrational moment, his mind filled with images of all of them living in the house together. It wasn't so much that he was out of love with Hannah, but that he was in love with Georgia.

He pulled off onto one of those side roads you never notice unless you have to, and stopped the car. He told Hannah what he was thinking.

She pushed her hair from her face and held it away for a moment. He could see the curve of her armpit. He could smell her.

"What?" she said.

He lifted both her arms and held them behind her head. He had always loved her smell, especially after she'd been crying.

"Cole," she said.

He took his hands from hers, but she kept her arms up. He reached under her shirt. She wasn't wearing a bra. She was damp between her breasts. He pushed her shirt up and bent to lick her there. She held her breath. He kissed her and licked her and nuzzled her as if he had all day. He'd do this until she was begging him for it, until she took off her own shorts and panties. He wouldn't think of Georgia once. One thing had nothing to do with the other.

"You love me," Hannah said.

He nodded.

Hannah was beneath him, naked. He was inside her and making her come with his hand. The familiarity of her body was heartbreaking and arousing.

"Did you hear?" she said. "We have mutual respect."

Cole came with her and rested his forehead against hers.

"Did you hear?" he said, meaner than he meant it. "It's too late."

When they got back from therapy, he proposed dinner out. She said she was tired. Mattie said she was too.

"C'mon," he said. "Second grade starts tomorrow. The evil Mrs. Ackley." He made two fingers into a hooked claw and went for Mattie's neck. "Ponderosa."

She slapped his hand away and tried not to smile. "Okay," she said.

Hannah said she'd sit this one out.

Ponderosa was Mattie's favorite. The buffet. The sundae bar. The waitresses who knew her by name. His theory was that if you kept kids from things, they'd just want to mess with them more. So from the time she was a toddler, she'd been allowed to explore the buffet bar, the soft-serve ice-cream machine, the ladies' room. She was particularly intrigued by the soap dispensers and the toilet paper. At the buffet bar, she was drawn to the stuff that looked like pink whipped cream with red Jell-O in it.

They took the truck, so Mattie could ride in the front and fiddle with the air vents, the radio knobs. He took the turn out of the driveway hard and she slid across the bench seat under her father's waiting arm.

"That's a COD turn," he said.

She stared at his boot on the accelerator. He was grateful she hadn't pulled away.

"Come Over, Darlin'."

She rolled her eyes. "Oh, jeez," she said.

Her mother said that too. He squeezed her shoulder. The air from the vent was blowing her shoulder-length hair across his face. "Did you know," he said, "that I can tell the difference between a redhead, a blonde, and a brunette by smell alone?"

She moved back to the passenger side. "Georgia's a redhead," she said.

He took her arm and held her wrist, then her elbow to his nose. "You do the left arm," he said. "It's closer to the heart."

"Hmm," she said.

He kissed the inside of her elbow. "Hey."

She took her arm back.

"You love your dad?" He poked her in the ribs. She squirmed against the door.

"Yeah," she said.

"Like love, or love love?"

She smiled. It was a game they played. "Love love? No way, José. Like love," she said. "Take it or leave it."

He took her hand and told her she was breaking his heart.

They pulled into the Ponderosa parking lot and headed for their favorite table by the window. It overlooked the freeway and the new-that-summer Hampton Inn. He and Georgia had spent opening night there enjoying free cocktails and movie channel TV.

"And," Cole said, leaning close, "I can also tell, just by looking, what bra size a woman is."

Mattie looked sadder than she should've. "That's gross," she said.

"Hey," he said, "I'm not the one who asked Georgia if she wanted to see your mama's titties."

Mattie reddened. "That was a long time ago. I was trying to say kitties."

The waitress came over and gave Mattie a sticker from her apron pocket. "You having the usual?" she asked.

Mattie looked suddenly nervous. She glanced at her father. "Is that okay? Can I get what I usually get?"

Cole laughed and looked from the waitress to his daughter. "Of course."

The waitress left and he asked what was wrong.

She looked at her silverware. "Mom says we can't afford things right now. Mom says we have to tighten our belts."

He looked at the buffet, watching people load their plates with chicken fried steak, fried okra, and biscuits and gravy, and iceberg lettuce salad. "When did she say that?"

"When I told her I needed a new riding helmet. She said to tell you she can't afford it. She said for me to ask you." Mattie reached down to the Barbie backpack she carried everywhere these days. "And I'm supposed to give you this." She pulled a paperback book out, and opened it to a page that had been marked with a Post-it. She looked at it before handing it over.

It was called *Divorce Hangover* and Hannah had marked a passage: "The new person may dull the pain of losing the familiar life for a time, but ultimately you have to experience the abyss alone. This is not a place where you can be with another person." She'd circled "another person" and drawn an arrow out to the margin where she'd written in block letters, the kind Mattie could read, "Cole/Georgia."

Goddamn her, he thought.

The waitress brought their drinks and a coloring book for Mattie. She nodded at the buffet. "Y'all help yourselves whenever you're ready," she prompted. He smiled at her and told her he was just enjoying watching her move around the restaurant. It was like his first course, he said.

Mattie sipped her milk through a straw. She wouldn't drink milk without a straw. The feel of milk on her lip weirded her out. She was the same way about impressions that the elastic of socks left on her ankles. When it was warm, she went barefoot.

"So I guess you're leaving us. Like Alison's dad," she said.

He watched her eyebrows move the way they did when she was thinking hard. She had white blond hair and dark brown eyes and eyebrows. He had never seen the combination before. He remembered how he and Hannah had talked about the way a third thing was created by loving each other. A space for the two of them to be better than they were on their own. The baby was going to be that third thing.

"Where'm I gonna live?" she asked. "Alison has two houses. She says she's lucky. She says she gets two of everything. Two Christmases."

He waited for her to start crying, but she didn't. She drank her milk and asked him questions he wouldn't bring himself to answer. What could he offer her? He was the man who had a line for everyone, and for her he had nothing, not even bullshit.

He found himself asking if she knew how many horses had

died in World War I. Five hundred thousand. A third of the horses
that had gone into battle.

She said, "I don't want two houses. I don't feel lucky." Her
voice was sharp, angry.

The mother at the next table glanced at them. He recognized
her from the feed store. He gave her a two-finger wave.

He stood up, leaving a ten to cover the drinks and a tip, and
gestured for Mattie to follow.

Their waitress came over. "Everything okay?" she asked, genuinely concerned. "Taking off before you eat?"

He nodded and smiled. He thought if he spoke he might fall
to the floor. The waitress shrugged and cleared their drinks.

Mattie remained sitting. "I haven't eaten my dinner," she said.

He reached down and tried to tug her gently to standing. They
were attracting some attention. "Let's go," he said. "We can talk
about this in the truck."

She looked at him. "Mommy says she can't *believe* you," she
said. She turned her head and gaze away. "*I* can," she said slowly
and carefully.

Cole just stood there.

The best thing anyone had ever said to him was, "You're an
animal man, aren't you?" And this, this right here, was the worst.

Georgia was still living in their barn apartment. The same one
she'd lived in since she started working for them five summers
ago. Winters she was back in Virginia, going to art school, and
working on her paintings, giving riding lessons to help pay the
rent. He didn't know whether he found her insistence on financial independence annoying or endearing.

That first summer the place had been a mess; Cole and Hannah hadn't had much time or money to fix up the apartment, and Georgia and Hannah had done most of the grunt work themselves. The toilet had been backed up since the dawn of time. Both rooms were covered with turquoise indoor/outdoor carpet that was permanently damp. When Hannah'd pulled up the carpet, she'd found a nest of baby mice smashed flat beneath it.

The two women had painted the floor and the walls. The plumber had solved the bathroom problems. Georgia had found a working microwave, hotplate, and office fridge at the Goodwill, and had spent the next five summers making the place hers.

At the beginning of last summer, even before he'd fallen in love with her, he had made her a bed, a futon frame to replace the milk crates and plywood she was using. It was just unfinished pine. Nothing fancy. It couldn't convert into a sofa or anything, but it smelled great, especially when it was particularly hot. She'd put it under the windows of the bedroom, and once they'd gotten together, they liked to lie there, listening to the horses on the gravel outside, looking at their clothes hanging together in her closet.

"That's nice," Hannah had said. "She'll appreciate it."

The memory of her complete trust made him guilty and angry, ashamed and injured.

Tonight, Georgia wanted to know about therapy and dinner with Mattie. The last few weeks, he'd felt like he was living in that Bill Murray movie about the day that keeps repeating itself. He'd live his day, then he'd relive it with Hannah, then he'd relive it with the therapist, then he'd go over the whole thing with Georgia. It was like running in sand.

They had showered and were lying on the bed. She was in that Japanese robe she liked. He was naked. He could hear the soft sounds of the horses eating the last of their evening hay. Georgia purposely spread the hay out under her windows. Every now and then one of the horse's heads appeared outside the screen, turning sideways to look in on them.

He threw his leg and arm across her body. "You know what I love about you?" he asked.

She put her hand up and pressed the horse's muzzle through the screen.

"You're bomb-proof." It was horseman's slang for the perfect temperament: steady, calm, amiable, well disciplined.

"You're comparing me to a horse again," she said.

"No," he said, pushing her robe up. "I'm comparing the way I feel about you to the way I feel about horses." He kissed her thigh. He pressed his thumb into the small of her back. Her skin was freckled, smooth.

She quoted, " 'A horseman afoot is a wingless, broken thing, tyrannized by gravity.' "

"What's that from?"

She shrugged. "I don't know. Somewhere." She took his hand and kissed it. "Tell me about therapy. Tell me about Mattie."

He had started with cutting horses. He'd been intoxicated and thrilled by that liquid quickness of a cutting horse following a cow's every move. Those shared moments of having the cow in your sights could feel like violence. Unbeatable.

"I got bored with cutting horses," he said.

"I'm sorry," she said. "Were we talking about cutting horses?"

"I started to feel penned in by my position on a cutting horse. Middle of the saddle, holding the horn, but not leaning on it, never slinging your weight here or there."

"The quiet Zen master wasn't for you, was it?" she said, turning to face him.

Cole could feel her forgetting about what she'd wanted to talk about. "Polo was different," he said, climbing between her legs, touching her with his mouth, being amazed by her wetness yet again. "Polo was like sex for the first time, every time."

She reached down and held the side of his face. "If things didn't go well today, maybe you should be with Mattie."

He pressed his hand here and there on her thigh.

She said, "Did you know that when Helen Keller put her hands on the radio, she could tell the difference between the strings and the cornets?"

He put two fingers inside of her. "Did you know that I talk to the horses about you? I'm crazy in love."

"You talk to the horses about everything," she said, closing her eyes, lifting her chin.

He looked down at her face. She kept her eyes closed.

Here was the thing. He hadn't known about happiness. He'd known about laughing and teasing, and the life he was supposed to lead. But he hadn't known about that sure belief that you fit with someone like lock and key. Until Georgia. But right alongside that knowledge was this: Why was his happiness worth everybody else's pain? Would what he felt ever be enough compensation for the pain he knew he was causing?

And what was this beautiful woman doing with him? He'd spent his life thinking about nothing but what he desired. Now he did nothing but wonder how to make himself into the person she'd want for the rest of her life.

Two months later, on a mild November day, Hannah moved out. That night, Georgia took Mattie for ice cream.

Hannah and Cole took trip after trip moving boxes to her new place—a small groom's cottage on a neighboring farm—not talking much except to say, "Put that there," or "Watch the door." Then the last car load was packed, and they sat down on the steps to the silly sunken living room they'd made fun of when they'd moved in years ago, and they both cried, and they held each other, and then Hannah got up and left.

∽ FOUR ∽

July 2000

WHEN MATTIE WOKE, IT WAS BARELY LIGHT OUT, BUT already hot. She kicked the covers off and stretched her legs tight for a minute. Her mouth was pasty, and her eyes felt like she'd been crying. She listened for sounds from the house. There were birds on the feeder she'd put up outside her window. There were chip-munks in the tree. She went to the window. Her mom's car was there; her dad's wasn't.

She could see dust playing in the light coming through the window. She hated that. It made her feel like things she thought were clean were actually dirty in invisible ways. Celia hated it too. They'd talked about it.

She went down the hall to check on Sam. The door to Cole and Georgia's room was closed. Hannah was probably still asleep in there; Mattie had heard her thumping around during the night. Sam was sleeping. His eyes were moving back and forth under his eyelids. His tiny bangs were stuck to his forehead. She

closed his curtains to let him sleep a little longer, and went back
to her room.

Her room was small, but she liked that it was almost a perfect
square. She liked that she had her own closet and her own window. When Georgia had moved in, she'd helped Mattie redeco-
rate. They'd gone for a farm motif, with an emphasis on horses.
She had horse sheets and a horse rug, and Georgia had painted a
mural on the wall with the most bare space, by Mattie's bed: a
rendering of the view from Mattie's window, of the big oak tree,
with feeder and chipmunks, the driveway, the gray barn. In the
mural, Blue and Mattie's pony, Stinker, had their heads out their
stall windows. Georgia had added pigs, cows, and chickens that
they didn't really have to liven up the driveway.

She picked out a pair of orange bike shorts and a pink-and-
orange tank top, and dressed carefully. She brushed her teeth and
her hair and changed the rubber bands on her back braces. She
checked on Sam one more time.

She drew some horses—a herd being corralled. She arranged
some of her glass animal collection as a model to copy. Georgia
had built her a display case for them. Kind of a miniature pigeon
roost, with more cubby holes than Mattie could ever hope to fill.
She spent hours organizing and reorganizing the collection. By
color. By species. By the person who had given her the animal.

She went downstairs to check the digital clock on the stove. She
wasn't getting how to tell time, and Cole and Georgia had
replaced almost all of the digital clocks with analog ones. The
stove's clock was built-in. It was eight thirty. Sam never slept this
late.

She opened his curtains; light filled the room. Even she
blinked. He hadn't moved. His head was still turned to the left.
His wrist was still cocked backwards at an awkward angle.

She rubbed his belly, and pushed his sweaty bangs away from his forehead. "Come on, Pink Bean," she said. "Time to get up."

He didn't start at her touch. He didn't move.

She leaned over and picked him up. His head fell backwards a little before she caught it. She took him to the window, rocking him gently, but firmly. She bounced him up and down a little.

She got a little more severe. Still nothing. He was breathing; that was it.

She carried him down the hall quickly, and opened the door to Cole's room. The bed was made. There was a bottle of Benadryl on the night table. Hannah wasn't there.

Something cold crept through Mattie's chest. This was one of those moments, she thought. The ones they were always warning her about when they let her watch Sam for a minute. "Be careful." "Don't leave him alone." The kind Lois liked to tell her stories about from the news. A ten-year-old who'd called 911 and saved his grandmother. A five-year-old who'd pulled his infant sister from the pool.

She felt like this was some kind of test, like there were cameras trained on her.

She checked the rest of the house, carrying Sam as gently as she could while going as fast as possible. She opened the door to the basement and called her mother's name. She stood out in the driveway and did the same thing, turning in a slow circle so that her voice would carry in all directions. As she called, something other than adrenaline began to move through her. It was the feeling she got when everything that could go wrong at school had gone wrong, and she would come home and try to explain it to her mother, and her mother would quiz her on what she could've done differently, how she could've felt differently, and even though normally she liked being the kind of girl whose mother talked to her this way, the kind of girl who everyone said was so poised and independent, she just wanted to scream. Sometimes all she wanted was sympathy and the promise that her mother would take care of things. It didn't matter that her mother couldn't take care of anything. The promise was all Mattie wanted.

She was angry. She was angry with her mother. And the reason she was angry was because she wasn't surprised.

Sam was heavy. And hot. A rash had broken out across his cheek and the bridge of his nose.

She went back in the house and put him on the couch. She didn't know what hospital Cole was at. She should call Lois. She picked up the phone. She sat there for a moment, the receiver to her ear, listening to the dial tone. She realized that she'd been waiting for something like this and hadn't known it.

She dialed 911, and when the dispatcher lady said, "What is your emergency?" she said in her clearest, most grown-up voice: "My name is Mattie Thompson. I live at two-forty-four River Road, and my mother has left me and my brother alone in the house. I don't know where she is, and I can't wake my baby brother up. I think she may have given him something."

At the sound of the sirens, she left Sam on the couch and waited outside the front door. There was a police car and an ambulance. The dust clouds they kicked up on the driveway were like the ones Cole made driving the truck and trailer too fast. The paramedics barely acknowledged her except to ask where Sam was. She pointed towards the living room and followed them in.

They laid Sam on a tiny stretcher. She didn't know they came in that size. They checked his breathing. One of them put a child-size airbag over his face and started squeezing. She thought of the

one airplane ride she'd been on. The other paramedic listened to
his heart with a stethoscope, then held his wrist. She couldn't
understand how the paramedic's big fingers could feel anything.
They hooked him up to a small box that beeped. They asked if she
knew what he might've been given. She told them about the
Benadryl, and went and got the bottle. Even walking into the empty
bedroom gave her the creeps. She almost expected her mother to
come out from behind an open door. She closed the door behind
her. When she handed the medicine to the paramedic, he asked if
she knew how much had been in there in the first place. She
didn't.

They asked if he'd had any seizures.

"Any what?" she asked, and then shook her head, and said she
wasn't sure; she'd been asleep for a lot of the night. The paramedic smiled. She should've stayed up, she thought. She shouldn't
have gone back to bed when her mother told her to.

They told her Sam would be fine, that he was just in a deep
sleep, that you had to take a whole lot of Benadryl to do serious
damage, but they were going to take him to the hospital anyway,
just to make sure. They'd found out which hospital Cole was at
and had filled him in. He was waiting there.

She registered that her father wasn't rushing back to her. She
remembered Georgia. She thought maybe she should go with her
brother. The police officers stepped in. They needed to talk to
her here. An investigator from Social Services was on her way.
Someone would take her to her father real soon.

She started to worry that she'd done the wrong thing. She
started to wish she could call the whole thing off and just sit with
Sam until he woke up on his own.

The ambulance left and they took her to the kitchen and asked
if she'd eaten anything. When she shook her head, the woman

officer got her a bowl of cereal and a glass of juice. Mattie helped her with where to find the bowls and the glasses, and the cereal. While she was getting them, the officer checked the other cupboards. She looked carefully at the fridge. She opened the freezer. She asked where the baby food was kept. She said to call her Tanya. She gestured at the man. He was Wayne. She didn't think it was normal for police officers to introduce themselves by first names. Whenever there'd been a police officer in assembly at school it had always been Officer O'Brien or Officer Pitts.

Mattie felt like she was in a play. Sometimes she was the director; sometimes she was the star. Sometimes, she was just watching.

The lady from Social Services came in without knocking. Tanya went to meet her out in the hall. Mattie heard low voices. Wayne stayed in the kitchen, standing at the counter, watching Mattie sit.

The new lady was black. Her hair was in tiny braids piled elaborately on the top of her head. She wore a series of beaded bracelets that went almost to her elbow on one arm, and a watch with giant numbers on the other. She was in sandals and wide pants that flopped around when she swung her legs over the bench. Her tunic matched her pants. She had six earrings in each ear and a nose ring.

She didn't look like the kind of person Wayne and Tanya would normally hang out with.

"Hey," the new lady said, kneeling down by Mattie. "I'm Debra. I'm from the Department for Community-Based Services, and I'm here to help you."

"Hey," Mattie said.

Wayne asked her to show him and the new lady around the house.

Debra examined things in a systematic way, as if she was dividing the place into small squares. She seemed especially curious about the cleanliness of things. She checked bed linens and towels. She took notes about the medicine cabinet. They all noticed the pile of clothes in the hallway. "Are these your mother's?" she asked.

Mattie nodded and remembered that her mother had been naked the last time she'd seen her.

Debra wanted to know where the laundry was done. Wayne smiled at her whenever he caught her eye. She could tell he didn't have kids. They finished with the basement and Wayne went to look outside.

Mattie and Debra went back to the kitchen table where Tanya was waiting for them. Mattie sat in the tall chair that her mother had painted for her. Mattie had insisted on keeping it at her father's house. It had unicorns on it and her name in silver glitter.

Debra asked a lot of questions. She asked them slowly and quietly, and she punctuated them with reminders that everything was fine now. Mattie recognized the voice from the sessions her mother made her have with the school psychologist after the divorce.

She didn't mind answering, but she had the odd feeling that they were the wrong questions, and she couldn't think of what the right ones might be.

Tanya raised her eyebrows when she heard Hannah's last name. "Baker," she said. "Like Judge Baker?"

Mattie nodded. "That's my grandpa," she said. She was used to him getting special notice. Before he became a lawyer and then a judge, he'd run a construction company. Everyone knew him. She explained the custody situation. She told about Georgia. She got the sense that Officer Tanya knew all this already, and Debra didn't.

She moved on to the story of last night. She left out the part

about finding her mother painting her nails. It seemed to somehow reflect badly on Mattie. She told about Sam being sick. She
told about the bottle of Benadryl on the night table. She told
about this morning and not being able to wake Sam, and not
being able to find her mother. As she told it, she began to feel
sorry for herself.

Tanya took notes in a long skinny notebook, with a serious-
looking black cover. Debra took notes on a yellow pad. She
stopped writing and looked up at Mattie. Mattie looked at the wall
of photos. Hannah had put them up, and Georgia had just
replaced the ones of Hannah with new ones of Cole and Georgia,
or Sam, or Mattie. If you didn't look carefully, it was like nothing
had changed.

Debra put her hand on Mattie's. She wanted to know how she
was doing. Whether she wanted more cereal or juice. Mattie was
fine. She didn't want anything, thank you, though.

Debra picked up her pen. "Has your mother ever done anything like this before?"

Mattie had lost count of the number of times after the divorce
when she'd woken up to find her mother out of the bed she was
supposed to be in. Sometimes she found her in the kitchen, a
cigarette glowing in the dark. Sometimes she found her on the
front porch, wrapped in that cotton blanket she liked so much.
Sometimes she couldn't find her, and she would prop herself up
in her bed the way she did when she had an asthma attack, and
wait, listening so hard she'd have to close her eyes to keep from
throwing up.

"What do you mean?" Mattie asked.

Debra put down her pen; it rolled a ways across the table
before stopping. Tanya closed her notebook, sliding her pen into

a special slot that was cool. Mattie imagined sliding her little finger into it.

"Well, has she ever done the kind of thing that's made you a little worried?" Debra explained. "The kind of thing you might not tell your dad or even your best friend?"

There were things she'd told Celia over the last two years. One Valentine's Day when Hannah had made a target out of a photo of Georgia and had made Mattie play darts with her on it. The time they'd driven over to Cole and Georgia's when Hannah knew they'd be away for a week and Mattie had watched Hannah stick the hose through a basement window and turn it on. The times Hannah had climbed into Mattie's bed wanting to know whether she thought Hannah was as pretty as Georgia, or telling her things about Cole that she didn't want to hear. On a school trip Hannah had volunteered as chaperone, and had fallen asleep in the aisle of the bus on the way back, and everyone had been so mortified that no one had said anything. Mattie got a stomachache remembering.

Most of the things she hadn't told Celia had to do with behavior of her own that she wasn't proud of. Last spring, after months of Hannah coming to spend part of almost every day at school with Mattie—for lunch, or to offer some extra adult help in the classroom—Mattie had asked her not to show up so often. Once, after Hannah had found out about Cole and Georgia, she and Mattie had been arguing about taking a bath together and Mattie had said she only liked to take baths with her father, because she love-loved him, and she only like-loved Hannah.

There were lots of times when she knew what her mother wanted or needed, but pretended not to, even if they were easy things.

Some things her parents had done she hadn't told anyone about.

The front door opened and Wayne was back. Hannah was behind him. She was in Georgia's robe. There was hay in her hair.

Everyone waited for someone else to speak.

Mattie said, "You've got hay in your hair."

"I was in the barn," Hannah said.

She could tell her mother was annoyed with her. She wondered if now the police would just tip their hats, and be on their way.

"I was just in the barn," her mother said again, to all of them.

"Well, we're glad you're back," Officer Wayne said. "But we'll need to follow through on some stuff before we take off." He plucked some hay off her shoulder. "Do you want to get dressed?"

Hannah looked down at herself like she was just now noticing she was in her robe. She held her hands out and flipped them palm up, palm down. They were dirty. She looked at Mattie, but Mattie couldn't feel her mother's look. Mattie imagined herself as a plant, or a table. A rock.

Her mother headed upstairs. Officer Tanya leaned close to Officer Wayne and whispered her last name to him before following. Debra stood as well and patted Mattie on the arm. "I'm just gonna talk to your mama," she said. "Back in a flash."

Wayne stood for a while by the sink, smiling that smile. Mattie invited him to sit down. He did; they regarded each other for a while.

She asked if he had kids, and when he said no, but he and his wife were hoping that the good Lord would bless them any time now, she just nodded, and said, "Uh-huh."

She drank the remaining milk from her cereal bowl, holding the bowl to her lips like a Chinese beggar she'd seen in one of her mother's photography books. She wiped her mouth with the back of her hand. They could hear footsteps upstairs.

"What's gonna happen to my mom?" she asked.

Wayne seemed taken aback by the question. "Well," he said. "We'll ask her some more questions, and we'll write a report that goes to Social Services, and—" He paused, twisting his wedding ring around on his finger. "There's a protocol we've got to follow," he said.

Mattie didn't want to ask what protocol meant.

The phone rang. She looked at Officer Wayne.

"You can get it," he said.

It was Cole. Sam was okay. Georgia had had surgery. She wasn't in a coma, but she wasn't awake either.

"Don't you want to know how I am?" Mattie asked.

"You're always okay," Cole said. "You're more than okay. You're my supertrooper," he said.

She twirled the phone cord around her finger and bent her finger until the cord made it go white. "She left us all alone," she said. "She gave Sam too much medicine."

"I know she did," her father said, sounding worn out or bored.

"She was in the barn," Mattie said. "She was in the barn the whole time and she didn't answer when I called."

"Is she back?" Cole asked.

She didn't answer.

"Are the police there?" he asked.

They'd had a dog for a week once when she was Sam's age. An Irish wolfhound—looking thing her father had found behind the feed store. He thought he'd make a good watchdog. Turned out he was scared of rain. Every time it rained, he'd try to chase down the thunder and the lightning. Pete and the neighborhood dogs would follow him, a whole pack of dogs running the fence line back and forth for the duration of the storm. Didn't matter, Cole said. He was still a good dog. Then the story went, baby Mattie had been crawling around on the kitchen floor and had taken an experimental taste out of the dog bowl. The dog had whipped around, and put her whole head in his mouth. The next day, her father had taken the dog to the vet and had him put down.

Last year, her mother had told her that wasn't the way it had gone. The truth was Cole *said* he'd put the dog down, but he hadn't. The vet had called, saying that Cole had dropped off the dog, but hadn't said what the vet was supposed to be doing with him.

"So," Mattie had asked her mother, "what happened to it?"

She'd taken him to the shelter. They hadn't had the heart to do anything else.

Mattie was crying.

Her father tried to coo at her through the phone. The voice he'd used to calm her when she was a baby and that he thought still worked. "Hey," he said. "I'm sorry. I'm sorry you were scared. But it's all over now. Everything's all right."

She held the phone out to Officer Wayne. "He wants to talk to you."

She sat where he had been sitting and watched him talk. She heard, "Yes, sir," and "Well, I can certainly understand that," and "Yes, well, we'll take care of our end. I can guarantee that," and "I wouldn't know; you'll have to talk to a lawyer about that one." She knew without hearing what voice her father was using.

She saw her mother and the other two ladies come down the stairs. Her mother was wearing a dress of Georgia's. It fit her differently. Mattie wondered whether she'd asked about Sam.

They went into the living room. Mattie could see Debra's back and part of Hannah's face. She couldn't see Tanya. Debra had her pad out. Hannah looked like she was trying to concentrate hard, like she did when she was working on those puzzlers she liked.

She watched and listened and knew that everything was not going to be all right. She had started something, and no matter what she did from now on, one thing would follow another. Her chair had wheels and she was being carried backwards down a long hallway whose end she couldn't see.

⟶ FIVE ⟵

May 1993

IT WAS MEMORIAL DAY, AND HANNAH HAD AN ALMOST THREE-year-old Mattie in the backpack because Cole had gone to pick up their summer help at the airport, after just barely finishing with the roof work on the barn apartment where the boys would be staying. For the last two days, she had been trying to paint the floors and walls, rescreen the windows, and get the refrigerator to work, all with a baby too big to carry around this way on her back.

Mattie had been good about it. With a toy or two to hold back there, she was fine, only occasionally shifting her weight too fast and throwing her kneeling or bent-over mother off-balance. And even then, if Hannah told her to stop, she usually did.

While she was waiting, Hannah was dragging magnets around, trying to get the last of the roofing tacks and nails Cole had strewn around outside the barn. Pete, the dog, was galumphing around in front of her, trying to beat her to the nails. He put them in his mouth and spat them out. He grabbed for the ones at the ends of the magnet. He was three, but still acted like a puppy.

To keep Mattie amused, she sang any song she could remember, from "Twinkle, Twinkle," to "Rosalita," to a nursery rhyme her mother used to sing her: " 'Clap hands, clap hands until Daddy comes home, because Daddy's got money and Mommy's got none.' "

Donna, her best friend, had told her it was awful and to quit singing it. Donna was into progressive parenting. She'd had her daughter, Celia, six months before Mattie, and that had given her status as the Expert. Of course, Donna's husband, Tommy, had just left her for one of Celia's baby-sitters and they were on their way to a divorce, so Hannah figured she wasn't the Expert in everything.

Mattie sang along and reached unsuccessfully for the magnet Hannah was using.

When Cole pulled up, there were the two Australians in the back, and in the front a red-haired girl no one had told Hannah to expect. Mattie squealed and called her father's name in a clear and happy voice. It always surprised Hannah to hear it, as if she'd thought she was going to be the only person calling out his name for the rest of their lives.

He came over and picked her out of the backpack. He kissed Hannah on the ear, and whispered, "Be nice. I'll explain."

He was the kind of guy who could get off an airplane with three or four "good people" he'd met on the trip. She had lost track of the number of dinners and drinks she'd served, the number of beds she'd made for people whose names she couldn't have remembered with a gun to her head. He was so much better at talking to strangers. It was one of the ways that they were a good match. She saw the number of beautiful women who were "good people" as proof of what a catch he was. They'd been together fifteen years now; they had Mattie; they were happy.

Georgia moved like she was walking underwater with something delicate balanced on her head, and Hannah couldn't get
over her hair. It was dark red and curly and came all the way down
her back, even in the braid she'd tied it into. Hannah was always
growing out her hair. Next to Georgia, she was the girl with the
wrong dress. The one who wore macaroni necklaces made by her
children.

Cole threw a polo ball for Pete into the darkness of the barn,
and everyone else followed the black dog, and Georgia stepped
up to Hannah. "Hey," she said in the strongest Virginia accent
Hannah had heard since she'd gone to college out there. "Nice
to see you." She put out a freckled hand.

"Hey," Hannah said, offering her own, smaller, sweatier one.
It made her feel cooler just to be touching Georgia.

"I'm with the blond one," Georgia said.

Hannah laughed. "So am I," she said. "The other one," she
added.

"Yeah," Georgia said.

The summer boys had towed girlfriends along with them
before. The boys were from Australia or New Zealand, Ireland,
or the wrong side of the tracks of Louisville. They were the youn-
gest of ten children. They were on thin ice with their fathers.
They were the polite kind of horsemen. They washed for dinner
and ate with their hats in their laps or under their chairs, and they
rose to say thank you and hello. They watched Cole like true
apprentices, learning from everything. The way he rubbed the
cheek of a horse, swung his daughter into his lap, did or didn't
speak to his wife. He liked to play with their attentions, leaking
rumors about himself until they couldn't tell his lies from his
confessions.

The girls who came with them were always smart and pretty, and usually rich, and all gone by the end of June.

Georgia was smart and pretty and rich. And Georgia stayed.

First, she was going to do temp work, but never seemed to get around to the application. Then she was going to help out in the barn, but decided she was sick of horses after years on the show-jumping circuit as a teenager. She was twenty-five; it was time to be a grown-up and not a groom.

Twenty-five to Hannah seemed a time warp away.

Hannah wanted to offer helpful suggestions, but every time she looked at the woman, trying to imagine what she'd be good at, or happy at, she came up empty. The one or two times Georgia had offered to lend a hand with dinner, it had taken twice as long. Another time Hannah had said she'd pay her for a couple hours of gardening and had put her to work spreading mulch. Georgia had seemed enthusiastic enough, but after one or two trips from the mulch pile to the flower beds, she'd wandered off, leaving the pitchfork leaning politely against the half-full wheelbarrow.

Hannah had told Cole, and he'd shrugged and said not to be too hard on her, she was probably used to a pretty different life than the one they could offer, and damn, wasn't she a looker? Hannah had played the part of the Offended Wife, but she'd wanted to agree, and it sent a little charge through her to know that she and Cole thought the same thing.

The Virginia Chandlers, he'd told her that night in bed.

Then Georgia was supposed to work for one of the guys on the polo team, Ron Bartlett, who owned Shucker's Oyster Bar in town. Cole had called him Rocket Ron since he'd shown up shirtless and in khakis and tasseled loafers for practice one day. "Cover that scrawny chest with its two sad hairs," Cole had said. "You're making the women sick." Rocket Ron had been delighted to be able to help Georgia out. He wore his curly black hair short in the front and on the sides, shoulder-length in back. It was called the mullet, Georgia informed Hannah. Guys like him were mulletheads.

She'd made them laugh about her interview. She'd been told to squat at the table and introduce herself to her customers. Tell them something about herself. She'd had to take a "menu test," which involved identifying which drinks went in which line drawings of which glasses. Mug? Martini glass? "Be careful," the assistant manager administering the test had said. "There are some toughies. Beware of your first instincts."

There hadn't been enough room on the application under "Education" for her to indicate that she'd gone to college, let alone that she was planning on grad school. They'd called her the night after the interview. She'd gotten a hundred. Everyone was excited to have her as part of the Shucker family. But she'd talked it over with Angus, her blond, and with Cole and Hannah, and had worked out that the gas and half-hour commute into Louisville kind of cut into the job's appeal.

"I mean," she said one June night in their living room, a leg slung over Angus's thigh, "my time's worth *something*, right?"

"Absolutely," Angus said, tracing tiny circles around her knee.

Hannah watched her husband watching the boy's finger. She turned back to the Duplos on the floor with Mattie. Pete was sprawled next to them, chewing on one of his own paws. She loved the way Mattie's tiny fingers tried to fit the chunky blocks together. Mattie's hands still looked like they had when she was an infant, as if someone had inflated them.

"You could work for Hannah," Cole said, getting up to put on k.d. lang, even though she was gay. She wouldn't be, he liked to say, if she ever met him.

"I could?" Georgia said.

"She could?" Hannah said.

He came and sat behind Hannah on the floor. He tossed a Duplo kitty towards Mattie. "Titty," she said. She couldn't say her *k*'s. After the cat had had kittens she'd asked Georgia if she wanted to see her mama's titties. Georgia had laughed and said no. No, thank you.

Cole put his hand under Hannah's tank top and squeezed her breast. "Mama's titty," he said. Georgia looked at him as if this was the kind of thing she'd come to expect from them both.

When they were first dating, he had liked to walk behind Hannah up stairs and put his hand between her legs.

Angus was blushing. Georgia was still considering them.

Cole laughed at them all, rolled onto his back, and laced his hands behind his head. He did a couple of quick sit-ups. "Hannah needs help around the house," he said. "With Mattie and meals, and there's all those boxes in the basement she's been meaning to unpack for about the last ten years."

Hannah said, "That's true." She didn't know how she felt about Georgia being the one to help. She didn't know what she could imagine Georgia doing. Something cool and slow moving. Something from another life.

Cole said, "We'll pay you two hundred and fifty dollars a week, same as Angus." He kicked Georgia's foot. "Not much for a Chandler, but better than having Rocket Ron breathe on you every night."

"Yeah," Angus said as if waking from a deep sleep.

Georgia didn't say anything, but it was settled, as if Cole was a fisherman who'd just thrown his net.

But Georgia continued to lose interest in what she was doing; Hannah would give her instructions to do something like get the recyclables ready for a trip to the dump, and four hours later, she'd find Georgia sitting in the garage making drawings of bottles and cans in her sketchbook. She thought Georgia might be more interested in preparing meals if she could fancy things up a little, so she presented her with a pile of wedding-present cookbooks that had barely been cracked, and suggested they try something new and different. Georgia flipped the cover of the book at the top of the pile back and forth and shrugged. "Whatever you want," she said.

Hannah suggested working on presentation.

She got some magazines for ideas and marked pages. Tiny bundles of fresh flowers in tiny glass vases on the table. Rose petals across the tablecloth. Napkin rings. Finger bowls and sorbet between courses. Angus was baffled. Cole made a lot of jokes. He asked if they wanted to be left alone, get a room.

"Hey," Georgia said. "This wasn't *my* idea." She waved a hand in Hannah's general direction. "Talk to your wife."

Cole held up his quail and asked what he was supposed to do with this. He said they'd be eating prairie oysters next. Angus asked what those were, and Cole told him: cooked bull's testicles. Georgia asked what raw ones were called. Cole cupped his crotch, and said, "Cole's Boys."

Hannah laughed, and when Georgia snorted, Hannah didn't know if it was at Cole or at her.

In private, he asked who the hell was paying for all this. She told him not to worry; she had the budget under control. She didn't tell him Georgia charged the bigger grocery bills to her parents' credit card.

Hannah hadn't realized how much she'd missed adult conversation since Mattie had been born. So even though everything about Georgia said *just passing through,* Hannah still wanted her there.

They talked boys. They talked parents. They talked Mattie. They put on music and Hannah made up dances. So what if it felt sometimes like Georgia was treating her like someone she might as well be nice to for the time they had together, like wary cousins at a family reunion. So what if Georgia was just passing time; she was willing to pass the time here and that was enough. It was more than enough. It made Hannah's insides take quick little lurches, as if she'd been running down the stairs and missed the last one.

When Georgia stumbled on Cole's pile of *Playboys*, Hannah suggested they write their own Playmate profiles. Ambitions. Turn-ons. Favorite Quote. Georgia's was from Voltaire, she said: "Marriage is the only adventure open to the cowardly." "No offense," she said.

When she left at night, the house filled with space, and Hannah rushed through her nighttime routine to trick the morning into hurrying up and getting there.

Sometimes she would ask Georgia to watch Mattie just so she could spy on them playing. Georgia bought face paints and painted dragons and unicorns on Mattie's cheeks, and when Mattie wanted a turn, Georgia closed her eyes and held her own face still for the out-of-control brushstrokes of a toddler. It was a stillness Georgia had never displayed for Hannah.

Once, when Mattie wanted to paint Georgia's whole body,

Georgia lay on the floor for her and took off her shirt. Mattie painted all she knew how to paint—baby faces and pigs—over Georgia's back and stomach and breasts. Hannah watched from the kitchen doorway, wanting to be in there with them, but unable to bring herself to move. She leaned her forehead against the doorframe, breathing around her cowardice.

Cole said he was glad things were working out, and wished he could say the same for the dimwits from down under. Donna said she was sure Georgia was very nice, but she really wished Hannah could see around herself for once in her life. Had she forgotten that Tommy was living with a woman who was also really good with children?

Lois, their cleaning woman and sometime baby-sitter, had the least patience for Georgia and anything to do with Georgia. "Morning," she'd say when Georgia arrived just after nine. "What time d'you wake up this morning?" Georgia would smile and answer, and Lois would say, "I was up at five. I fed the chickens and the horses. I mucked out stalls. I made breakfast for Jimmy and bagged his lunch, and I went to church all before I got here at eight."

Or Lois would pull Georgia into the bathroom she'd just cleaned, saying, "Look at this." She'd make Georgia get in the shower and check the tile from top to bottom. "Have you ever seen a shower as clean as this one?"

Georgia was polite with her, but it was the politeness of someone used to dealing with servants. Even Hannah could tell it was politeness designed to make Georgia feel better about Lois rather than the other way around. Hannah liked Lois, and wished she could summon more loyalty, but she laughed at Georgia's imitations of Lois's heavy accent, and told stories of her own. How Jimmy drove the neighborhood kids around in the back of his

pickup until he hit a bad bump and one five-year-old was cata-
pulted out. So, Lois had told Hannah, Jimmy had stopped for a
while.

How Lois had come to work one day and announced that
there'd been a visiting preacher at the church, who'd said that
August 15 was going to be the end of the world. The moon would
turn to blood, the rivers would overflow, sinners would self-
combust. The date had come and gone, and Hannah had resisted
pointing that out to a silent and sullen Lois. For Georgia, she
changed the end of the story and gave herself a one-liner that it
took her days to think up.

Hannah didn't care who she sacrificed for the sake of her new
friendship. It was like what Cole had said about training racehorses. You picked a rabbit, a slower horse you always put against
the one you had the higher hopes for, breaking the horse's heart
over and over for the sake of the one you thought was going to be
the winner.

From nine to after dinner five days a week, Hannah had a
companion. The hours she used to spend waiting for Cole to get
back from the barn, the polo field, a horse-buying trip.

She felt like she felt about Cole: all the ways in which she
wasn't the focus of his attention made the moments when she was
that much more electric. Around nearly any moment there was
the warmth of being chosen, or the promise of what might be.

One Thursday, Mattie was taking her afternoon nap, and Hannah
and Georgia were trying to fix the screen on the screened-in
porch. There were a bunch of small tears in several of the panels,
and Hannah was trying to avoid having to replace them. Georgia
said trying to fix it was dumb. She'd pay for the new panels. That

first time in the grocery store Hannah had hesitated long enough for Georgia to push her gently aside and offer her own credit card. Hannah had protested, but Georgia had put her hand up and smiled the smile she used with deliverymen and waitresses. Hannah had barely managed a thank-you in the parking lot.

This time, Hannah had a plan. She put Georgia on the inside and she went outside, on the other side of the screen. Pete chased a bee behind her, caught it, and spat it out, rubbing his muzzle with his paw.

Georgia sat cross-legged on the indoor-outdoor carpet and regarded her.

Hannah pulled a needle and a spool of gray thread from her pocket.

Georgia said, "*That's* your plan?"

"Shut up," Hannah said, frowning as she tried to thread the needle.

Georgia tipped back onto her elbows and stared up at the ceiling fan. "Think of someone you admire," she said, "and list their traits that appeal to you."

Hannah said it sounded like one of the exercises from Donna's get-over-your-husband-betraying-you books.

Donna had shown her her Divorce Workbook, the notebook she was supposed to do her divorce exercises in. "Have fun with this," the instructions said. "Buy a notebook—spiral, loose-leaf, diary, whatever appeals to you—and use it for just this purpose. Choose a color and style you like, and perhaps even a pen with an unusual color ink." Donna had chosen hot pink. "You deserve the time, energy, and attention it takes to work through a divorce hangover." Hannah had tried to be supportive, admiring the photos of Celia pasted to the inside cover. But the whole thing had made her pity Donna more than she liked to pity a best friend.

"God," she'd said to Cole in bed that night, "can you imagine?"

"It works," Georgia said. "You make as specific a list as possible and that increases your chances of finding your perfect match."

Georgia didn't sound worried about finding her perfect anything.

"I'm married," Hannah said, closing one eye to thread the needle.

"Yeah, well, I'm not," Georgia said. She said she was going to get paper and pencil. The screen door to the kitchen banged shut behind her.

Hannah gave up on the needle and thread and sat down on the grass. Pete came over and nosed her hand. She petted his head. He had a little bump at the top of it. Cole said that's where he kept his brains. The first person who'd come to mind when Georgia had said think of someone you admire was Jackson. The second had been Georgia. If she had been a different kind of woman, she might've asked herself some more questions. She was not that kind of woman. She didn't want a tour of the places her questions would take her.

She took the needle and pricked the tip of her index finger. She squeezed, and a drop of blood beaded, alive looking.

She indexed Cole's admirable traits. How much he touched her. She'd seen on nature shows how all kinds of mammals caressed. Dolphins nibbled, whales rubbed each other with their flippers, moles rubbed noses. He loved taking inventory of the places on her body he said got shortchanged in their lovemaking. The backs of her knees. Her shins. The tops of her feet.

She wished he touched other people less. He hugged male friends. He put his arm around women at parties. Even at polo: he was always coming up alongside the only woman player at the club and poking her lightly with his mallet. He handled Mattie like he was rubbing a dog's face. He wished people could be more like animals.

He'd described Georgia as bomb-proof, the best kind of horse, more than once in Hannah's presence.

The one time Georgia had heard him, she'd said, "What kind of women let you get away with this crap?" But Hannah could tell she was flattered.

Georgia was back with a yellow pad and a silver pen. "Number one," she said. "His butt has to look good in jeans." She wrote as she talked.

"That's not a trait," Hannah said. She was still pricking her fingers, one by one. Pete sniffed them and then moved away towards the woods.

When Cole wanted oral sex, he said he thought the dog could use a walk. When he was only after sex, he'd say, "Hey, Hannah Banana, there's no cover charge tonight at the Club Zucchini."

Hannah smiled. Poor Donna, she thought.

"What?" Georgia asked.

Hannah told her.

"What's wrong with you guys?" Georgia said.

Hannah was pretty sure she was joking.

"What are you doing?" Georgia asked. She was already on to the next thing. She was looking at Hannah's bleeding fingertips.

Hannah laughed and wiped her hand on the grass. "Nothing," she said. "Just playing." She stood, spooling up the gray thread. She announced she was going to get stronger thread.

On the way back she looked over Georgia's shoulder at the list. Sense of humor, kind eyes, strong hands. She was surprised at the ordinariness.

Cole had all of those traits. She pointed that out.

"You're right," Georgia said flatly. She ran her finger down the page. "Maybe he's my perfect match."

Hannah laughed, and after a minute, Georgia did too.

Hannah said, "I read a story once where the guy took a needle and thread and *sewed* the name of the girl he loved across his fingers." She put her own fingers to her mouth, brushing them back and forth like her lips were sunburned. "Whatever that trait is, *that's* what I want," she said.

Georgia said, "You would," and it made Hannah want to forget about the boys and hole up there, just the two of them, eating quail, playing with Mattie, sewing their names beneath their skin.

She found some thick black thread, a larger needle, and the rest of Cole's pot. Every night for as long as she'd known him, he'd started with beer, moved to whiskey, and ended with pot. If he'd left the bong by his bed, he'd start the morning with a hit as well. At night, she sometimes joined him, mostly she didn't. It aggravated her asthma, and all it made her feel was sleepy. It didn't put her in the mood. When she complained that all she could do when she was high and they made love was lie there, he said he didn't mind.

Every six months or so, gripped by some sudden desire to be a different person, he vowed to quit cold turkey. He'd ride out to the far end of the back pasture or down to the river and dig a hole for whatever pot he had left. Alcohol and chew from now on, he'd announce proudly when he walked through the door. One time, right after Mattie was born, he'd lasted a week. He'd been in his new father mode. He'd spend minutes standing over tiny Mattie in her bassinet, shaking his head and saying, "I don't know. If anything happened to her, I don't know who I'd kill first, the person responsible, or myself."

Usually, in a matter of a day or two, he was out there on his hands and knees, trying to use a baffled but game Pete to track his treasure.

The four of them had gotten high a couple of times together. It made Angus look kinder and more harmless than usual. It made Georgia laugh genuine laughs, and made Hannah laugh, and made Cole suggest threesomes.

"Threesomes?" Angus had said. "Where d'ya get three?"

Once, Cole had taken both women into a hug, rolling his face between their necks. Georgia's expression had been blank, as if she were waiting for Cole to pass, like the weather. Then it wasn't. First, it made Hannah want to take Georgia by the shoulders, get close to her face, and make her understand: being married to Cole wasn't the same as being Cole. Then she understood that Georgia didn't think Hannah was like Cole. Georgia thought Hannah would walk miles to get to Cole, which was much, much worse.

Years ago, they'd been on the road with the horses and Tommy and Donna, and the men had convinced the women to swap for the night. It had been a night like these, full of drinking and smoking, and Hannah feeling like she was invisible, and the new couples had gone into their motel rooms giggling and whispering. Hannah and Tommy had gotten Hannah and Cole's room, and she hadn't been able to keep herself from looking at all of his stuff strewn around. His Resistol, his shaving kit, the copy of *Blood Horse* he'd been reading in the bathroom just hours before, that leather-and-silver bracelet he'd forgotten to put back on after his shower.

She and Tommy had tried. They'd sat on the edge of one of

the beds and kissed, and he'd touched her breast, but Hannah had felt like she was in the seventh grade. So they'd finished a bottle of Maker's Mark and had played cards until Cole and Donna came pounding on the door.

Cole had come right over to Hannah, taken her in his arms, and kissed her.

When she left that motel, she'd left the whole night behind, like putting a file in a drawer and locking it away. Though sometimes, she took it out.

They got stoned, and Hannah threaded the needle, and they put their faces close to the screen and passed the needle back and forth through the tiny squares of the mesh.

The sun dropped behind the trees. Pete came out of the woods. Hannah checked on Mattie, who was awake but playing quietly in her crib. Hannah backed out of the doorway, knowing that if Mattie saw her, she'd demand to get out, but if she didn't, she could be happy on her own for at least another hour.

The screen looked like the rehabilitation work of an accident victim. Black thread draped on both sides. Georgia sat, still cross-legged, in front of the mess. Hannah sat next to her, their knees touching.

"Well," Georgia finally said. "What can you do?"

Hannah was happy. "We gave it our best shot," she said.

Georgia considered her. "What can you do?" she repeated.

Dinner was pasta. Hannah was in charge of the water.

Mattie was on the kitchen floor stacking nesting blocks into towers and knocking them down. The boys were still at the barn.

Hannah could see them through the kitchen window, taking some of the new horses into the round pen for their first training sessions. She recognized the gray that Cole had told Mattie was her horse for the summer, the one she was supposed to root for in matches. The gelding's name was Court Recorder, which in Mattie's mouth came out Tort Torder. It was better than what she called the truck and trailer.

They'd gotten a late start, and had Tom Petty cranked on the stereo in the living room, trying to get their still-stoned limbs to move faster. Georgia loved the CD; she made Hannah get quiet and listen to the choruses of "Into the Great Wide Open" and "All or Nothin'," and Hannah thought for sure she was trying to tell her something, but she didn't know what.

The phone rang in the middle of all this. "Don't get it," Georgia said, but Hannah had never been able to let a phone ring.

It was Donna. "One woman," she said, "had a subscription to *Hustler* sent to her husband's office. Another steamed all the labels off of the bottles in his extremely valuable wine collection. Another put bleach in his eyedrops."

Since Tommy had moved out, Donna spent a lot of time on the message board of an Internet site devoted to revenge fantasies of divorced or soon-to-be-divorced women. There was a little box next to each of the fantasies that was checked if the fantasy had actually been carried out.

Georgia was singing along with Petty's twangy whine.

Hannah watched her shake some spice into the sauce and stir. To Hannah's stoned mind it seemed that if she stared hard enough at Georgia's back she could move her further away or closer at will.

Donna was talking about a Japanese woman, the former

Mrs. Tanaka, who was arrested for having made over a hundred thousand crank calls to her ex over two years. Her monthly phone bill was half her salary. Her record was two hundred calls in a single day. On the day the police entered her apartment, she was on the phone.

"That's horrible," Hannah said. "Listen, I'm in the middle of dinner, can I call you back?"

"Oh, sorry," Donna said. "Yeah, sure, call me back."

Hannah promised herself she'd remember, but knew she probably wouldn't, and she could tell from Donna's voice that Donna knew it too.

Georgia did a little victory dance. "Ha," she said. "Taste this." She held out a spoonful of her sauce. Hannah put one hand over Georgia's and guided the spoon to her mouth. It was a thick, meaty sauce and she smiled and told Georgia it was perfect. She didn't tell her that getting stoned gave her the taste buds of an eighty-year-old. She rolled the sauce around in her mouth and tried to get flavor from texture.

The boys were heading down to the house; they were shadow puppets against the twilight. The timer for the noodles rang and Hannah set up the colander in the sink. Georgia was dancing in place by the stove, stirring a little cream into the simmering sauce. "Oh, yeah," she said to herself. "I am good."

Hannah turned to take the pot from the stove as Georgia did a little dip and shimmy. They bumped each other, and boiling water and noodles hit the linoleum and splashed up onto her daughter's tiny hand and foot.

Mattie screamed. Hannah shrieked.

Cole appeared in the kitchen and took charge, brushing Hannah aside.

"It wasn't her fault," Georgia told him as he soaked Mattie's hand and foot in a bowl of cool water and then wrapped them in gauze.

He picked Mattie up and bundled her into the back of the car. Mattie was arching with the pain, screaming so long and so loudly that sometimes the screams disappeared into silence, her face still a mask of suffering.

He wouldn't let Hannah in the car with them.

Georgia drove her to the hospital. They watched Cole's tail-lights dip and rise ahead of them. Hannah thought about her daughter's expression. The surprise, and the sureness that her mother would fix it. It was the expression of a childhood dog hit by a car, lying there on his side, his one eye telling her he trusted her, and would wait right there until she made everything better.

The emergency room doctors had resoaked the burns, spread salve on them, and had given them instructions to take her to their family doctor in two days' time.

They had some questions for Hannah. Had anything like this happened before? Was Mattie particularly accident-prone? What, exactly, had happened? Two different doctors, a nurse, and someone in a suit had asked. All three talked to Georgia as well, in a separate room. While the two women talked, Cole went with another nurse and Mattie to X-ray for what the nurse said was a routine scan. By the time everything was done, Hannah was so drained that she didn't even have the energy to ask Georgia what she'd said.

Later that night, Georgia had driven her home again, this time in front of Cole's car, with Mattie in the backseat, and had touched her cheek before going down to Angus and the barn apartment.

Hannah had hovered behind Cole, watching him carry a sedated Mattie to her crib. Later that night, he'd told her she was stupid, and she'd returned, naked, to their bedroom, ready to agree with whatever he wanted to call her, just so she could lie next to someone. They'd had sex, which she'd taken as proof that things were better.

She fell asleep almost before he'd pulled out of her.

She woke to the bed's quick, hushed movements. The clock was on his night table; she didn't know how long she'd been asleep. She listened, waiting for her eyes to adjust. She heard his breathing. He was masturbating. She was lying next to him. He had gone to sleep after making love to her and now he was masturbating.

She held her breath and listened. She felt his movements through the bed. Mattie's accident had been that evening; they had been in the hospital that evening. She thought of what she could turn around and say to him. She knew she wouldn't, because through the whole night, the spill and the trip to the hospital, the implications of the doctors and nurses, Mattie's expressions and Cole's expressions, all she'd been able to come back to was Georgia. Georgia on the porch. Georgia in the kitchen. Georgia singing, her mouth like hands around the words of that song. Somehow this mini-obsession had taken shelter under the umbrella of the bigger one. So Cole, she thought, Cole with his hands on himself was what she deserved.

They put off sorting through the boxes in the basement, using Mattie as an excuse. But Hannah wanted to be upstairs, in the sunlight, shorts pulled up high, legs stretched out in front of her, gin and lemonades within arm's reach, Georgia by her side. That was the kind of girl she wanted to be that summer, even more after the accident than before.

But she'd remembered photo albums in some of those boxes somewhere, and wanted Georgia to see them. She liked the idea of Georgia pointing out what a good photographer she could be. See, she could say back, I'm an artist, too.

So they left Mattie with Lois. Upstairs it was August, and the cool dampness was welcome, like getting to stand in front of the open door of the fridge. Every day since the beginning of the month, she'd woken thinking: *She leaves in thirty days. Twenty-nine. Twenty-eight.* This morning she'd thought: *five.*

The daybed positioned under the laundry chute was piled high with dirty clothes. The play area corner was a disaster. Hannah headed for the back end of the room and the boxes that hadn't taken priority when she and Cole had moved in ten years ago. The ones without kitchen items or current clothes, CDs or toiletries, wedding presents that had to be displayed.

They worked for hours, making piles of things to take upstairs, give away, throw away, repack. Georgia made fun of her high school yearbook photo. She'd been voted Most Likely to Marry a Horse. They unearthed her glass animal collection. Hannah took extra care with the tiny row of ducklings in the family of ducks. "Mattie will like those someday," Georgia said.

Hannah pulled out the shoe box filled with little nothings from her first few months with Cole. Notes he had left her: *See you at four.* Doodles he had done on restaurant napkins that she had slipped into her pocket after he'd paid the check. A series of pencil sketches he'd done of her after he'd noticed her, but before he'd made his first move. When he'd given them to her, she'd been thrilled at the thought that someone had been watching her without her feeling a thing. A paper cigar band that he'd once slipped on her finger under their boss's dining table as he leaned over and whispered that he wanted to be inside her.

Georgia studied Cole's sketches. "I didn't know he could draw," she said. "He's good." She looked up at Hannah. "How'd you guys meet anyway?"

Hannah told her.

"Did you always look like this?" Georgia asked.

"That's very nice," Hannah said.

She was still looking at her. "No, I mean you don't really seem like Land the Bad Boy material." She held her own hands against Cole's sketches and considered them. "*I'm* more that kind of material," she said.

Hannah didn't argue. When she tried to look back and figure out how she'd gotten where she ended up, events and decisions blurred into one another, impossible to see through. What had made Cole want to marry her? What had made her say yes?

"What's this?" Georgia asked, putting down the sketches and holding up a pillowcase.

Hannah blushed, and lowered her voice, and said it was the pillowcase from the hotel room where Cole had made her come with his mouth for the first time.

Georgia nodded matter-of-factly, going back to the box.

The room had spun. She'd had to focus on one corner of the ceiling. Cole had insisted she take the pillowcase. She'd said, "I don't steal linen from hotels." He'd said, "Well, I do," and had tugged the case off the pillow.

Watching him stuff it into her bag, her stomach had done renegade little flips.

Georgia pushed the laundry on the daybed aside and dumped the rest of the shoe box out next to it. She sifted through it. "You are a sad, sad case, Hannah Baker Thompson," she said.

Hannah came and sat on the other side of the little pile. "I am not," she said.

"The guy who won't let you ride in the car to the hospital with your daughter," Georgia said. "The guy who blames you for everything."

Hannah felt tears starting. She'd never said anything about Georgia's dip and shimmy.

She'd be whatever Hannah Georgia wanted.

She told her about the night of the accident. Even about the next morning when she'd found hand towels hardened with cum in the back of the closet. She said she didn't know whether they were all from that night or whether he'd been at it for weeks.

Georgia came over and took her face in her hands. Hannah's legs sank into the fabric of the couch like a spill. She had no idea what would come next. Georgia kissed her. For Hannah it was like trying to stare at the sun. She closed her eyes. Georgia laid her back on the daybed and tugged off her shorts. She bent Hannah's legs, and swung them over her shoulders. Things from the shoe box fell onto the floor. Hannah could feel some pressing into her back. Her eyes stayed closed. She wanted Cole to know. She couldn't explain her wishes to herself. Georgia's mouth on her was like sound. It was like water or like love.

When she was finished, they kissed for some minutes, tasting each other, and then Georgia pulled back, touching Hannah's cheek with her fingers. "Listen," she said. "I don't want you to get the wrong idea from all this."

Hannah's eyes were still closed. She thought she'd keep them that way.

"I mean," Georgia said, "let's not tell anyone about this." She tossed Hannah's shorts into her lap. "Think of it as a going-away present," she said. "For both of us," she added.

And Hannah was not offended or much saddened, because she didn't believe in all that much. Knowledge, she'd already come to believe, wasn't power. Knowing one thing didn't mean you had to learn everything. So days would come one after another and she'd try to be grateful for what came next, take what she could get, and not ask for more.

∽ SIX ∽

July 2000

SAM WAS FINE, BUT HAD TO SPEND THE NIGHT IN THE pediatric ICU. Hannah and Mattie went over after Wayne and Tanya finished. In the car ride, Hannah didn't say a word. Mattie tried not to let it bother her, and reminded her mother that her father would probably be at the hospital.

"What's your point?" her mother snapped.

Mattie stared out her window, hating her tears.

Celia wouldn't have liked the pediatric ICU; Mattie found it interesting, though the smell bothered her. It was how the house smelled after Lois had done the floors. It looked like a nursery, or a creepy day care center. There were cribs, and those other, smaller things that they put newborns in. Her father called them crispers. There were nurses with teddy bears and bunnies and lollipops on their shirts. There were balloons tied to the ends of some of the cribs. There were the same kind of cutouts on the walls that she remembered from preschool and kindergarten. Letters of the alphabet, kittens and puppies, piglets and calves.

But there were wires and tubes weaving in and out of the crib bars, and the cribs were metal, and there were some crispers with tops and lights like the ones in the kitchen of Ponderosa. The orange ones whose heat you could feel if you got too close. There were babies the size of Mattie's forearm.

Sam was hooked up to beeping, adult-sized monitors. He had an IV coming out of one arm. A bag the size of his torso hung from the stand next to his bed. Her father was watching the clear liquid drip down the plastic tube into his son's arm.

When he saw Hannah, it was like he didn't recognize her, and then like he did.

Mattie had seen her father angry lots of times. At traffic, at bad officiating in football games, at misbehaving stereos and VCRs, at horses and children he thought should have more sense. His anger came and went quickly, and she'd understood for a long time that he got angriest with himself. When he couldn't find the hat he wanted, or when he forgot to duck his head going up the stairs, or when the truckload of hay didn't arrive for the third straight day because he hadn't paid for last month's order, or when he missed an easy goal in polo, he threw whatever was within reach and cursed himself and yelled up to the sky to just take him out right there and then.

She'd seen him throw the TV through the open doors to the deck. He'd broken so many remotes, they didn't replace them anymore. He'd slammed a jar of mint jelly down on the glass-topped deck table so the whole top collapsed at their feet. They'd just had time to grab their plates and hold them up. His favorite curse was, "Fuck me." He said it softer each time, usually while banging his fists against his temples, or slapping his cheek with his open hand.

It made her cry, but then he felt worse, so she tried not to. Or tried not to let him see. Things that made him angry one day wouldn't the next, so she tried to remember that none of it would last long.

She'd never seen him look at anyone the way he was looking at Hannah.

He moved Mattie behind him and put his face inches from her mother's. "Do you know what a fuck-up you are?" he whispered.

Mattie stared at her brother and his tubes and wires until they blurred out of focus.

"This time I don't give a fuck," he said. "This time you're on your fucking own."

Her mother made a snorting sound. "Oh," she said, "what will I do without all your support?"

Mattie tried to hear Sam's machine's sounds as distinct from all the others in the room. She imagined her head as a water balloon under a tap.

When she tuned back in, her father was saying, "I don't care who your father is; actions have consequences." And her mother was crying and saying, "You're right, they do." She was saying it like *he* should know better.

Mattie reached out and unplugged the wire closest to her. The green screen went black. Its whirrs and beeps were replaced by a soft alarm. Both her parents stared at it. Nurses arrived, and Mattie and her parents backed away, giving them room to fix everything. Her mother watched for a minute and then left. Her father's fingers twitched against his thighs. Mattie watched the nurses and imagined their hands on her aching head, and then she sat down for what felt like the first time all day.

She wasn't sure whose house was worse, her mother's or father's. Protocol, it turned out, meant more visits, announced and unannounced, from the Department for Community-Based Services. Two houses meant double visits.

Her mother said that all she cared about was Mattie and acted like all this was Mattie's fault. Her father pumped Mattie for information to feed his lawyer. Her mother did, too. Everyone had lawyers again.

Mattie was desperate for school to start, but that was a month away. She was supposed to be working on a summer assignment, a story about her family, but she couldn't bring herself to think about it. She was sick of family.

She was too embarrassed to spend all her time at Celia's. And even there, Donna kept looking at her with those Poor You eyes that Mattie imagined could leave marks. Ever since Donna and Tommy had gotten undivorced and remarried, Donna looked at everyone that way.

All Mattie wanted was to be invisible, to move from house to house like a barn cat. After the divorce, after she'd stopped wetting her bed and proven that she wasn't going to fall apart and become some kind of bad kid who didn't shower and refused to do her homework, things had started to go her way, and she'd started to feel like even if she couldn't have things back the way they were, she still might be able to manage. But now the last people she wanted looking at her were staring all the time, though it was like they were looking through her, to see each other.

What she wanted most was for everything to be over, one way or the other. Both parents kept reassuring her that they would take care of all this, that she didn't have to worry about a thing, that it practically didn't even involve her. She didn't believe them, but she let herself be comforted anyway.

If she had to pick, her father's house was a little better. Georgia was still only moving every so often and the only sounds she'd

made had been moans and grunts. Her father had to take care of
Sam and run the polo operation and worry about his wife. Hannah
had nothing but Mattie on her mind.

The court-appointed psychologist was not going away. They'd
been staring at each other for what seemed to Mattie like way too
long. She wished she could read the clock on the desk. The doctor
was small and blond with freckles across the bridge of her nose.
Her face was so small it made her eyes look huge. Her parents
had already had their meetings with her. Neither of them had told
Mattie much about how it had gone. Her mother had been miffed
that someone this tiny and this blond was going to be making
decisions about her parenting capabilities. Her father had said
she was a looker. Then he had said to just be herself and tell the
truth. Then he had added that Mattie should remember that what
she said could really make a difference in how all this turned out.
He'd said that part in the waiting room. He was still out there
waiting to take her home.

She sat in the Creamsicle-colored swivel chair. She thought
the doctor looked like one of those sixth-graders she could sometimes imagine talking to. Her name was Britta. They had a water
filter at home with that name. She couldn't imagine that anything
she said here could make a difference, and she'd told herself she
wouldn't say anything at all.

She was supposed to be drawing a picture of her family. Britta
had said she'd heard that Mattie was a really good artist. There
were markers and crayons in a plastic bin on the table in front of
her. There was a stack of clean white paper, the kind Hannah used
in her printer. Britta was sitting next to her, waiting.

Mattie wondered if her parents had had to draw pictures.

She looked over at Britta. "Which family do you want me to draw?"

Britta said, "That's totally up to you. Whatever you want to do is great."

Mattie pulled in her chair and peered into the bin of crayons. They were old; so were the markers. Some were missing their tops. They were the thick, stubby kind.

She could see a holder on Britta's desk with six pencils in it. All new, all sharpened. "Do you have a pencil?" she asked.

Britta handed her the whole thing.

Mattie took a sheet of paper from the middle of the pile. She bent over it, leaning so Britta couldn't see. She put everyone outside the front doors—like the Christmas card Donna and Tommy sent every year. She'd have to draw two pictures. She started with herself and Hannah because that was fewer people, and the front of Hannah's house was easier to draw. She sketched the front porch, the pot of geraniums, the metal garbage can with Potpie's food in it, the screen door. She used a new pencil to do the cross-hatching of the screen. She put Hannah sitting on the edge of the concrete porch. She put herself standing next to her.

As she was starting on Cole's house, Britta asked if she minded some talk while she drew. Mattie shook her head.

Britta asked if she had ever been to someone like her before. Mattie nodded.

"Great," Britta said. "Then you have a good idea of what to expect." She paused. "I love the way you did that tree," she said.

Mattie was good at birch bark. She always put a birch tree somewhere in her drawings.

Britta went on. "So did anyone explain to you what this is all about?"

Mattie nodded.

"Well, let me tell you what I think it's about, and of course if I get anything wrong, you just tell me, okay?" She passed Mattie the electric pencil sharpener. "Okay, so as I understand it, your mom and dad have been divorced for a couple of years now, and you've been sharing time with them."

"Joint custody," Mattie said.

"Right," Britta said. "Joint legal and physical."

Mattie had no response, so she nodded.

"So it sounds like your dad thinks that you'd be better off with him more permanently, and he's asking the court to change the custody agreement, and your mom disagrees."

Mattie didn't say anything. She knew that much, but she wondered if she was going to find out things she didn't know.

"So my job," Britta said, "is to help come up with the best solution."

Mattie put Sam on the porch swing, next to Georgia. She put him in the onesie with the pea pods on it. The fat in his thighs and arms was hard to get right. She looked at Britta. "Should I put in Georgia even though she's in a coma?" she asked.

Britta said she could draw it however she wanted.

Mattie wanted to say that sometimes more instructions made things easier.

Britta recrossed her legs and took a swig of her Diet Coke. There was another half-empty bottle on her desk, and next to it, two almost full bottles of Crystal Light. "Now, this is what I'm guessing, and you jump in anytime. I talk to a lot of kids who are in this kind of situation. Not exactly like yours, but you know, the whole divorce thing. And I would say that most of them are pretty fed up. I'm not sure how I would deal with it if I was your age." She looked at some papers in a folder on her lap. "You're gonna be in fourth grade this fall, right?"

Mattie looked at the folder. "Fifth. I was in fourth last year."

"Oh, right," Britta said. "My goof."

Mattie said, "How old are you anyway?"

Britta laughed. "How old do I look?"

Mattie didn't much like it when adults answered with another question. She tried to be generous. "Sixteen?" she guessed. She wasn't sure about numbers.

Britta laughed, but she was blushing. "Well, thirty-two, but everyone always thinks I'm younger. I guess I'll be glad for that when I'm sixty."

Mattie went back to her drawing. She started on Cole, putting him behind the porch swing, pushing Georgia and Sam.

Britta went on. "Anyway, most kids feel pretty confused. I know I would. They get asked a lot of questions, and they're not sure how to answer. The worst is when parents are fighting, and you get caught in the middle. That happen to you?"

Mattie glanced at her and then nodded. A million times she'd been in the middle of fights. In the Wal-Mart parking lot. Mattie and Hannah had waited half an hour for Cole to arrive, and once Mattie got in his car, he'd screamed through his open window that he hoped Hannah was happy, that with the money she and her judge father had left him, he'd be able to feed her daughter every other day. Then he'd turned to Mattie, and said, "Tell your mother what you ate for dinner three nights ago." Mattie hadn't been able to remember. He had thought she was picking sides, and had said, "Fine; you want to be your mama's little girl, then let her and her father's servants feed you," and he'd reached across, opened her door, and sent her back.

Britta made a humming sound and nodded. "The toughest part, I think, is that most kids just want it all to be over. They have dreams about everyone getting along, or things going back to how they used to be."

Mattie's heart was beating a little harder. If she concentrated, she could feel it beneath her shirt.

"I don't think I've had one kid come in here happy with the situation." She leaned a little closer to Mattie. "Between you and me, most of them are actually kind of pissed off."

Mattie tried to imitate her humming sound.

She finished herself in the drawing. She was sitting on the edge of the porch, looking at the swing. She slid both pictures towards Britta, received her compliments, and said she guessed Britta wanted to keep them.

Britta said that would be great, if she didn't mind. She flipped the pictures over and penciled a number one on the one of Hannah's house, and a number two on the other one.

"So," she said. "I really liked talking to you. How would you feel about coming back to talk again sometime?"

Mattie knew this was Britta's thing. She knew Britta did this with every kid who came in here, but she liked her anyway. "No, thank you," she said in her most polite voice, and then asked if she could use the machine to make copies of the drawings.

Her mother was in the waiting room when she came out. Britta looked more surprised than Mattie was. Hannah looked nervous. She was kind of dressed up.

"Cole had to take off. Something at the hospital, I think," she said, more to Britta than to Mattie.

Britta looked at Mattie.

Mattie shrugged; there hadn't been a regular schedule since

the night Hannah had disappeared. Her mother had even put Lois on hold. Her father had been on the phone even more than usual, and he'd been useless on the polo field. Guys who'd hired him to play in tournaments at the end of the summer were changing their minds. He told her he didn't care; he needed to concentrate on Georgia and Sam; but he cared, she could tell.

She headed for the door. On her way out, she heard Britta say she'd be calling about the family interview in the next day or so. Her mother said anytime would be fine, in a voice that was too high and too enthusiastic. Mattie was embarrassed. The heat as she left the air-conditioned office annoyed her.

"So," she said. "Does Grandpa know that doctor?"

"What's that supposed to mean?" Hannah asked.

Mattie scanned the parking lot, trying to find the Buick. "Where'd you park?" she asked. "It's hot," she added.

"Hello?" her mother said, tugging on Mattie's backpack.

"I just asked," she said, readjusting her backpack in exaggerated ways. "Dad says the whole thing is fixed. Grandpa knows everyone. He says it's like the office boy suing the CEO."

"Oh, he does, does he?" Hannah started. "Well, I'll tell you, the thing about your father is—" She broke off, staring. Then she palmed the top of Mattie's head, and tucked a wild piece of hair behind her daughter's ear. "You know what?" she said. "Grandpa doesn't know that doctor, and I think we should just go on home."

She knew that wasn't what her mother had started to say, and she also knew that the decision her mother had made was the right one. But she couldn't stop herself. "Well, he knows the judge," she said.

Hannah looked sad, like it took all she had to keep herself from doing the wrong thing, and convincing Mattie to follow her lead was beyond her.

"The one you're fighting in front of."

"I know who you're talking about," her mother said wearily.

Mattie spotted the broad tail of the car ahead of her a couple of rows. "They play golf together," she said.

"Yes," her mother said. "They do. You're right."

But Mattie didn't feel like anything about her was right.

They got to the car and there was a guy in the front seat. He was dark haired and dark eyed and looked as different from her father as another man could look. Last night, Mattie had snuck downstairs and watched *Predator* on TV. When Arnold Schwarzenegger had come face-to-face with the alien, he'd said, "What the hell are you?" in a way Mattie had really liked.

Hannah opened her door for her. "This is Jackson Ellis," she said. "He's an old friend."

Jackson waved at her from the front seat.

"Who's Jackson Ellis?" she asked her father two days later at his house.

"Jackson Ellis," her father said. "Jackson Ellis," he said again.

"I know his name," she said impatiently.

"Jackson Ellis was the first guy your mama gave it up to," he said. He was smiling.

Jackson was over a lot. He was a lawyer in Indiana. He'd just moved back from the East. He was giving her mother legal advice.

"What's the matter with the lawyer you've got?" Mattie asked.

"Nothing," Hannah said. "This is like a second opinion. A *free* second opinion."

"Dad's from the East," she said.

"You're right," her mother said.

Mattie was supposed to be setting the table for the three of them. Jackson had been to dinner every night that week, and who knew what went on when she was at her father's. The house was a lot cleaner. Sometimes she couldn't find stuff.

She hadn't told her father. She didn't know what she'd say if he asked. Hannah had dated one guy in the two years since the divorce. Ted. Mattie didn't even know his last name. He lived somewhere like Mexico or London. When he went back to wher-ever he was from, her father had commented that Mattie didn't seem all that down about the breakup. "Yeah, well," she'd said. "I'm not really a sentimentalist." He had repeated the comment to Georgia and his friends about a million times.

She centered the napkins and the plates, and then stared out the window, the forks and knives a metal bouquet in her fist.

"Dad says you should just pull that sock out from under the mattress if you need more money." She let the cutlery fall on the table like a round of pick-up sticks. Potpie leaped out from under the table. His claws made skittering sounds on the linoleum. "He says you must be doing something with all that money your mama and papa give you."

Her mother came up next to her and set the forks and knives in their places. She got three glasses from the cupboard and handed two to Mattie. The kitchen was almost small enough for them to stand in one place and reach anything. After the divorce, her mother had said she needed to feel like she could touch all the walls.

She told Mattie the table looked great. Mattie saw it all as just stuff that was supposed to be on a table.

Her mother sat in one of the chairs that didn't have a setting in front of it. The light from the window made it hard to see her face. There were fresh flowers, arranged that afternoon. They'd picked them from the garden.

"Your dad just has his things," Hannah said. "They're things that may or may not be true, but they're things that he absolutely believes in, like some people believe in God. And he's never gonna let them go.

"I can't control what he hangs on to," she went on. "I can only control my reactions to him. I can only control me."

She sounded like she was reciting instructions.

Jackson's car pulled up in front of the cottage. It was new and clean and sporty looking. Red. Mattie had never had a new or clean car. Both of them watched him slide out. He looked like the gymnasts she'd seen in the Olympics, but he didn't move like them. He moved like if he wasn't careful, he'd break something in his way. She imagined her mother kissing him.

Hannah got up and wiped her hands on her apron. "And sometimes," she said, "I can't even do that."

Jackson tapped on the frame of the screen door, and called, "Hello? It's me," and Mattie watched her mother go greet him, and then she sat down, feeling like she was climbing onto the school bus for the first day of kindergarten.

With him around, her mother seemed better. Like the night she'd disappeared had been some kind of dream, and someone watching had said, "Oh, I know what you need," and had sent Jackson over.

Maybe it was that that made her realize that her father had been angry less with Georgia around. With Georgia in the hospital, he was angry more. And maybe it was that that made Mattie go to the hospital.

She got Lois to give her a ride. Lois called every few days, just to check in, to remind her that if she needed anything, she should call. Mattie never called, so Lois was delighted to hear from her. She'd been the one adult Mattie could count on. When Mattie had been at sleepaway camp last summer, Lois had sent a coconut cake for her birthday. She'd put extra eggs in so that it would still be moist. Mattie's friends were kind of scared of Lois. She was stern and had been known to get after them with segments of Mattie's Hot Wheels tracks when they misbehaved. But her rules and her love were sure things, and even as a small child, Mattie had known enough to be grateful.

When Mattie asked her not to mention this hospital visit to anyone, Lois had raised an eyebrow, but that was it. She dropped her in front of the emergency room entrance, and said, "So I don't suppose you'll be wanting me to come in with you."

Mattie smiled and thanked her for the ride. The automatic doors had opened, and she was halfway through before she turned around and asked when she should meet her for the ride home.

Lois waved her hand vaguely. "I'm just gonna sit in that lounge with the air and the TV and watch my stories. When you're ready, I'm ready."

Mattie had been to Georgia's room once before, with her father and Sam, a week after the accident. Her father had fussed around the bed, pulling at sheets and blankets, moving wires, brushing back Georgia's hair. All sorts of things she'd never seen him do before. She'd felt like she shouldn't be watching. Georgia's eyes were closed, but Cole said that if you held her hand, she could feel you. Mattie wasn't sure about that. And bringing Sam had not been a good idea. He kept reaching for Georgia, crying when she wouldn't reach back. Her father had said, "I know how you feel, buddy. I really do."

Mattie had told him that the place weirded her out and had asked if she had to go back. One good thing about that night with Hannah had been that he let her do what she wanted even more than before. Now he went by himself, when she was at Hannah's, or left her and Sam with a sitter.

Georgia had a private room, with a view of the parking lot. Her parents had wanted her brought back to Virginia, but Cole had reminded them that her home, husband, and son, were here. The compromise had been that her parents were paying for things like private rooms and specialists.

He'd brought Georgia's favorite quilt from home, the pillow she liked so much she traveled with it, the first painting she'd done for him—a small watercolor of a spot by the river at the back of the farm. Mattie and Cole used to go down there to play *Wild Horses and Wilder Horsemen.*

She wondered who took care of her hair. It was brushed and braided, but not the way Georgia did it. There was a ribbon at the bottom of the braid. Georgia made fun of ribbons.

Mattie pulled a turquoise chair over. It was a lot heavier than it looked, and it made a screech against the floor. She froze and held her breath before she remembered that she didn't have to.

Georgia had the same wires and tubes that Sam had had, and more. There was a thing that looked like a Japanese lantern moving up and down with short gasping sounds. There was more than one bag hanging from her IV stand. There were white rubbery stickers peeking out of the neck of her nightgown. It was the nightgown that matched the robe Hannah had borrowed that night.

Wires came out of the rubber stickers like vines. Mattie

thought of botany projects at school. An avocado pit balanced with three toothpicks in a plastic cup. The way the sprouts and the roots started outgrowing the little cup.

She moved the photo of Cole and Sam on the night table, and set the glass animal she'd brought next to it. It was a small red dragon Georgia had given her last year. She'd said she knew Mattie was way into horses, but she might find that she wanted something to like that her parents hadn't liked before her. Then she'd told her some things about the dragon's power that Mattie couldn't remember.

She sat. The turquoise chair had looked soft, but it wasn't. Even with the air conditioning, her bare thighs stuck to the vinyl.

Should she say hi? Was it like when Sam had been inside Georgia, and Georgia had told her that he could hear them? When he comes out, Georgia had said, he'll recognize your voice. It was one of the best things anyone had told her.

What was she doing here? "What am I doing here?" she whispered out loud.

Georgia's chest rose and fell. She didn't answer. Sometimes her face looked like she was listening. Like someone at a concert.

She figured she didn't have to answer her own questions right now. Coming here had seemed like the right thing to do, and for now that would have to be enough.

Some days, Mattie found herself with the time and the privacy to do whatever she wanted. Some days she drew. She copied her favorite Calvin and Hobbes cartoons. She'd done about twelve versions of the one where Calvin has transmogrified Hobbes into a tiny duck, and Hobbes points a wing at him and says, "You, my friend, have made a big mistake." She also liked the one where Calvin has to sing the apology song to Hobbes. And Hobbes says, "You're not doing the dance." And the final frame of a Sunday one of Calvin and Hobbes playing their unidentifiable games. It showed Calvin streaking by, saying, "The score is still Q to 12."

She wished she were as funny as Calvin and Hobbes.

She was also working on illustrations for a book she and Celia were writing about a place where horses were a part of the family. The fathers trained them, the mothers fed them, and the foals were invited into the family tents to be looked after by the children. They'd named it after a song they liked.

Some days she read. She'd finished the Harry Potter books. She liked true stories. She read one about a black girl who'd gone to an all-white school. Her grandmother had seen it and had asked why she was reading it. Hannah had asked if reading about black people didn't count. Her grandmother had told her to get off her self-righteous little pony and not put words in her mouth.

At her mother's, she read in the hammock under the willow. At her father's, she read in her room, on her bed, lying on her stomach. At both places, she read in the bath. Her dad could read while he was showering. He held the magazine outside the curtain and lathered up with the other hand.

She made floor plans for rearranging the rooms she had or imagining other ones. All the rooms were up high in houses she hadn't known yet. She wanted to have windows on four sides and low bookshelves underneath them. She wanted cupboards specially designed for her toys and clothes. She wanted deep, shallow drawers that slid out on silent runners for her art projects. She wanted slots for her markers and pens. She loved that everything could be put away behind closed doors and drawers. It didn't

bother her that she didn't have these things yet, because she
believed she still might.

Britta wanted them to do something normal. It was the home visit
ordered by Social Services. They were being observed in their
natural habitat.

Mattie and her father had nodded, and then stared at each
other. She wasn't sure her father knew how to be normal since the
accident.

Something you do a lot together. Something you like, Britta
had prompted. The three of them had already played a board
game Britta had brought. Sam had sat in his Johnny Jump Up and
jumped and watched. The game looked like Britta had made it
herself, and Mattie was impressed with the work. It was a Greek
mythology thing. She knew about Greek myths from school. Cole
was Theseus; Britta was Ariadne, and Mattie was the Minotaur.
Theseus and Ariadne had to find their way out of the labyrinth
before the Minotaur ate them. Mattie won three times in a row.
Every time she needed a six, she got one.

Now he suggested a riding lesson. Mattie shrugged and said
okay. They hadn't had their usual lesson since the night her mother
disappeared. Cole had played in Sunday polo games, but he
hadn't gone to any practices. The summer boys were doing more
work than they had all summer. Today was Monday, day off.

Britta was on her feet and thrilled. She didn't ride, and Mattie
had noticed that anything horse brought on this reaction.

The teenaged girl, Riona, who'd helped Cole out in the barn
on weekends since forever was on hand to keep an eye out for
Sam. Cole carried him to the barn on his shoulders. Mattie

reached up every now and then to touch his foot. She saw Britta
notice.

As she was tacking up Stinker, her pony, she started to get a
bad feeling. Cole had been talking to Tommy earlier in the day
about some paper test he'd had to take at Britta's. There'd been a
lot of multiple-choice questions. "Four fucking hundred," she'd
heard him say. Hannah had had to take the same test, and he was
sure she'd done better. "She's the one with the degree," he'd said.
Then, "I don't know. MMPP. MMPD. Something. They don't
even tell you what the letters stand for." He'd made fun of the questions. One of them was about constipation. Another asked if he'd
like being a florist. "How the hell do I know?" he'd complained to
Tommy. " 'I like repairing a door latch'? What the hell?"

She took the saddle pad off to do more grooming. She hunted
in her grooming box—rubber curry, stiff body brush, soft dandy
brush, hoof pick. Her father had made her the box; she'd painted
it red. He'd spent days instructing her in how to groom. It stimu-
lates oil glands and circulation, he'd said. And it was a time to
check for cuts and sores.

She could tell he was trying to be on his best behavior. He was
usually good at charming people. She could tell he wasn't sure
about Britta. She decided to brush out Stinker's tail. She used a
regular people brush for Stinker's mane and tail. Regular people
brushes didn't break off as much hair. It was easier if the brush
was a little wet, but she didn't want to leave the stall.

They were all watching her from outside the stall. Riona was
sitting on an overturned water bucket until she was needed. Cole
was talking like Britta was here to look at horses for sale. He
described the work he'd done on the barn. He talked about his
plans for the future. He looked at Mattie like he'd just remembered

her and added that the horse life was good for kids to be around. They learned about hard work and caring for animals and people.

He gestured at Stinker. "Now, that one's not pretty. He could drink out of a fifty-gallon drum and still keep an eye on you. But he's a good pony."

"What do you mean?" Britta asked.

Mattie answered. "He's long. He's long in the face."

They all looked at Stinker's head.

"I like it," Mattie said.

Britta nodded. "Me too," she said, and asked her some more about Stinker. Where had she gotten him? How often did she ride?

Cole said, "We've had a once-a-week lesson since Mattie was six." He picked a dangling crosstie up and hooked it back up. "She's never had a lesson with anyone but me." He smiled. "When you've got the best in your own backyard, why look in somebody else's?" He took Sam off his shoulders and set him down between his feet in the barn aisle. "I picked him out for her," he said. Sam picked a pellet out from under the toe of Cole's boot and squeezed it between his thumb and finger. Mattie glanced at Britta, then went to work on Stinker's ears. She cleaned out his crusties with a soft cloth, then she smeared in petroleum jelly to keep the gnats away. She skipped picking his hoofs, though she knew it was one of the things her father would notice. She was supposed to do it to avoid thrush. Her father had once lifted a horse's foot rotten with thrush and made her smell it. Now every time she picked up a hoof, she could smell the rotting frog, that dark liquid.

"Here's the thing," her father said, resting his hand on Britta's shoulder. "There are all kinds of horses—plain horses, vanilla ones, good moving ones, and scorpions. And there's nothing better than a good mare, but a good mare is rarer than a fan in hell."

Mattie rested her head against Stinker's flank and breathed in his horse smell. Her dad wasn't from anywhere near the South but spoke like he'd been born on a ranch and raised by cowboys. When he was nervous, it got worse. Stinker twisted to look at her, then went back to hanging his head over the stall door.

"And there's nothing worse than a bad mare," Cole added. "A bad mare is worse than the worst kind of woman. I saw one who stripped the buttons off the front of a man's shirt with her hoofs. The only safe place was on her back."

"I see," said Britta neutrally.

He peered over the stall door. "C'mon, girl. It's gonna be next week by the time you get this animal ready." He turned to Britta. "Mattie'll walk out of the house into six inches of snow without her shoes on if I don't remind her," he said. "I don't know how many lunch boxes she's forgotten at school. Now I just give her paper bags; I don't think Hannah's wised up yet."

Mattie tacked up, remembering to put the saddle pad slightly ahead of where she wanted it, then sliding it back to smooth Stinker's hair. She was doing the things she was supposed to be doing without anyone else noticing.

She opened the stall door and led Stinker out, holding the reins like she was supposed to, standing on the horse's left side. She stopped halfway out and asked Riona to pick Sam up. The teenager stopped twirling her belly button ring, leaned over, and pulled Sam into her lap without getting off the bucket.

Cole rubbed Stinker's nose vigorously and whispered something into his ear.

Mattie and Stinker led the way to the first pasture, where they'd made a kind of makeshift outdoor ring. It didn't have a fence, but

Cole had put stubby stumps of wood where dressage letters would've gone and there were a few rails and posts. The polo boys used it for exercise work when they weren't using the round pen.

When she was nervous, she didn't ride well, and that made her father annoyed. Today would not be a good day to ride badly.

Maybe because of Britta he would just have her do easy stuff. She gathered her reins and turned Stinker to the right down the circular path worn in the grass. Her father took his position in the center of the ring and told her to go ahead and take her stirrups off.

It was not a good sign. If he'd said to cross her stirrups, that would've been one thing. It would've meant part of the lesson, maybe a small part, would've been without stirrups, and then he'd let her take them back. Taking them off completely meant they weren't coming back on.

She pulled on her reins gently and sank weight into her seat to stop.

"You can do it at a walk," Cole said. "No reason to stop and start a horse if you don't have to."

Britta was sitting on the grass outside of the circle. The teenager and Sam were making their slow way towards them from the barn.

When Cole changed horses between or during periods in a polo game, he had his groom hold the new horse on the sidelines, and he cantered up and just swung one leg over the new horse, and pulled the other leg up and over the old horse that the groom was already leading away. He would never have let her mount that way, but she understood that she was supposed to wish he would, that it was the cooler way to do things.

She hadn't been on a horse in weeks. She was a pretty good rider, better than Celia, but she knew he wished she were less cautious. In the pool, with the football, even when they played board games, he was always pushing her to do again something she'd gotten hurt at. One winter, when she was five, on vacation in Florida, it had rained four and a half days. Her father got so mad, he made them all get out on the beach anyway. It wasn't actually raining, but it had just stopped and looked as if it was about to start again. There was a lot of wind and the waves were twice her size. The sky was the same color gray as the water. He got after her about getting in, and she wouldn't, so he'd picked her up and carried her out to where the water was about up to his waist. He'd dunked her a few times, and was laughing and congratulating her, and he put her down where she could stand, and turned around to holler to Hannah.

She didn't see the wave. It pulled her down like she was nothing, and her dad's arms weren't anywhere, though she swept the tumble of water around her like she might find them by accident. She hit sand, and tried to keep her mouth closed, but couldn't. Then a hand gripped her ankle and pulled her up and out of the water, dripping like a fish. She remembered seeing her mother, upside-down, yelling and scared. She remembered her father turning her right-side up and carrying her back in and saying to Hannah, "Why the hell didn't you tell me the wave was coming?"

Her legs without the help of the stirrups felt like they were nothing but a lack of muscle. She wondered if Georgia's legs felt this way to Georgia.

"Remember," her father said. "Horses are intelligent; if you ask one to do something he was going to do anyway, he gets insulted. You hurt his feelings."

He took his hat off and smoothed his hair back with his hand. Women liked her father's hair. It was blond and thick and different shades in different places. If he let his beard grow, there was red in it. She heard women at the polo field talking about him all the time. His shoulders, hands, eyes, butt. It seemed like there wasn't a part of her father that wasn't worth talking about. He did have nice eyes.

He put his hat back on and said what she'd heard a million times before. "So all you need to know is what the horse is going to do anyway, right?"

She nodded.

"Posting trot," he called, and she thought, *So this is how it's gonna go*. But she didn't expect him to set up the cavalette. She knew better than to ask for her stirrups back before she jumped it.

Britta asked whether this was a good idea.

"She's my daughter," he said, pacing off the placement of the ground rail. "Hannah might not ride anymore, but Mattie does; it's a thing we do together, and she's better at ten than Hannah ever was." He made a tiny readjustment to the rail. "What do we say, Mattie?"

Mattie said, "There are a billion Chinese who don't care whether I make this jump or not."

He laughed.

She liked making him laugh.

"Damn right," he said. And then he picked up her stirrup leathers and said that she should go ahead and take these back.

She knew she was going to fall before she did. She always knew. Sometimes she gave up. He could tell when she did. It annoyed him way more than the falling did.

This was one of those times. "Half-seat," he called, and she did her best to get up and forward in the saddle. Even with her stirrups, her thighs were trembling before she turned down the center line to approach.

Stinker trotted over the ground rail no problem. Her father

called, "Straighten the line of your back. Look up; what are you doing, tying your shoes? Get your butt out of the saddle. I want to see light through there."

Her legs were just too tired to keep Stinker between them. The pony ducked out to the left, and she went to the right. She landed on her back and arm.

Britta was standing.

She lay on the grass. The blades pricked her skin. She imagined ants crawling on her. This was another thing that angered her father—if she didn't get up right away. But she never could. It was as if once she'd given up trying to save herself from falling, she had to give herself to it completely. She also thought she'd get more sympathy this way, even though that never happened.

He was holding Stinker, who had stopped almost immediately to graze. "Oh, for God's sake," he said. "Get up. You're not hurt."

Britta helped her to her feet. She brushed off the back of Mattie's jeans and shirt. "You know," she said, "it's much later than I thought; I've really got to take off." She turned to Cole. "I wonder if you guys might walk me out."

He led the pony over to them. "She's not hurt," he said to her. "It's not enough to ride well. You've gotta learn to fall well—on your feet." He put his hand on Mattie's shoulder. "You're not hurt, are you?"

Mattie shook her head, and Britta patted her back and said she was sure she was fine, but she still had to go.

Cole called Riona over and traded Sam for Stinker with her. He seemed ready to smile. "Don't worry about it, Mattie," he said, putting an arm around her. "You'll get it next time."

She knew how important this had been for him. It was one of the only things besides Georgia he'd been able to concentrate on since the accident. She'd rarely seen him in a situation that he couldn't make go his way. She felt a little sad for him, but also knew that if Britta hadn't been here, she'd have been out past dark doing it until she'd done it right. She didn't always mind; when she finally did get it, and she usually did, she felt his warmth more than she would've if she'd gotten it on the first try. She liked the feeling. It felt like he'd been doing what he'd been doing for her. It reminded her of love.

Late that night, she couldn't sleep. For the past few weeks, she'd been falling asleep okay, but waking up at three, unable to go back to sleep until five or six. Mostly she stayed in bed, staring at the ceiling or trying to make mysteries out of familiar shapes in her room. Sometimes she got up and wandered around the living room or kitchen. If she was at her father's, she checked on Sam.

Tonight, she turned down the hall to her father's room. The nightlight in the hall was on, and she turned it off on her way past. There was a small light coming through his partly open door. He was probably reading a magazine. He didn't read books.

There were sounds. There was breathing. A girl's voice said, "I bet," and then there was no more talking.

She leaned forward and looked. Her father was naked, on top of the covers. Riona was bent over his penis. She had it in her mouth. She was naked too. Her knees were bent. Her butt was in the air.

Mattie knew about blow jobs. There were jokes about them at school. Her father's face bothered her more than what he was doing with his body. One hand was over his forehead. It scared her. Here he was, her father, looking like something she'd never be able to know. She told Georgia about it on her next visit to the hospital.

Mattie was getting used to being watched. She didn't like it, but she was getting used to it. She even looked forward to seeing what jewelry Debra was wearing, what color head scarf. The second DCBS visit went the way the first had—a tour of the house, questions about how much she ate every day and what her favorite foods were and had she had any accidents recently. Then Debra had asked her to please excuse her mother and her, but they were going to have a chat. She hadn't done that the first time, so Mattie was curious.

The two women went outside, to the picnic table under the willow. Mattie didn't like to sit at it because of the splinters and the bird poop. She kept an eye on them from just inside the front door.

Depending on the wind and the positions of their faces, she could hear what they were saying. She heard her mother say, "What now?" and "Okay." She heard Debra say, "It must be hard," and "I am too." And, "Well, one of the issues of concern is a pattern of behavior." She talked for a while longer. At one point, Hannah leaned forward, and said, "When you have asthma, sometimes you go to the hospital."

Debra pulled a paper out of a folder and showed it to Hannah, pointing out something with her finger.

Hannah stabbed at the paper with her own finger. She said, "Someone in your office isn't checking out their records carefully enough."

She held the paper pinned to the table for a moment longer and then handed it back. Debra hadn't moved.

Mattie was tired of this whole thing. She went to her room, rolled under the bed, and pulled the edge of the quilt down until she couldn't see a thing.

One day that August, she and Celia spent the whole day in the pool. It was an aboveground circle, and a long time ago, Cole had showed them how you could get a real whirlpool going. It was easier if you had a lot of people and if some of them were grown-ups. He used to do it with Mattie on his shoulders. But Mattie and Celia managed. They stayed close together, one behind the other, and used the edge of the pool for balance as they ran around and around as fast and as strong as they could. The trick was to figure out how to keep from getting too dizzy before the whirlpool was where you wanted it. They laughed and laughed. They held hands like they were passing the baton in a relay race. Then whoever was the leader would scream, "Now!" and they'd let go of each other and the edge, and let themselves be swept around and in to the center of the whirl. They were quiet and closed their eyes for that part. They let themselves fall underwater.

Afterwards, they'd take a break and lie on their towels on the concrete and talk about what all it had felt like. Celia said like going down a drain. Mattie said more like a tornado from the inside. Celia said cotton candy in the cotton candy machine. Mattie said flying. Celia said they should stop talking about what it was like and just do it again. And Mattie would stand up too, realizing even before it was over that it was going to be one of her best days ever.

She wasn't supposed to know when the court hearing was, but her mother had it marked in red and circled on the kitchen calendar.

August 20. She pretended not to know until her mother was almost ready to leave, and told her Jackson would be staying with her for the afternoon.

"Jackson?" she said, even though he was standing right there. "What happened to needing free second opinions?"

Her mother didn't even blush; she just said he wasn't going to court with her.

"I bet," Mattie said.

Jackson blushed.

She wondered who was watching Sam. She'd forgotten to ask her father when he'd called that morning to ask whether she was rooting for him. Sure, she'd said, glancing over her shoulder at her mother making pancakes.

Hannah was dressed up in a suit that Mattie had never seen before. Pieces of her hair that always fell across her eyes were pulled back in barrettes. They were Mattie's old ones. Her mother had shoes with heels on. It made her look like a different kind of mother.

They were all in the tiny space by the front door. Potpie was at their feet staring up at them expectantly. Jackson held her mother by the shoulders and told her she looked great and kissed her on the forehead.

Mattie tried to imagine a mother who always looked like this. She couldn't, and decided that she wasn't going to like anyone who could.

Jackson asked if she wanted to say anything to her mother.

Her mother looked at her like she'd almost forgotten she was there. She tried to think of something. If he hadn't asked, she would've. What was she supposed to say? *Good luck getting me? Hope I never see Dad again?* For the first time since this had all started, she wondered what she would do if she were the judge.

"I'll see you later," she finally said, and her mother said, "Yeah, see ya later," not unkindly.

They watched the Buick's rear bump down the driveway and out of sight. She looked up at Jackson and gave him her best the-ball-is-in-the-air-and-you-better-run expression.

He asked how she'd like to spend the afternoon.

This, she'd learned by now, was how lawyers talked.

"Just 'cause you're watching me," she said, "doesn't mean you need to do stuff with me."

"No," he said. "I'd like to. Really."

He was wearing khakis, a polo shirt, and white New Balance sneakers. Play clothes, she thought.

"Well, what are you good at?" she asked. They were still outside. She could hear the bees in her mother's flowers. Potpie stood on top of a pile of mulch.

Jackson seemed really bothered by the flies.

"Do you want to go inside?" she asked.

He nodded and held the door open.

They sat at the kitchen table in their usual dinner places.

"I can speak French," he said.

She didn't know what to say. At least he wasn't trying to prove that he was hip to what fifth-graders did for fun. She and Celia had a name for guys like that.

"So, how'd you meet my mom?" she asked.

He didn't seem to mind. "We went to school together. Nursery, elementary, junior high, high school."

"Wow," she said. "You've known her even longer than Dad."

He picked his chair up beneath him and rearranged it about two inches.

"Some people say that was their problem," she said. "That they'd known each other since they were practically kids."

He laced his fingers on the table in front of him. His thumbs tapped each other. "I'm sure it was more complicated than that."

He was talking like she was a dumb kid. She hated him more.

"Guess *you* better hope so," she said.

A bee stumbled and buzzed against the screen.

"I can bake," he said. "Want to make cookies?"

"It's too hot," she said. Her mother never made cookies. Her mother never baked. "So what happened between you and Mom anyway?" she asked.

He looked like he was giving his answer some thought.

"Do you really want to know, or are you just giving me grief?" he asked.

She reddened. "I really want to know," she said.

He put his hands flat on his thighs and looked at her like he was going to give her some straight answers. "I wanted to marry your mother," he said. "She wanted to marry your father." He looked sad. "It's not that complicated a thing," he said. "Happens to people all the time."

"So you went away," Mattie said. "And now you're back. Why'd you come back?"

"She said she needed me."

Mattie raised one eyebrow. It was something she and Celia had worked on. "That's it? So you just spent the last whatever many years sitting around waiting for her to call? That's kind of loserish."

He smiled. "I guess you could look at it that way," he said. "I'm sure some people do, but here's the thing: Your mom and I are made for each other. I wasn't going to find that anywhere else. Believe me, I'd spent a lot of years looking, and I met some nice women. I almost married one. But I didn't. Your mom was here. I came back."

Mattie thought things like that were cheesy, but something about what he'd said made her a little sorry she'd asked.

"We can make the batter now, and cook them later when it cools off," he said, as if they'd never stopped talking about cookies.

It occurred to her that he might be here a long time.

"No, thanks," she said.

He stood up. "Well, mind if I go ahead?"

She shrugged.

He seemed to know where everything was. He was making chocolate chip with nothing fancy in them. Figured, she thought. She sat and watched for a while. He had an interesting way of creaming the butter. That was the part she hated the most about making cookies. The sun dipped and filled the kitchen. Their eyes were the same color. Her father's eyes were green. Her mother's were blue. How she had gotten brown eyes was a mystery.

"So," she finally said, "if you're Mr. Second Opinion, what do you think is going to happen?"

He made a well in the batter and poured the bag of chips into it. "I know your mother loves you a whole lot," he said.

She hooked her feet behind her chair legs. "That's not what I asked," she said.

He was holding the bowl in the crook of his arm, the mixing spoon in the other. He was wearing Hannah's apron. She tried to imagine him as her father.

"What do you want to happen?" he asked.

Angry tears shot to her eyes. She turned away from him. The sun from the window made it worse. "Why does everyone keep asking me that?" she said, trying to keep her voice from sounding like a little kid's. "I'm sick of it." But she knew she wasn't crying because of that. She was crying because no one had asked. Not one single person. And she was crying because if someone had, she

wouldn't have known what to say. *Poor me,* she thought, hating herself. *Poor, poor stupid me.*

And when her mother got home, she told Mattie that the hearing
hadn't gone well. Apparently, even with lawyers, nobody could
make a decision. The thing both her parents had said wouldn't
happen was going to happen. The judge wanted to talk to Mattie.

∞ SEVEN ∞

October 1989

HANNAH SAID HE WAS GOING TO HAVE TO CUT OUT THE JOKES about pregnant women. Cole had no idea what she was talking about. He asked why, and she stared at him until he smiled, and then she smiled with him.

She told him in October. She said she'd known for weeks, but she'd wanted to be sure, so she'd waited for the doctor's test. He hadn't even known she'd gone to the doctor.

He told her he'd quit with the jokes, and he knew it was a miracle, and it was what he'd been after her for a while about, but, he said, poking at her between the ribs, she couldn't tell him she was going to be beautiful, because she just wouldn't be. Pregnant women; they just got fatter and fatter. You didn't do it for the looks.

"What do you do it for?" she asked, quieting his hands against her still-flat belly.

He took in the feel of her small hands on his bigger ones. He took in the softness of her low belly. "There's something inside you that the two of us made," he said. He leaned down and ran his tongue under her upper lip. She shivered. That always got her. He smiled. "It's that simple," he said.

That night, they'd had good sex. Having sex with her pregnant was even better than when they'd thrown away her diaphragm a year ago and started trying. He imagined she was softer, fuller than before. When he came, he felt like he couldn't be deeper inside her. He wondered what it felt like for the baby.

Lying there afterwards, her leg slung across his, he'd remembered trying, years ago, before he'd met Hannah, to get his degree at the community college back home. He'd shown his father his first English paper, and his father had said, "This is good. Who wrote it?"

His father had an old back injury. When he bent to pick up something, he genuflected. He used his knuckles to rise from the table.

He'd woken her up. "Again?" she'd said, laughing. "Already?"

"Are you scared?" he'd asked.

"About miscarrying again?" she asked.

He hadn't been thinking of that. "Yeah," he said.

"Sure," she'd said. "I'm scared about everything. Aren't you?"

"Shit, no," he'd said. "Kids. They can't be any harder than horses."

Two months later it was Christmas Eve, and they were at her parents' place with friends and cousins, uncles and aunts, and they were going to make their announcement, and he was fighting that feeling that he got when a horse wasn't behaving and he couldn't figure out why.

Pell, her father, was a lawyer, a kind man with gray hair and a stoop to his walk that he managed to make regal. His face was a plain of ridges and divots. It made Cole think of training surfaces after a day's work. He tried to remember that before Pell had been a lawyer, he'd run a construction company. He tried to remember that at some point Pell had been someone he could've talked to.

Pell handed him a beer with a glass over the top of it, and asked how the horse business was holding up.

Cole put the glass on a nearby table, being sure that there was a napkin underneath, and took a long swig from the cold bottle. "Pretty good," he said. "I can't say I can complain."

Pell had lent them over $50,000 to buy the house and farm and get the business going. That had been over six years ago, and though no one had said a word about it, Cole felt sure Pell and his wife, Aurelia, spoke about it every night, concern for their daughter on their soft white faces.

"Well, that's good," Pell said. "I'm glad to hear it. I really am."

At the end of October, Hannah and Cole had sold their stock. The entire operation, foals to grannies. The plan was to cut some corners over the winter, and restock in the late winter and early spring, in time for him to train them for the summer season. He didn't like to recall her expression when she'd said, "Great plan, honey, and I don't think we need to share this with Daddy, do you?"

Pell moved off to get drinks for some newcomers, and left him by the piano in the living room. No one ever used this room except for parties. It had a fireplace with built-in bookshelves on both sides and space for two oil paintings of ancestors only Aurelia could identify. She was from South Carolina; you could hear it in her voice. She drank straight gin in a tall glass and pretended it was water. She bought Hood ice cream for the family and visitors and Häagen-Dazs for herself. With each serving, she marked the outside of the carton with a marker, forbidding the rest of them from sneaking a scoop. She had an older sister who drove her nuts. When she talked about her, she puckered up her mouth and made her voice high and tinny. Betsy was perfect; Betsy was the good girl; Betsy made her sick. He thought Aurelia was at her best when she was mocking her sister. Aurelia had been charmed by him at first.

He caught her eyes across the room and gave her a two-finger wave. She nodded, then took the arm of the man standing next to her and introduced him to a stout woman sitting in the corner. The living room furniture was creamy and salmon pink and seemed too small for its stuffing. He could never get comfortable perched on top of the slippery sofa or matching chairs. All Hannah's other boyfriends, he knew, had grown up in houses like this. The whole place made him hungry. Whenever he visited, he ate twice as much as usual and never felt full.

The piano filled one end of the room. Silver- and velvet-framed photos of Hannah in various stages of childhood covered it. There'd been a boy, older, who died of crib death at six months. Hannah had shown him family photo albums including the tiny boy, and then he turned a page and the tiny boy was gone. It had bothered him, and he'd avoiding looking at any more family albums.

French doors opened, in the warmer months, to the back patio and the long backyard. There were neighbors you couldn't see behind the age-old magnolias and dogwoods.

He scanned the room. It was the same group every Christmas. For a while he'd had to deal with seeing Jackson Ellis, but he'd taken a job out East last summer. Cole liked to think of the two of them in a Western, and the move out East as the other guy being run out of town.

The son of one of Pell's partners was across the room. Cole

had gotten high with him last year. The year before, he'd put his hand beneath the guy's sister's skirt as she walked up the stairs. Being in this house made him do things like that. That's what he'd told Hannah when the sister had ratted him out to her. As far as they knew, the sister hadn't told anyone else.

Aurelia was at one end of the room with one of the newest members of the firm, a Jewish guy from New York. "That's not what I meant at all," she was saying, her hand fiddling with her long strand of pearls. "Some of the people I actually know are Jewish." The small group around her roared and she smiled politely, unsure of what she'd said to bring on such happiness.

He slipped out one of the French doors and lit a cigarette in the darkness of the porch. It was cold. For him, the smell of winter was tobacco and cold, cold air. He wouldn't last long out here.

"Hey," a voice said from the other end of the porch. "Those'll kill you."

It was a woman's voice, and his heart did its thing.

"I'm counting on it," he said.

Hannah came out of the shadows, and his heart did something else.

She was bundled in her winter coat, which already looked like it didn't fit. He took her in his arms and rubbed her back. "Not that I know anything," he said. "But aren't you bigger than you're supposed to be?"

She kept her face buried in his chest. "Thanks," she said, but he could tell she wasn't annoyed. She was pleased with her bigness. She saw it as the opposite of miscarrying.

He flicked his cigarette out into the darkness. There were patches of snow on the broad yard. He reached a toe out and the frozen grass crunched beneath it.

"Mama's gonna find that tomorrow," she said.

He undid the belt on her coat and slipped his hands under her sweater. Her mother gave her a new Christmas sweater every year. You were supposed to wear last year's to this party and the new one to Christmas Day dinner.

"I'm sorry," he said. "Let me apologize."

The tininess of her waist always surprised him. He loved that she didn't wear a bra. He ran his hands up and down her sides and thought of smoothing a horse's forelegs before wrapping them for games.

"How's it going?" she said, nodding towards the party on the other side of the glass.

The light inside was yellow and warm. "The usual," he said. "I'm trying," he added.

"I know you are, baby," Hannah said, reaching down to lift her skirt up over her hips. From inside, she'd look like a woman with a coat on.

Cole moved them a little deeper into the shadow of the house. He unzipped his pants and hiked her up onto her toes, pressing her back against the wall. Her eyes were closed. She looked like she was wearing mascara, but he knew she never did. The white-wash of the bricks was flaking off on her coat. The position was awkward. He turned her around, lifted her coat, pulled her hips towards him, and slipped in easily.

She took in a sharp breath.

"Sorry," he said, already moving inside her. Her hips were warm under his cold chapped hands. He could see her father at the piano. He was playing. Her mother was singing. Christmas carols. He knew the playlist, beginning with "Jingle Bells," and ending with "O Come All Ye Faithful."

"Slower," Hannah said. "I'm going to crack my head on the wall."

He moved his hands from her hips to her shoulders, and pulled back on them with each thrust. "Better?" he asked. She nodded. Her cheek was against the brick. In the wild there was always a dominant mare. The stallion skirted the herd and defended it, but the dominant mare was in charge of everything else.

He didn't want to go slower. He wanted to fuck her. And through the wall of this house, the people she had come from. He wanted to fuck them all.

He leaned over and whispered what he was thinking in her ear.

"I know," she said, like she was soothing a child. "I know, baby."

He knew her girlfriends couldn't figure out how someone like her had landed someone like him, but what they really should've been asking was what he asked himself all the time: What had he done to deserve her? And when was he going to fuck it up?

So she said what she said, and he loved her like he never had before. *It's okay,* she was letting him know. *You won't mess up. And even if you do, it's still okay. You're my baby. You're always, already forgiven.*

He had expected her to keep riding, and he reminded her that it could be done. Cece, the only woman in the polo club, had ridden until the day she delivered twins. But Hannah didn't seem to want anything to do with horses anymore. One day she was getting up with him at six to do the morning chores, and the next she was in bed until nine, holding her stomach with one hand and head with the other. She potted and repotted plants in the sunroom. She took long junk-store drives to find child-sized furniture, even though he'd told her he'd make whatever she needed. She spent hours leafing through magazines. He hadn't noticed how much he'd liked her down at the barn with him until she wasn't there anymore. And it bothered him how easily she could give up something he'd thought meant so much to her.

But he couldn't figure out how to voice any of those feelings, so he started to spend more time at the barn, even though there was less to do. He made his phone calls from the tack-room phone. He worked up resentment about the distance she was putting between them. He made himself feel better by relegating her saddle and bridle to a back corner of the tack room.

Things were happening that winter; he could feel it. After a particularly good performance in a tournament in August, he'd gotten two calls from Argentine players and owners about coming down to play high-goal with them for the winter. They'd called again right before Christmas. He would be their American ringer, they'd said. The four-goaler who played like an eight-goaler. They'd described their setups. They'd described the polo. They'd said Hannah was welcome, and then they'd described the women. Down here, they'd said, it is for an American man what it is for an Argentine in your country.

Cole couldn't count the number of blond ladies who'd passed him over for the import Argies, their upper-crust parents looking on in horror. He liked the idea of evening things out. It made him feel patriotic.

Before the Argies had called, he'd talked to a polo friend in Virginia about going in on a polo breeding operation. Enough of getting racehorses that hadn't worked out at the track. Enough of converting cutting horses. Why couldn't there be a standard breed of polo pony mixing the speed of thoroughbreds with the stamina of quarter horses? Lots of people had been doing it on a small scale for years. He had a bigger operation in mind. The friend in Virginia would supply the capital—Oren Chandler, of *the* Virginia Chandlers; Cole would supply the know-how and generate the interest. He'd sell the idea to the horse world. With a few renovations, they could run the whole thing from his farm right here. He'd already started on the round pen and a breeding shed. He was waiting to hear from Oren about buying new horses. Hannah could help; he'd hire a few more guys, and he'd never been afraid of hard work. The best thing about the idea was that no one would expect it from him. It'd be like the 100—1 shot winning the Derby. He could just see their faces. He imagined handing his father-in-law the $50,000 plus interest.

Thinking about all these percolating plans made the emptiness of the barn less noticeable. He took small, circular walks around the almost-completed round pen. Buster Welch had invented the round pen after not being able to get a line of song out of his head. "A string with no end." A place where the logic of a horse's motion could be allowed to run its course. Fifty feet across. Solid wall eight feet high. He tested the sand surface's cushion by bouncing up and down lightly on his toes. He walked the aisle smelling clean stalls every day and thought of the lack of horses as an opportunity, as something like his time coming. It was the same way he'd begun to think of the baby. He imagined himself and Hannah passing their baby between outstretched arms. One end of a circle meeting the other. Whatever'd been missing would now be found.

She didn't ask about his plans, so he didn't share them. It made their time together more quiet. Since she was pregnant, there'd been a general hush about her, as if she was in a giant soap bubble that if she moved too suddenly would pop, setting her gently back on the ground.

She still asked questions about his day, his life, his thoughts, but when he started to answer, he could feel her drifting, like the asking had been all she could do for one conversation.

So he watched her blue eyes darken and drift and her body shift and change.

When he was ten, his family had gone on the one and only vacation he could remember them going on. They went to the tip of Cape Cod. It rained for three days, and when he couldn't stand another round of gin rummy in the motel room, he snuck out the bathroom window and went down to the beach in the storm. He'd thrown what he could find into the gray water. When he ran out of rocks and sticks and shells, he threw handfuls of wet sand. The rain wouldn't let up, and his T-shirt and camp shorts were plastered to his body.

A retriever appeared, collarless and as wet as Cole. He dropped a small plastic football at Cole's feet. It was red and black and dimpled with the dog's teeth marks.

Cole threw it into the water. The dog leapt in, clearing the first wave, getting swamped by the second. He righted himself, panned the water for the ball, and started swimming. Cole threw and the dog retrieved for what seemed like a long time. Cole stopped worrying about getting in trouble. He just threw, and the dog just fetched. Life was that simple.

And then the dog lost his bead on the ball in the waves, and the ball got too far out, and Cole called the dog back in, and they stood there together on the beach, watching the ball bob and drift farther and farther out of their reach.

He imagined what their child would do for them. Quiet his worries. Reassure them that they'd done the right things. Reassure Hannah that she'd made the right decision about Jackson. About Cole. With their child in the world, any mistakes that they'd made could be unmade.

He reminded himself that she still did for him what she'd always done. Meals, laundry, cleaning. They still rented movies, took walks after dinner, made love on the living room floor. She never said no, but that soap bubble quality was there all the time. He couldn't blame her for it. He figured it had to do with losing the pregnancy before this one. He figured it was something he couldn't understand. It made him want her more, not less.

The Argies never called back. On a bitter day in February, his feet as close to the space heater as he could get, he called one of them, carefully figuring out the time difference in Buenos Aires. When the guy didn't recognize who was calling, Cole hung up.

Oren strung him along for months. He knew he was being strung along, but what were his choices? So he played dumb, voicing loud agreement and understanding to the guy's empty reassurances and excuses. Occasionally, he continued to sell the idea, half-full of self-hatred for fighting a losing battle, half-sure he could bring the guy around.

Hannah walked in on one of these conversations, and looked at him funny, but didn't say anything, and after finding what she needed, headed back to the house, one hand massaging her lower back through her layers of winter clothes.

Later, at dinner, she asked what was up.

"Nothing," he said, smashing peas and mashed potatoes onto the back of his fork.

"I don't believe you," she said. She was eating a baked potato with a side of tuna and had a jar of baby onions in front of her.

The jar annoyed him. "Well," he said.

"What's wrong?" she asked again.

"Nothing," he said.

"Are you going to make me pull this out of you?" she said. "Are you going to make me guess and guess?"

Two things that they'd been able to rely on in their over ten years together: his moods and her attempts to pull him out of them. He'd come to rely on those attempts. They were a sign of her love. Her pregnancy seemed to have made her both more and less patient with him. So he told her about the Argies and about the idiot Chandler boy, handing his embarrassment and humiliation to her like a piece of himself he wanted her to hold, and she listened, and didn't zone out.

When he was done, she pushed her plate away and reached over and placed her hand on his forearm. "Look," she said. "It's their loss. You'll find something else. I know you will."

And it didn't matter whether she was right or wrong. What mattered was that he'd handed her a piece of himself, and she'd cupped it in her hands. It was the sexiest thing she could've done.

When Oren called in March and said he'd just have to wait until next year, see how things shook out, Cole took the tack room apart. He overturned the desk; he ripped saddle racks from the wall; he pulled bridle hooks from the ceiling. He unzipped his pants and pissed on the whole mess, and then he walked back to the house, told Hannah to pack her bags. The Chandler boy had come through with the first ten thousand after all, and they needed to go buy some horses.

On the road, things seemed better. They'd always liked road trips, felt they were good at them. It put them both in more generous moods.

From a pay phone on the way to their first stop in Alabama, he called his sister, Kate. She was teaching at Harvard now—a biochemist, and she'd just gotten some big science grant. His father had told him about it when Cole had called to tell him about the baby. Cole played up the biogenetic part of the breeding operation, swore that she'd triple her money in the first year, and thanked her from the bottom of his heart.

He drove, and they listened to Johnny Cash and Elvis, and he kept Hannah stocked with ginger ale and Chee·tos and they talked about the horses and horse friends who were ahead of them on the road. They cursed the drivers in front of them who didn't know how hard it was for a truck and trailer to come to a sudden stop, and they waved and honked their thanks at the ones who did.

They stayed in motels with indoor pools when they could find them and made love in both beds and stayed up watching bad movies on Showtime and HBO. He got high in the truck so she wouldn't have to inhale any of the smoke and then made her come with his mouth so that both their heads could be spinning.

They pulled into barn after barn, auction after auction. He tried more horses; she watched. They held hands and talked about judging horses, about how there was no such thing as the perfect horse. How learning to judge horses meant learning to compromise, deciding which faults you could live with and which you couldn't.

They ate dinner with friends they hadn't seen in years. They touched each other under tables. They snuggled under cold covers at night in guest beds and pullout couches and relived the high points of the visits. How Carlos had said about that one mare, "She will turn on a dime and give you some change," in his particular mix of Dominican and Texan accents. How Bill Edwards had watched them at the table and had said to Missy Edwards,

"Just look at these two. Damn; I want some of what they got." How Missy Edwards had laughed her big laugh, and said, "Well, come on over then and fill up." They were reminded of how much they loved Teddy Cashin, and decided that if it was a boy, it'd be called Teddy.

They kissed each other's naked bodies and marveled at the changes in hers and what those changes did to him. Her legs, he told her, were better now. Her back, he added, was something else. He imagined them as Bonnie and Clyde, Sid and Nancy, that couple from *Sugarland Express.* He imagined she would do anything for him.

"Would you do anything for me?" he whispered to her across stiff motel pillowcases. "What do you think?" she whispered back.

On the way back, the trailer loaded, there was a scuffle at the head of the rig. To determine the damage, they had to unload nine horses to check out the tenth and eleventh. They pulled into the wide empty parking lot of a boarded-up car dealership and took turns leading their new brood off the trailer. They tied them to the side of the trailer facing away from the highway, but the animals still nickered and raised their noses, nervous at the sounds and smells of the busy road. He kept up a conversation with all of them as he unloaded. He spoke softly and calmly, as if they were all back home gathered around a campfire.

Numbers ten and eleven had lingering resentment in their eyes, but hadn't done any serious damage. Eleven was frothy with sweat and his skin quivered as he high-stepped off the ramp. Ten looked too proud of himself for his own good. "Here's our troublemaker," Cole said to Hannah, handing her the lead rope. He said it like he admired him. "Let's give them both a little walk around, and then reload," he said. He believed horses got into trouble standing still. A good walk could avoid a lot of problems.

He followed Hannah in a big random serpentine around the lot, enjoying the quiet. There was something about watching her lead a horse around that made his heart move and his throat close. She had loved horses. He knew that for sure. He tried to remind himself that her turning her back on horses didn't mean she was turning her back on him.

He let them walk longer than he needed to. The other horses snorted and shuffled and eyed them from the trailer.

He said, "We better head on." And Hannah looked back at him as if she could've led him around forever.

He loaded number eleven first, telling him things were going to be fine now; he'd worked it out with that bad boy. Then he took number ten from Hannah and while she loaded the rest, he walked in smaller circles with troublemaker and had a little chat. He knew enough about horses not to tell this proud gelding what he needed from him. Instead, he asked, with his hand on the smooth space between the horse's eyes, whether the horse could help him out. They had a few more hours to go, and he needed his help. Will you? he asked low and clear. Will you?

When Hannah was ready, he took the gelding in a small circle and started up the ramp. No go. The horse backstepped, pulling hard against the lead rope. Cole hung on to his end, but didn't insist. There was no point in going head to head with an animal this big. Instead, he told him everything was fine, and tried again. This time the gelding's head was high and back before he even had one hoof on the ramp. The other horses regarded the action from their places in the trailer.

"You're gonna act like a baby, we're gonna treat you like

a baby," Cole said, and told Hannah to go get the long lunge line on the floor of the truck cab.

She held the horse while he ran the line from his halter to the crossbar at his place in the trailer, and then he took the line back out, keeping it slack, but ready to use. He took the lead rope back from her and told her to push on the horse's rear. She did. He pulled gently on lead rope and long line. The horse snorted and stopped with three feet on the ramp. Cole praised him, petted his neck. "Praise him," he instructed Hannah. "But keep your hands on him." "Good boy," Hannah said and pushed a little stronger. The horse kicked out twice. The second one caught her between her belly and her hip. She let out a soft, "Oh," and fell to a sitting position, her hands on her belly.

"Goddamn," Cole said, still standing on the ramp. "Are you all right?"

She looked like any pregnant woman feeling her belly. "She's kicking back," she said. "I'm getting it from both sides."

The horse seemed to have instantly settled. Cole walked him up the ramp and tied him into place. He hung his head and his ears went limp as if he were ashamed. Cole praised him, closed up the back of the trailer, and went to squat by Hannah.

He lifted her jacket and shirt. There was a bruise already, but nothing too serious. "Looks like you're fine," he said.

She was pale. "I guess," she said.

He stood and offered her a hand. She took it and he pulled her easily to her feet. He held her hand and led her to the passenger side of the truck and helped her in.

Pulling back onto the driveway, he was trying to remember what he'd felt when he'd watched her go down. He had an anxious feeling, but he couldn't pin it down. It floated and moved from his gut to his fingers, from his chest to his head.

"I think I better stop at an emergency room," she said. "Just to be sure."

"Really?" he said, genuinely surprised and concerned.

She didn't say anything.

"All right," he said, scanning the side of the highway for one of those blue hospital signs. "Keep your eye out."

It wasn't until he was standing next to her, holding her hand, watching their baby thrash and kick on the ultrasound monitor that he remembered what he'd felt. He'd felt relief. Like he'd been told to miss a turn and go back to Start. Like all bets were off and anything was possible.

"You're hurting my hand," she said quietly.

He loosened his grip, stroking the top of her hand with his thumb in time to his thoughts: *This is my life, this is my life, this is my life.*

They came back home owning forty new head, and he settled down to wait for the spring grass to come in, and she settled down to wait for this baby. And they hung on to the good they'd had on the road, and he thought: *This is my life, and it's a good one,* and he told her that whenever he thought to. She'd smile and put his hand to her moving belly and remind him how lucky they were, and how that toast he'd made at their wedding had been right; they did make each other better people. "And you," he'd say to the baby. "You're going to make us the best that we've been."

In June, two weeks overdue, she went into labor. It lasted almost all day, but once she'd had the epidural and was out of pain, he wasn't nervous anymore. She took a nap. He kept one eye on the TV hanging from the ceiling and another on the monitor they'd hooked up to her. He watched the contractions make jagged little peaks on the thin strip of paper spilling out of the machine and checked to see whether she could really be sleeping through all this. It made him laugh. He imagined telling people about it afterwards. He watched all of *Gaslight* before she woke up. He smiled at her.

"Listen," she said. "I know about the money."

"What money?" he said.

"I know about Kate and the Chandler boy and the whole breeding thing not working out." She looked bored at having to go over all this.

Something connected his gut to his chest and pulled.

"You've gotta give that money back," she said. The needle on the machine flew to the top of the paper. Her expression stayed. "It's not yours. It's Kate's. She earned it for her own work."

He pointed at the paper. "You're having a contraction."

"How do you expect me to pay her back?" he asked quietly.

She smoothed the blanket over her belly, careful not to dislodge any of the monitors. "You'll have to sell the stock," she said.

"And if I sell the stock," he said, "how do you expect me to make a living this season?"

She glanced at him and then away. "There are lots of jobs," she said. "You're a grown man. You can do lots of things. When you make some money, you can go back to whatever you want, but now's not the time to be borrowing money." She leaned over and took his hand. She petted it. "It would just be a whole lot cleaner if everyone paid their own way," she said.

The cable in his chest broke, whipping through his body.

"What about your family?" he asked. "You don't seem to have any trouble borrowing from your family."

She looked at his hand and spread his fingers apart one by one. "I paid Daddy back last week," she said. "I sold some of the shares Granddad left me."

He took his hand away. "You did that because of Kate's money?"

She looked disappointed in him.

"Glad everyone's relying on their own money here," he said.

She lay back against the pillows and closed her eyes. They sat there like that for what seemed to him way too long.

The doctor came in trailing two nurses behind him. He checked Hannah out and announced it was time to push. Cole held her hand or her head; each nurse took a leg. She pushed and pushed.

"Well," the doctor said, rooting around on his tray for the appropriate tool. "This baby just doesn't want to move."

Cole scanned the doctor's tray, imagining uses for those things having nothing to do with babies.

The doctor tried the regular forceps, and when those didn't work resorted to the thing that looked to Cole like a miniature toilet plunger. The doctor gripped and pulled. The plunger came flying away from the baby's head, sending a spray of who knows what around all of them. Everyone was splattered. Cole looked down at himself. The wall behind him was covered. The chair beside him was covered, but he himself, was completely clean.

The doctor gave it another try and in a matter of minutes, Cole had a baby girl. Mathilda Baker Thompson. But already the hope that she'd make them better people seemed like it was moving away from him at a steady canter. Because what he now understood about Hannah was that she was a player right along with him, and they were each making move after move, unable to stop, unable even to recognize the game they found themselves in. So the next day, when he placed a careful chair beneath the hospital room's doorknob and crawled into her bed with her, running his hand gently up the curve of her thigh, her side, stopping with his palm resting against her neck, she didn't say a word. She didn't even try.

∽ EIGHT ∽

October 1988

JACKSON'S BODY WAS NOTHING LIKE COLE'S, BUT IT WAS familiar in its own way. It held childhood and reliability and first love and things that seemed like they'd belonged to another Hannah in another life.

It was October of 1988. Hannah had been married for nine years. Jackson had been back in her life since the spring. She'd confronted Cole about some rumors about him and the woman at the feed store. He'd denied everything and said it was about time they thought about starting a family. Jackson had never really gone anywhere. He'd been working for her father's firm since graduating from law school. And last spring she'd looked up and there he was, right in her line of vision.

They went to Jackson's place, just blocks from her parents' house, or sometimes, when he could convince her to let him splurge on her, they went to fancy hotels in Cincinnati or Lexington. He'd just been made partner at the firm and had more money than he knew what to do with. "Why," she'd ask him time after time, "do you want to spend the money for a whole night in a hotel when we're only going to be there a couple of hours?"

Because she asked questions like that, he'd tell her, coming around to open the car door for her in another driveway in another hotel.

He liked her practicality; he liked her emotional pragmatism, but he treated her like a horse he was trying to bring in from pasture: sugar in the outstretched hand. She wasn't used to feeling that way. Since hitching her star to Cole, she was more like a golden retriever: *Here I am. Here I am. Pet me, pet me, pet me.*

Today they were at his place. In ten years, it would look like her parents' house and the houses of her parents' friends. It was new. The paint colors were historically accurate. The moldings were clean and well painted. The blinds moved smoothly on their tracks. She could open the windows with one hand.

It was a Tuesday. Cole was at a meeting with the banker in town. Hannah needed to be home by four. It was two. Jackson had taken the afternoon off. Yesterday, she and Cole had thrown away her diaphragm, the culmination of his let's-start-a-family campaign. His idea had been to have sex every day for two months, and if they got pregnant, they got pregnant, and if they didn't, they didn't. He'd been pleased with himself, and Hannah had resisted saying something catty about the feed-store woman. Instead, she'd said, "How's that any different than our regular sex life?" and he'd looked even more pleased with himself, and had taken her in his arms, put his nose in her hair, and said, "Don't you want to see what you and I could make together?"

Her heart had done its thing, and she'd given in.

She understood that it was not the smart thing to have done. She tried not to think about it too much, though when she did, she thrilled herself with her dangerous behavior.

She hadn't told Jackson. He was sleeping next to her under his matching sheets and duvet in masculine combinations of dark greens and blues. They'd just made love. He always made love under the sheets. He couldn't sleep without something covering him. Sometimes she uncovered herself and they slept like a new pair of shoes S-wrapped in tissue paper in a shoe box.

Cole's feet hung off the end of every bed they'd slept in. Jackson had a good two feet at the end of his. His legs were short and strong. His torso was solid and strong. She knew these things without having to look. His neck was solid and strong. His head and face were what you'd expect to find at the top of a body like his. Intelligent eyes so dark they were almost black. A round face, a soft mouth. He adored her body. He could spend hours on her shins. He got a glassy look when he looked at her naked, like he was on drugs. Sometimes, with Cole, she felt like all her curves were in the wrong places, but he was with her for other reasons anyway.

The light in Jackson's house was a deeper yellow than at her place. As he slept, she tried to figure out whether it was the window glass or the actual sun. It looked more gilded, more full of the good things sunlight was supposed to bring.

A starling, then a jay, took turns on the feeder outside. She could still feel Jackson inside of her. She was wet from him. He made love in careful and caring ways. It brought back slow dances with him in high school. Even her short arms could've gone almost twice around his skinny waist. He hadn't been much taller than she, and he'd talk quietly into her ear while they danced, usually about basketball or music. She imagined what their child would be like. A sober little boy who looked like his father. She imagined what her child with Cole would look like. A boisterous, poised little girl who would have Cole's hair and eyes, and take

her mother's side in all disagreements. She imagined Cole watching her give birth to Jackson's son. All these thoughts made her
feel things that she didn't think people on the edge of being
mothers should feel.

She reached under the covers and stroked Jackson's thighs and
penis with her fingertips. She cupped him in her hand and felt
him grow without waking. She folded the covers back and watched
him sleep. She thought about taking his picture. *See,* she could
say, *you* can *sleep without the covers.* She thought about what the lawyer
in him would say to that.

She climbed on top of him and fitted herself against him, moving slowly. She imagined herself as Cole, sexually voracious and
risky. She leaned over him, her small breasts pressing against his
curly chest hair, and whispered, "Hey, wake up. I want to fuck."

She never called it that with Cole.

He opened his eyes and took her face in his hands. "Don't call
it that," he said.

When they'd started this whole thing, she'd forbidden love
talk. This was not about love, she'd told him right from the
beginning. And even if it was, that didn't matter. She had a life;
she had a husband. That wasn't what this was about. She told herself she'd been up-front and honest with Jackson. He'd known
going in what he could and couldn't expect from her. So now she
shook her head as she adjusted her hips, putting herself around
him. "No, baby," she said, thinking of the baby that might be
inside her, thinking of how she hadn't called Cole baby in the
longest time. "It's *like* love."

Her mother had some questions. Hannah was helping her do her
fall decorating. This involved pumpkins and squash and Indian

corn and strings of dried red peppers on the front porch, and
dried flowers cascading out of the cornucopia horn Aurelia had
gotten at the Christmas Tree Shop. She didn't come from money,
and she'd made a life out of decorating on a four-dollar budget
before she'd met Hannah's father, and she didn't see the
necessity in stopping just because she'd happened to marry a
lucky man.

Aurelia was plucking at the dried flowers. Hannah was arranging cranberries and floating candles in a shallow glass bowl. Outside, a team of workers was raking the massive lawn. One of them
was under her favorite tree, the shagbark oak. His feet disappeared into the pile of yellow-green leaves. She recognized him as
someone from her high school.

"What's the story with Jackson Ellis?" Aurelia asked, snipping
the ends off a bunch of lavender with her garden scissors.

Hannah poked at the floating cranberries with her finger, then
licked it. "What do you mean?" she asked, trying to sound calm.
Since the first time she'd slept with him, she'd been waiting for the
moment when she'd have to explain herself. But it had been more
than five months, and no one had asked for any explanations.

"I'm not an idiot," Aurelia said.

"I didn't say you were," Hannah answered.

"But you thought it," her mother said. "You think it. I know
what you and Cole say to each other when you leave this house,"
she said, without anger.

"Cole and I barely talk about you," Hannah said. And it was
true. Talking about her parents made him crazy.

"How nice," Aurelia said, without looking up, her South
Carolina accent just that much stronger.

Hannah rolled her eyes.

"Don't roll your eyes at me," she said.

Hannah dumped the candles into the bowl. Some of them bobbed upside down. "How do you do that?" she asked. She knew most people in this world were more perceptive than she was, but she found it unpleasantly jarring every time her mother turned out to be one of those people.

"It's a gift," her mother said, stuffing the bunch of lavender between the black-eyed Susans and the eucalyptus branches.

Hannah's father walked in carrying the Sunday paper in one hand and his reading glasses in the other. He was wearing the slippers that she had gotten him when she was ten. When the daffodils appeared, he put them on the top shelf of his closet. When the leaves started to fall, he took them down again. The fact that he still wore them could move her to tears.

He smiled and kissed the top of her head. He surveyed the table's mess. "Must be fall," he said. "Thank God you do this, Aurelia. I'd likely lose all track of where I was in the world."

Aurelia snapped her garden gloves at him, but she was smiling, and Hannah knew that in his own way he was telling the truth for both of them.

"We're discussing what Hannah ought to do about Jackson Ellis," Aurelia said.

"Mama," Hannah said.

Pell cleared his throat and shifted his paper from hand to hand. "Well," he said. "I've always liked Jackson Ellis." He cleared his throat again and left the room.

"So have I," Aurelia said. "So have I. So I think you better just make up your mind. If you're going to go, you go, and do it before you have kids. You're lucky Cole hasn't wanted kids already."

It maddened Hannah that their childlessness was always attrib-

uted to Cole, never to her. But she never corrected her mother
on it. There was no point in correcting her mother on anything.

"I'm not sleeping with Jackson Ellis," Hannah said.

Aurelia lowered her head and waved her hands around her
ears like she was shooing gnats. "Oh, for heaven's sake, Hannah, I
don't want to know about that." She reached across and touched
Hannah's arm. "I just want you to know that Jackson Ellis is much
more suited to you than Cole ever was or ever will be. You
should've married Jackson years ago."

Hannah looked at her mother's delicate hand and fought back
her usual arguments.

"You were meant to be with someone like Jackson," her
mother added before going back to snipping and plucking. She
stopped suddenly and looked up, her shears in midair. "Jackson
is the kind of person you're supposed to love. And not because
he's the good provider and the safe choice. Jackson thinks about
you before he thinks about himself. Cole Thompson is all about
desire. That's a disastrous quality in a life partner. You know
that better than anyone. Even you know that to be God's honest
truth."

And she was right; Hannah did, better than she knew almost
anything.

When she miscarried the week before Thanksgiving, she told no
one except her doctor. She hadn't told anyone she was pregnant.
She didn't know who the father was, and she'd spent two weeks
worrying the question like a rock in her hand. She'd thought about
getting rid of it. She'd thought about staying with Cole and having

it with him. She'd thought about leaving for Jackson and having it with him. She'd prayed for all her decisions to be made for her. And now one of them had been.

She was by herself in the house, standing over the kitchen counter, when the first cramps came. She felt as if she were being pushed roughly from behind. She steadied herself against the counter and waited for the next round. When it came, she put her head on the counter and held her back with one hand, her belly with the other. For an instant, the pain brought back the abortion she and Cole had had before they were married. It had been Cole's idea; she'd wanted the baby. The first time they'd arrived at the clinic for the abortion, the nurses had sent her home, her ambivalence way too clear. The second time, she'd convinced them all. She'd made Cole's desire her own, even convincing herself for a while. The pain, she thought, standing at the kitchen counter, is punishment. And relief.

She drove herself to the doctor's office. She could feel the blood seeping through her underwear. She dragged a saddle blanket from the floor of the car under her butt. She was torn between driving fast and driving slowly to be safe. She ended up riding the accelerator and the brake like an old woman.

There was the tiny nut of a baby on the ultrasound screen.

"Well, there it is," her doctor said. He moved the vaginal ultrasound probe around a little.

She found herself embarrassed at the blood that must've been getting on everything.

He stopped moving and put his hand over her cold ankle. "I'm not seeing a heartbeat," he said quietly. He kept his hand on her ankle. She was glad for it. "I'm sorry," he said.

His nurse, waiting at a discreet distance in the corner of the room, looked sorry too. The doctor told her to take her time getting dressed, and he'd meet her in his office to talk about what to do next.

When she was alone, she hunted around in the drawers under the exam table for a maxi pad. With her underwear turned inside out and lined with a pad, she felt almost clean.

She had two choices. She could do nothing and wait for nature to take its course. That meant waiting for the body to expel the tissue on its own, the doctor explained.

The tissue, she thought.

That could take a few days, or even a week or more. Or she could do a D and C right now. She'd be uncomfortable for a day or two, but then fine. And, the doctor added, could the nurse get in touch with anyone for her?

She told the doctor Cole was out of town, but her mother was on her way. She lied, and took door number two. She found herself in another room, with a primitive-looking machine that seemed to consist of an oversized glass jar and an assortment of clear tubes. There was a red bucket in the corner marked Medical Waste in white letters. There was a mobile of biplanes over her head. The nurse was back in her corner.

The familiarity of the scene was disturbing and reassuring. She anticipated the doctor's explanations before they came. She heard the sound of the machine before it was turned on. She reached for the nurse's hand because that's what she had done the last time. The pain was as she remembered it, and she was surprised as the details of the first time came back. She would've said she'd banished them, put them away. It felt like a double failure, and she let anger at Cole ride through her in long, reaching strides. But with each grab and pinch at her insides something else jockeyed into position. Anger at herself. A person like her didn't deserve to be a mother; a person like her deserved this. And the pull of her baby separating from her self was just right, equal parts blessing and curse.

Jackson wanted to marry her. It was the week between Christmas and New Year's and he was on his knees by his dining room table. She was sitting in her chair. A take-away dinner from the gourmet place on the corner was spread out in front of them. There was wine. There were candles. Outside, the branches of the spruce swept the window.

"I'm already married," she said, refusing to take the ring box.

"Not happily," he said from his knees.

"Happily enough," she said.

He put his head in her lap and waited for her to stroke his hair. "There isn't enough happiness for you," he said, sounding just like himself.

"I have just the right amount," she said, surprised again at the softness of his thick hair.

After the miscarriage, she'd started using her diaphragm again. She'd tell Cole both things, she thought, at some point.

"You're part of that happiness," she said. It seemed like a nice thing to say. So many years with Cole had made it harder to remember how to play any game but their own.

He stood up and went back to his chair, slipping the ring box into his shirt pocket. It bulged there above his heart. She'd read a book recently about the symbolism of everyday objects. There'd been a chapter devoted to engagement rings. The chapter had ended with a woman who'd been unhappily married for fifty years saying that she'd come to understand that her ambivalence towards her ring had signified ambivalence towards other things. Hannah had laughed out loud. "Duh," she'd enjoyed saying to herself. "Duh, duh, duh."

Jackson was playing with the dripping wax on the candles. It was the one obvious way he reminded her of Cole. She watched him for a minute. Why couldn't she have another life? she thought. She didn't even have to think to imagine years with Jackson spreading out in front of her. She worked harder to imagine what her time with Cole would then become—a blip on the otherwise smooth and patternless lawn that her life should have been and now would be again. She'd tell stories about him at dinner parties that she and Jackson would become famous for throwing. He'd be her bad boy, the boy in the leather jacket whom every girl wanted. The other wives would smile knowingly and blush and Hannah would smile with them and take Jackson's hand to her mouth, kissing him knuckle by knuckle.

She took a piece of wax from the pile he had going by his plate. She pinched the piece into the shape of a heart and slid it back across to him.

He picked it up and balanced it on the end of his index finger.

"Can I think about it?" she asked.

He kept his finger out. It was like he was pointing a gun at someone across the table.

"I'm giving you all I can right now," she said, sounding meaner than she meant to. "You deserve way better than me," she added. It was what Cole used to say to her in the first few months together. Did she want to be with Cole, or did she want to be Cole?

He folded the heart into his fist and held it on the table like he was going to throw dice. "There's no better than you," he said simply.

He believed that, and it broke her heart in all sorts of ways for all sorts of reasons. He valued her more than she valued herself. She had been presented with someone like that, and, still, she was hesitating.

After that, she couldn't stop herself from keeping a running score sheet in her mind. She pictured it like a page from a bookkeeping ledger. Every experience became an asset or an expense.

She and Jackson picnicked by the river and he rose suddenly from their blanket, waded in up to his khakied thighs, and came out cupping a drowning bee in his hand.

Cole went out of town for two days without telling her where and left a silver bracelet she'd admired in a store window the week before under her pillow.

Jackson reduced a hotel clerk who'd screwed up their reservations to tears.

Cole woke her in the middle of the night, threw a coat over her nightgown, carried her to the barn, and told her to keep her eyes closed. When she opened them, she'd been placed carefully in a warm stall banked high with clean straw, and a newborn foal was in her lap, awkward as a greyhound.

Some days the men surprised her, some days they didn't. She stopped trusting herself to know which column behavior should go in. She was looking through a kaleidoscope. Everything depended on the position of the lens and angle of the light.

For a week in February, she moved in with her parents, telling both men that her mother was sick. Cole said he didn't see why she had to spend the nights. Jackson said he'd be happy to pay for a private nurse.

She lay on her twin bed still made up with those pink chambray sheets and waited for the comfort of her old room to

reappear. Stuffed animals whose names she'd forgotten, her
Brownie uniform folded and stored in a clear plastic bag, the
Around the World doll collection her father had added to one
by one every birthday: all of them turned out to offer not comfort but more of the suffocation she'd been feeling in both her
men's houses.

A week into her stay, her father appeared in the bedroom doorway and waited for her to open her eyes. She had a fantasy of him
announcing he'd solved everything. And why not? she thought. It
could be like when she was a kid, and would come home with a tale
of woe from school and her mother and father would listen and
cluck sympathetically, and tell her to do this, and not that, and
she'd feel better even though she knew she might never take their
advice.

Why couldn't somebody appear to take care of her? Her eyes
were still closed, but tears were running down her face to her ears.

He shifted his weight, making the doorsill creak. "Your
mother sent me up," he said.

She squeezed her eyes tighter, making the tears run faster.

"Not really sure what she expects of me," he said. He jingled
the change in his pocket. "I'm not going to tell you what I think
you should do," he said, as if arguing.

She opened her eyes. "I wish you would," she said. "I wish
someone would." Just expressing the desire made her cry harder.

His face was a flickering screen of different emotions. He'd
spent his life giving her what she asked for. But every time she had
trouble making a judgment, coming to a decision, she'd been
offered the same expression. How, his face always said, had a
daughter of his not inherited the decision making that came so
easily to him? He was baffled.

French or Spanish lessons, violin or piano, ballet or gymnastics, sweet sixteen party or trip to Europe. All the way back to home-work sessions at the breakfast table where she tried to decide which letter came after the *A* in apple. He'd get that face and then he'd walk her through how one made the right decisions. Sometimes he used paper and pencil. Sometimes he drew in the air with his hands. And she had tried; it wasn't that she grew petulant and sassy and gave up. She followed his pencil with her eyes; she lis-tened to his careful words, and understood them. But at the breakfast table, and for her whole life, when she tried to do it on her own, her mind shut down with the hisses and clanks of a fac-tory going dark.

Lying there crying under the eye of her kind father, she couldn't think of a major decision she'd made on her own.

And then she could. She saw herself, a college senior, at the sorority's pay phone, making the unexpected call to Cole. Saying yes to Cole. That was all her own. It had been some kind of tip-ping point. She'd been making smaller versions of that decision over and over ever since.

Her father's hands were still in his pockets. He hadn't stepped into her room. Her mother's sounds came from downstairs. He raised his toes and lowered them. "Making decisions isn't a com-plicated thing," he said. His eyes were filled with love for her. "What will make you happy?" he asked. "That's all you have to know."

In his voice it sounded so easy; it always had, but to someone who'd spent most of her life finding herself in places she hadn't sought out but had been handed, it was like listening to a foreign language.

It wasn't a matter of knowing *what* she wanted. It was a matter of knowing *how* to want.

Had she said yes to Cole because she'd believed he would make her happy? Why had she wanted him? Her mother had been right: Cole was all about desire, and there was nothing like being the object of that desire. Girls glanced his way. Girls wanted him. All those girls must've known something.

She wiped her face. Her inability to know how to want had its source in a lot of things, but one of them was the precise, gentle man in front of her.

"Well," he said. "I can see I've certainly made things better up here. I suppose I'll go downstairs and receive your mother's disappointment."

Hannah smiled. Her nose was running. "I'm okay," she said. "I'll be down in a minute."

"We're looking forward to it," he said, turning and closing her door behind him.

In March, Cole stopped in midlovemaking and looked down at her. "What the hell?" he said. "I can feel your diaphragm."

She'd been waiting for this.

He propped himself on straight arms above her. He was still inside of her. He was still hard. "Got something you want to say?" he asked.

"Is there anything I could say that would make you lose an erection?" she said, not expecting an answer.

"Don't be a wiseass," he said. "You could tell me you don't love me enough to have a baby with me. You could tell me that all that talk about wanting to see what a person made out of us would be like was just junk," he said. He was genuinely hurt.

It seemed like all she was doing this year was hurting people. "I don't think that'd do it," she said, knowing she was making it worse. The affair seemed to make her more aggressive with everyone.

He rolled off her.

It was the middle of the day. That was the joy of the off-season; they were around each other in the middle of the day with nothing to do. The windows were open. She could smell new grass. She imagined large nests of garden spiders hatching in her garden.

"I want to have a baby with you," she said. "I'm just not sure now is the right time."

He stared up at the ceiling fan. "You got something else you're working on?" he said.

She'd always thought her parents' money was the only way to feel any pull over him. Even when she'd started up with Jackson, it hadn't occurred to her that this would hurt him, though she knew now that she'd hoped it would. Proof that she mattered. The beam of his headlight trained right on her, blackness everywhere else.

She touched him on the arm and told him about the miscarriage, and he looked exactly like he should've looked, said exactly what he should've said. She told him how it had made her think of that abortion from years ago, and he looked exactly how he should've looked, did exactly what he should've done. And maybe because he was doing and saying all the right things, she told him about Jackson, and he said "Oh," and "I just talked to him at the Christmas party," and "Well, what do you think you'll go ahead and do, then?" And "Goddamn, Hannah. I didn't think you had it in you."

And then he just lay there, his legs crossed at the ankles, his hands lighting and holding a cigarette.

She watched him and thought of all his one-night stands and longers that she knew about and the ones she didn't. That was just Cole; it didn't mean anything about the two of them, she always told herself, because that's what he told her. She wondered what she wanted from him. Had she started back up with Jackson because she wanted to get what was missing, or because she'd wanted to incite it in Cole?

But he didn't say anything, so finally, she said, "I do have it in me, and I don't know what I'm gonna do."

The next week, there was urine in Jackson's car. He could smell it, and figured it was kids playing pranks, or a confused animal.

The week after that they came back from their favorite hotel in Lexington and found the back window open. Nothing was missing, but the house had been gone through. You could feel the disturbance rather than see it. He called the police, and she didn't tell anyone that she could smell Cole in the air. While Jackson gave what little information he had to the patrolmen, she walked around the house following the scent of tobacco and sweat.

When the police left, Jackson told her with a smile that the officers had assumed they were married. Then he told her that they'd said the two of them should be careful. This kind of thing was worse than a straight-up robbery. This was the kind of thing someone really off liked to do.

"I'm sure it is," she said. Her stomach was like choppy water.

He stood there looking at her. His expression was one she hadn't seen before, at least not directed at her.

"What?" she said.

He waited a moment longer. "What do you think?" he said.

She shrugged.

He shrugged back at her, then pulled her down onto the living room rug and started undressing her. "Let's reclaim the house," he said.

They'd made love in the living room before, but not like this.

He didn't get a couch pillow for her head, or a blanket for under her hips. He took her skirt and panties off, and sat back on his heels to take in her half-dressed body. "How can you stay with this guy?" he said.

She closed her eyes. She felt like she'd been avoiding his question her whole life. She thought about trying to explain the ache she felt in her joints when Cole's attention turned elsewhere. It was like he'd asked why she needed the cells in her body, the ligaments.

"I haven't decided yet," she said.

"That's what I mean," he said.

When she asked Cole about it, he said he'd wanted to smell her in that guy's house. He could tell, he said, which rooms she spent the most time in. He'd smelled the sheets, he said. He'd smelled the seams of the living room chairs. The fringe on the fireplace rug.

That they'd wanted and done the same things thrilled her. He was dangerous, she thought. So was she, and not just because she'd chosen him but on her own terms.

She got pregnant the second time while using the diaphragm. The doctor said she could do an ad for fertility.

This time she had an abortion. Again without telling anyone, again in that same room. Because this time she knew who the father was.

On a clear Saturday night in April, she stood in the darkness of Jackson's porch watching him move around the living room. She'd

decided a week earlier that she was staying with Cole. Jackson
didn't know. Neither did Cole.

His front windows were a triptych of yellow light. She could
hear Bruce Springsteen. She squatted in the shadow of one of the
pillars. Her nose was cold, but she couldn't see her breath.

He was opening cartons and unloading and arranging books
onto a wall of shelves he'd just had built. Every so often he inter-
spersed the books with an object he pulled out of one of the
boxes. All the stuff had been in his basement for years. He'd told
her he was glad to be getting them out into the air.

He stood with his hands on his hips, surveying the shelves.
They were cherry, with walnut trim. He ran his hand along
the edge of one. He was wearing his at-home project clothes:
black soccer sweats and a blue long-sleeved T-shirt. There was a
glass of bourbon on the coffee table. There was a pizza box on
the floor. She could see the flicker of the TV from the family
room.

He paused over a Paul Klee book. He loved art, she thought.
He loved photography. She saw some glossy coffee table books
about guitars. He added them to the stacks around his feet. She
didn't immediately understand his sorting system.

He looked glumly at the torn dust jacket of a tall thin book.
She thought she recognized a Cowboys uniform on the cover. He
added it to a stack of football books he thumped onto the bottom
shelf, and then dusted them with a rag he pulled from his back
pocket. The gesture of a magician.

He sipped his drink and scanned the piles. Some were chest-
high. Some were piles of one. He tapped his fingers against his
thigh to the music. He tapped his toes. He was wearing white ath-
letic socks.

He went into the TV room and stayed there for a while. She

compared the living room without him to the living room with him. "Oh, man," she heard him say. She knew he was watching the Final Four. The Hated Kentucky was playing tonight.

He came back in hefting two unopened boxes and squatted to set them down next to the shelves. Then he got distracted by an open box to his left, pulling out two brightly painted Mexican sculptures, a fish and an armadillo. The armadillo was missing a front leg. He set it on a shelf and went into the kitchen. It tipped over while he was gone. He came back with a chopstick and a knife. He eyeballed the chopstick against the other front leg, sawed it with the knife, and twisted it into place. He arranged it so the chopstick leg was hidden by the fish.

Hannah was getting cold. She hadn't planned to be outside this long. Cole was at a polo tournament in Tennessee. She'd planned to surprise Jackson, give him the bad news as easily as she could. But now here she was on his porch with no plans to move one way or another.

He was on the couch, his feet up on the coffee table. Taking a break or finished? He flipped through a magazine. Minutes passed. He tossed the magazine onto the floor and looked around. He seemed surprised to find himself in the midst of this mess. He pushed at a box with his knee. He peered into another as if it held someone else's belongings.

He went to the stereo. He squatted in front of his CD collection, deciding. None of them seemed to please him. Hannah shifted her weight from foot to foot in her squat. Van Morrison came muffled through the windows.

He wiped his brow and the back of his neck with his rag and then attacked one of the taller piles. He shelved them at eye-level, the tallest at either end until the shortest met in the center like a suspension bridge.

He leaned a photo of himself and his twin brother at eight in front of a book called *Volcano!*

She thought she should go. She could give him the bad news later. She stood. He was putting his boyhood collection of Peanuts cartoons on the top shelf. He kept them from toppling with the skull of a hornbill. He ran his hands roughly through his hair, like it was a long drive and he needed to stay awake.

The shape of the windows, the darkness of the porch, the quiet of the front yard all made her feel as if she were watching a movie in an empty theater. She moved towards the big center window, squinting at the light. He propped what looked like a framed tarantula against his Jim Harrison collection. A Brownie camera went in front of Edward Weston's journals. A cow skull faced a horse skull on the bottom shelf.

She was close to the glass. She'd always wanted to do this at the movies: get so close that it wasn't just her looking at them. Two dogs barked at each other down the street. She backed away.

Jackson turned, wiping his hands on the rag, and pushed the empty boxes aside with his foot. He looked up, smiling at something. She kept her eyes on him. He couldn't see her. She strained against blinking. And she returned the smile.

Jackson wanted to know if there was anything he could say to change her mind. In the midst of being utterly destroyed, that was the sentence that came out of his mouth. At the same time that she knew it was sentences like this one that were the reason she was leaving, she also knew that they had been the reason she had gotten with him in the first place.

It was late April and they were in his garden, sitting uncomfortably in his wrought-iron patio furniture. The wildflower patch was just coming to life. She noted that his azaleas looked healthier than hers did at home. He had his legs open wide; his fingers were laced, his arms hung between his legs. Cole was waiting for her back at the house. They'd gone over what she should say.

Jackson looked up, a sudden idea across his face. "What is it that you want?" he said. "I can offer it."

She shook her head. "You can't," she said. "It's why I love you, but why I can't be with you," she said.

His head was back down. "Now she gives me love talk," he said.

She turned her glass of lemonade around and around on the table.

"What the hell, Hannah," he said. "I'm doomed."

The "what the hell" sounded like Cole. The rest didn't.

"No, you're not," she said.

He nodded. "I've known you since nursery school," he said. "Where else am I going to find those kind of years," he said. It wasn't a question.

She closed her eyes and took in the smell of the magnolia, the fresh mulch she'd watched the gardener spread last week. It was spring, but it was post-Derby spring. The Pegasus Parade, the balloon race, the Oaks. It was post-everything. She tried to recall the color of the saddle pad on the horse she had favored at Dawn at the Downs. She opened her eyes. "You'll find it in a girl who's crazy about you," she said.

"I want *you* to be that girl," he said. He leaned forward and looked at her in a way that suggested he could make her. It almost made her change her mind.

Sparrows hopped beneath the table, picking at the crumbs from their half-eaten sandwiches. An ant went for something the birds had overlooked.

"Why can't you be with me?" he asked, sadness and bitterness spread across his face.

She marveled at her power.

He didn't wait for her to answer. "You weren't thinking about it," he said. "You said you were, but you weren't."

The words felt harsher coming from him. "That's not true," she said weakly.

His rage was doing things to his face and hands. He was speaking the way he spoke about a client's innocence or guilt. "You knew going in that you weren't leaving," he said. "You treated me like a jerk, and I let you."

Arguing with someone who'd known her since nursery school seemed pointless.

"It's exactly the way you and Cole work." He was sitting on his hands. "It's pathetic." He sounded equally enraged at her and at himself.

"What kind of woman stays with that guy?" he asked. "Tell me." He wasn't angry with himself anymore.

"Jackson," she said.

"No, really," he said. "Jesus Christ, Hannah, we made fun of girls like that in high school. We felt sorry for them."

She knew what he was talking about. All those girls who went out with the football players, tried to work their way up to the quarterback. All those girls who ended up in tears in the hallways. Why are they surprised? she and Jackson used to marvel to each other. How can they be surprised?

She tried to think of arguments that would sway his lawyer mind. "I'm not one of those girls," she said. "He doesn't treat me like a jerk. I know what his flaws are. He knows what mine are. We make each other better people." Out loud, the arguments sounded silly and unconvincing.

"You are so much better than who you are with him," he said.

She didn't have anything to say to that.

He snorted.

"You know how love is," she said. She did sound like one of those girls. "Everything else is like being outside a locked door," she said, registering the cruelty and truth as she said it.

She could feel his love strung between them. "What's wrong with you?" he asked.

He looked like a good explanation might make him feel better. "I don't have to explain it to you," she said.

This wasn't going the way she'd planned when she and Cole had talked about it. "I just do," she said, standing and brushing crumbs from her skirt.

He stayed sitting. "Well, then you're sick," he said. "You're both sick."

She wasn't sure she could explain it to herself. But all those years ago, she had chosen Cole, and he had chosen her. And his choice had made her into something she'd never imagined being. You didn't just walk away from something like that.

This time she snipped her diaphragm to pieces with her kitchen scissors in front of him, both of them watching the jagged rubber pieces fall into the bathroom wastebasket. When she did it, she thought of what she could say to her mother and her father and everyone else who thought they knew who suited her best and why. She thought with pride of how she'd turned out different from the way anyone had expected.

When they began to make love, Cole asked if she was sure. And she said, "I said I was staying. If I'm staying, there's no reason not to."

And he said, burying his face in her neck, "I'm a dead man without you."

And she thought, *I've become the kind of woman who's got Cole Thompson saying things like that.* And there would be a pregnancy to make him say even better things. And a baby that would be all blessing, no curse.

"Say it again," she said, holding his head with her hand.

And he did.

Look at me, she thought. *Look at me.*

NINE

August 2000

THE MEETING WITH THE JUDGE HAD TO BE POSTPONED another week. Something in the judge's life. Mattie was glad, but then she wasn't. More waiting wasn't good. Everyone wanted to have a little talk or a private chat. Just tell the truth, Hannah and Cole both said, but she knew what they meant.

Now she was at her mother's working her way through a pile of rental movies, all Westerns. She'd already seen *High Noon* and *My Darling Clementine.* She liked the part where Clementine and an all-shaved-and-perfumed Henry Fonda stands on the porch and Clementine breathes in, and says, "Smell those desert flowers," and Henry Fonda has to say, "That's me."

She noted without interest that the hero always turned out to be the guy who'd given the horse a lump of sugar. She noticed in *True Grit* that the girl's name was Mattie.

Her mother stood behind the couch watching her watch the end of *The Unforgiven.* "Are you going to watch TV for the rest of your life?" she asked.

"I might," Mattie said, rewinding. She readjusted Potpie on her lap. He opened one eye, then closed it, sighing.

"Not on my watch," Hannah said.

Mattie turned up the volume a notch.

"Mattie," her mother said sadly.

Mattie remembered something Lois had said on their most recent trip to the hospital: it didn't help to add insult to injury. She hadn't explained. She'd just said, "Just do your bit to ease things all around. Not more than your bit. Just your little bit."

Without turning around, Mattie said that she'd watch this one and then do something else.

Her mother sighed and said that sounded good, and came around to sit on the couch for the end of the movie.

The movie ended. The TV screen went blue. The VCR started rewinding on its own.

She liked just sitting there next to her mother. It seemed normal.

"So," Hannah said. "How're you doing?"

"Good," Mattie said.

"Do you want to make Sculpey?"

"Maybe," Mattie said, not moving off the couch. She held Potpie's ears up and waved them. He let her.

"Do you want to play a board game?"

"Maybe," Mattie said. Her mother always won.

"How are things going at your father's?"

She felt a combination of wariness and excitement whenever one house asked about the other. She tried to keep still, to keep her insides from moving in their underground ways.

"Good," she said, trying to sound like there wasn't a lot she was leaving out.

"How's Georgia?" her mother asked.

Her father had told her he was meeting with the doctors to talk about some idea they had. Something that might help. "The same," she said.

Hannah sighed as if she knew what that meant. "Must be hard on Cole," she said.

Mattie couldn't remember the last time her mother had said something kind about him. She never called him Cole anymore. Always "your father." Her skin sent off tingles of warning, like the time Celia had dared her to touch the electric fence around the back pasture.

Her mother just sat there. She reached out to rub Potpie's curled back.

Mattie felt like her whole life was spent waiting for what would come next.

"You know," she said, "I didn't mean to name him Potpie."

"Oh?" her mother said. "What did you mean to name him?"

She palmed the dog's head. "Fatty."

Her mother smiled and put her hand on top of Mattie's on top of the dog's head. "How does your father seem?" she asked.

He was losing weight. He checked himself on the scale in the bathroom every morning. He nicked himself twice a shave. He let phone calls go unreturned. He wasn't going to Saratoga this month. She couldn't remember an August he hadn't gone. She'd gone with him once. She remembered large shade trees and a good breeze. The only place he seemed like himself was the barn. She'd hung out down there just to be around a dad she recognized.

"Hello?" her mother said.

"Ask him yourself," Mattie said.

Her mother looked over at her. "*You* don't seem so good," she said.

Mattie didn't say anything.

"I found your sheets," her mother said.

Mattie had wet her bed three times in the last two weeks. She'd balled the dirty sheets up and stuffed them in the back of her closet. She'd known her mother would find them, but she couldn't think of what else to do.

Last year, she'd been poking around in Hannah's room and found a box of condoms in the nightstand drawer. She opened one up and took it out. She'd been so grossed out that she'd flung it across the room. It had landed in the corner behind the closet door. She'd known she should've thrown it away, but she couldn't bring herself to. She couldn't even bring herself to touch the wrapper. When her mother asked about it, she said she didn't know anything. She'd said it until her mother had stopped asking.

Now she thought about lying again.

But her mother was already talking. "I'm not mad," she said. "I'm worried. You're quiet. You're using your inhaler way more than usual. I hear you up at night. You're not eating well."

She didn't know which was worse: having her mother's attention or not having it. She pulled Potpie closer. "*I'm* fine," she said. "You're the one who's not acting like herself."

It was true. Hannah was paying closer attention, looking at her all the time. It was like her mother had turned into someone quieter, someone who moved slowly.

"I try all the time not to be like myself," her mother said. She didn't seem to expect a response. "Maybe you should talk to someone," she said.

"I'm *always* quiet," Mattie said.

She went to the trunk in the corner of the living room. Potpie looked offended and then resettled on Hannah's lap. At the bottom of the trunk was her parents' wedding album. She pulled it out.

"Oh, Goose," Hannah said. "What are you doing with that?"

Mattie knew the only reason this had survived was because the school psychologist had told her mother that it wasn't a good idea to destroy *everything*. At least it wasn't a good idea *for Mattie*.

They had looked at it once way before the divorce. They'd giggled making fun of those earlier versions of Hannah and Cole. Hannah in her homemade eyelet dress, her crown of daisies. Cole in his royal blue cowboy shirt and good jeans. Her mother had said she'd always thought Robert Redford would play him in the movie. Mattie hadn't known who Robert Redford was, but she'd agreed anyway. Cole had walked by and heard them, and had said, "Too damn short. Nothing but a wannabe." He'd stood in front of them and struck a movie-star pose. He'd swung Hannah up out of the couch. They'd sung a song and danced around the living room. Mattie had sat on the couch, waiting for them to finish and sit next to her and go through the album and tell her the stories behind the pictures. And they had.

She'd rediscovered the album hunting around for something to do with Jackson the day of the hearing.

In the back, Hannah and Cole had stuck a copy of the ceremony. She'd read it for the first time last week. "I've got some questions," she said.

Her mother put her head back against the couch and closed her eyes.

Mattie started to read from the beginning.

"I was there," Hannah said.

"Okay, okay," Mattie said, flipping to page two. "You wrote your own vows, right?"

"Mattie, I really don't want to talk about this," she said.

"Grandma says you wrote your own vows," Mattie said.

"You talked to Grandma about this?" Hannah said.

"So what does this mean?" Mattie read aloud. "I promise to make everything as simple as possible and no simpler."

Hannah opened her eyes. She glanced at the page in Mattie's hand like she was refreshing her memory. "Your father's idea," she said. "Something he'd read."

"He read it," Mattie said. She leaned back, triumphant. "Dad doesn't read that kind of stuff," she said.

"I guess he used to," her mother said.

Mattie was quiet. She was trying to figure out what exactly her questions were.

"Why do we have to talk about this?" her mother asked. "Do we have to talk about this?" She was asking like she had no say in the matter. She was getting those spots on her neck she got when she was angry or sad.

"It's what I want to talk about," Mattie said. This was not what Lois had meant by doing her bit, but her mom for the last month was making doing her bit harder.

"It's not what I want to talk about," her mother said. "I'm sorry," she said. She was trying to stay calm, but picking at the skin around her thumbnails.

I'm making her do that, Mattie thought. With sudden clarity, it occurred to her that you didn't just have to wait and see which Hannah was going to show up.

She said, "It's just a question. *You* wanted to talk and now you won't."

Her mother shifted in her seat. Potpie stood and shook himself, his ID tags jangling. He jumped off the couch and resettled with his back to them.

"It's not fair," Mattie said.

"You're being a kid about this," her mother said.

"I *am* a kid," she said.

"You know what I mean," her mother said.

"You know what *I* mean," she said.

Potpie marched off to the kitchen. They could hear him at his water dish.

"How can talking about this be something that'll help you?" her mother asked.

"Forget it," Mattie said. "I'll ask Dad."

Her mother threw her hands up to her head and made her breaking-point noise. She put her hands in her hair and made fists.

"Okay," she said. "You want to know about those vows? Here it is." She took a breath. "When your father left, he gave me a complete inventory of why he was in love with Georgia and not with me." She pronounced "When your father left" as if she were speaking to a deaf person. "And he said, 'As simple as possible, but no simpler.'"

Mattie felt like she'd built a sand castle that hadn't turned out right.

"I said, 'You're using our wedding vows? You're using our wedding vows to leave your wife and your daughter?' I told him he should be ashamed of that, if nothing else."

Her mother took one of Mattie's hands and was quiet for minutes, doing nothing but stroking and stroking the top.

"I'm glad he said what he said," she said quietly. "I'm glad he took it away, put it back where it had come from in the first place."

Mattie wanted to say she was sorry, or stupid. But she didn't. She just sat there and let her mother stroke her hand.

—————

That night, she wet her bed for the fourth time. She stripped the bottom sheet off, balled it up, and put it in the closet. She put a new one on without taking apart the whole bed.

She was ashamed of what she'd caused in her mother that afternoon. She didn't know why any of that was making her cry.

She thought of her mother and her father and everyone behind them walking up the aisle. She thought of herself as one of those people. She thought of all of them walking onto God's fingertips, down the length of his fingers, and into the big curve of his cupped hand.

Her father opened the bathroom door and held up a handful of notebook paper. "What is this?" he asked. Sam crawled in behind him, making a beeline for the toilet paper.

She was reading in the bath. She was used to her father ignoring the closed doors of bathrooms. He liked having bathroom chats. When she was little, he liked her to sit in there on a stool while he took a shower, or shaved, or pooped. He called them buddy poops. Sometimes she still did buddy poops, not because she liked being in the room with him but because she knew he was right, these were their best talks.

"Paper," she said. She went back to her book. She was reading a grown-up book she'd found at the library. The whole thing was narrated by a horse. She'd thought it was going to be cheesy. It was turning out to be great.

"What's *on* the paper?" he said, leaning on the edge of the sink. She squinted. "I can't see it," she said. "Lines?"

"Don't sass me," he said, but he didn't sound mad. He started to read. "Things I Know," he said. "Number one—"

She threw her book at him and climbed out of the bath. Sam startled and whimpered. "Are you going through my stuff?" she said, grabbing for the papers.

He held the papers up above Mattie's head. She climbed up on the toilet and banged her shin.

From the seat, dripping wet, she said, "Give me those."

He kept his arm up. "You can't bully a horse. You sweet him into going where you want him to go."

She got off the toilet, sat on the floor, and started to cry. She couldn't believe she was crying. "Can you please just act like a normal father," she said.

Her father put the papers on the counter and squatted by her. "Goddamn, Goose," he said. "Why're you crying?"

He was always astonished by it.

"What do you want?" she sobbed.

"I want you to be happy," he said.

"You want me to stop crying," she said.

"That too," he said.

"Quit going through my stuff," she said.

"Quit going through mine," he said.

Her stomach did a twist. She did go through his stuff when he wasn't in the house. She'd found his stack of *Playboys*. She'd found a list of phone numbers with names she didn't recognize. She'd found a giant Ziploc bag of pot. She'd found a glass bottle with tiny white pills in it. The yellow label said Zip in letters like lightning bolts.

He passed her a towel and told her to wrap up. She threw it over her shoulders like a cape and Sam sucked on the edge closest to him. With Georgia in the hospital, he'd had to go to bottle feeding. Now he put everything in his mouth just to see if something came out of it.

"What do you do with a list of stuff you know?" he asked. "Who even comes up with an idea like this?" he said.

"It's better than a list of the stuff I don't know," she said, wiping her nose on the towel. She was getting cold.

"What don't you know?" he said. "You're my Super Smart Girl." He wasn't mocking her.

She wiped her nose harder. Sam put his head under the towel. She wrapped it tighter around her.

"Like what the judge is going to ask. Like what's going to happen to Georgia. Like why you do things to Mom."

Her father threw a face towel over Sam's head. Sam pulled it off. Her father threw it on.

"I didn't know you thought about Georgia," he said. "I think she thinks about you. I think she thinks about all of us." He reached over to let the water out of the tub.

Did he mean that in her sleep, Georgia thought about them?

"She's better than she was last week," he said. "She's responding to all kinds of touch."

He'd been saying that for weeks.

"She's gonna be fine," he said.

"You don't know that," Mattie said.

The drain gurgled and sucked. Sam crawled over and pulled himself up to watch.

Her father asked if she remembered watching *Pinocchio* when she was three or four.

"Is this an answer to one of my questions?" she said.

"When you were three or four, you were watching *Pinocchio* for the four-hundredth time, and you got to the part where the boys go to Pleasure Island. You turned to me, and said, 'Why do they want to go to Pleasure Island if they're going to get turned into donkeys?' And I said, 'I guess they don't know they're gonna get turned into donkeys.' And you said, 'They don't *want* to know.'"

Mattie said, "Mom told me about the whole wedding vow thing."

His face registered that he didn't know what she was talking about. She watched him catch up. "Your mother's sick," he said. "Maybe she can't help it, but she's sick." He rubbed his palms up and down on his thighs like he was rolling dough. "What all did she tell you?" he asked.

She looked down at her towel-wrapped body. Which part was her mother? Which part her father? Which part sick, which part okay?

"Once," he said, "at the end of the first summer Georgia worked for us, your mother and I were driving home from a party and she asked if I thought about having a serious relationship with someone else, would I think about having it with Georgia. And I said I would. I said she'd be the first woman I'd think of."

"You're gross," Mattie said.

He scooped Sam onto his shoulder like a bag of feed.

"Your mother knew lots more than she said she knew," he said. "She didn't *want* to know," he said, imitating three-year-old Mattie's voice.

"So?" Mattie said.

"So it's a good thing to be clear on what you want, on what you know. Whatever the judge asks you, you say what you want, not what you think someone else wants," he said, closing the door behind him.

She picked up her book, splattered with water. She dried the cover as best she could with the corner of her towel. She reached up to the counter and got her papers. They were wet too. She held her book and her papers and felt sorry for herself.

She had nine pages of things she knew. She turned to the last page and read: *Most animals sneeze straight down their noses, their mouths closed. Dogs have a sweet tooth. Greek soldier horses had a special sandbox to roll in. Human hair will keep deer away from your garden.*

She read back through the other eight pages and confirmed that everything on her list came from her mother or her father. She didn't know anything without them.

Celia invited Mattie for a four-day weekend to her lake house. Hannah didn't want her to go, but she said she'd ask Cole. He said he thought it would do her good. They went back and forth about it on the phone without any shouting, and she got to go.

Tommy and Donna had a van, and the two girls voted to sit in the way-back. Tommy had already removed the backseats to make more room for all the stuff, but when Mattie said she'd like to sit back there, Donna gave him a look, and he mussed Mattie's hair, and said, "You got it, girl."

Celia whispered, "See, I told you; all you're gonna have to do this whole weekend is ask." The two of them watched him unload the bags, the cooler, the folding chairs, the tent, the towels, the sand toys. They watched him reinsert the backseats and remove the middle row, then reload the stuff.

He brushed his hands off on the back pockets of his jeans, and asked if that was what she had in mind. Mattie nodded, and said thank you. He said, "No problem. Anything else, just holler."

In the car, they listened to Celia's Walkman with two sets of earphones. They played their Game Boys with their power-link cord. They snacked on the individual-sized bags of Doritos and Chee·tos that Donna had a whole drawer of at home and that Hannah didn't allow. They drew; they read Calvin and Hobbes out loud to each other. Mattie fell asleep against Celia's shoulder. They didn't talk about her parents except when Celia said, out of the blue, that when she told Mattie's father a story, she always felt like she should stand up. Mattie let it go.

The lake house was from Donna's side of the family. Her family had lived in Kentucky even longer than Mattie's grandfather's. And they were even richer. Tommy said he came from money too, the stolen and squandered kind. Without Donna, Mattie had heard him say once, he wouldn't even have piss, let alone a pot to put it in. Tommy was her father's best friend, and sometimes he reminded her of him.

The house was big, and Celia's room was at the other end of a long hallway from her parents'. It was like being by themselves.

There was a broad stone patio out back shaped like a half-moon. There were plants that smelled good and were sturdy enough to stand the occasional soccer ball kicked through them. There was a long, sloping lawn down to the lake. There was a croquet set. There were two bocce ball sets. There was a rope swing, a floating dock, and a raft. There was cold, dark water and tall pines that made sound something it wasn't anywhere else.

She was scared of the rope swing. She couldn't shimmy up it the way Celia could. Mattie had to hang on to it and climb up the side of the bank with it, trying to get as high as she could without letting the rope go. She didn't like to hang on with one arm and do Tarzan yells the way Celia did. The whole thing embarrassed her. She didn't think anyone would be making her go off the rope swing on this visit.

They spent the daylight hours in their bathing suits. Mattie had brought three, Celia four. They traded one-pieces and mixed and matched bikinis. "You could be sisters," Donna said every morning. "How's my sweet girl doing?" Tommy always added, and they knew he meant Mattie, and Celia didn't care.

They ate strawberries and melon and pancakes and waffles on the picnic table out back. They dabbed maple syrup on their lips and waited for the hovering bees to alight and had competitions to see who could stand it the longest. They drank what they wanted of their milk and their orange juice and then made potions out of the rest, and Donna didn't mind if she had to tell them twice to bring in their dishes before they ran down to the lake.

Mattie had gone to the other side of this lake once two years ago. A business friend of Cole's had invited them for the weekend. A guy interested in a large purchase of horses. "You may never have to work again," was what he'd said. Her mother had been skeptical, but her father had figured it was a weekend on the lake.

It had rained solidly for three days; the other guy's two sons were older and spent their time ignoring Mattie or tormenting her. The guy's wife only had conversation having to do with food. The cabin was one of those wood-paneled ones with wall-to-wall carpet that you don't like to go barefoot on. The kitchen cabinets had those fake forged-iron handles that were supposed to make it feel country. The toilet clogged when Mattie flushed, and she didn't tell anyone.

Her parents barely spoke to each other, and later she figured out that the weekend had come after her father had told her mother about Georgia. The guy bought one horse that he returned within a month.

"This is really great," she said to Celia. They were working on their tans on the floating raft.

"Switch," Celia said, and flipped over onto her back.

They were doing fifteen minutes a side. Sometimes they got too bored or too hot to last the whole fifteen minutes, but they were trying. Celia could tell times. She had a watch with a timer that could go underwater. The sun made Mattie's eyes hurt even though they were closed. She put her arm over them.

"You're gonna get a weird tan line across your face," Celia said.

She knew about these things. She'd already picked out her fifth-grade wardrobe. She'd gone back-to-school shopping last week. Mattie had reminded her mother, and her mother had said, "Damn, damn, damn," and the subject hadn't come up since.

"I don't care," Mattie said.

The raft rocked lazily. Across the lake, someone was trying to start a motor over and over.

"I'll still like you," Celia said. "I'll like you no matter what," she added.

Celia was great.

"I'll like you no matter whose house you end up in," she said.

The motor turned over and stayed on; there was applause and two whoops. Mattie imagined her head as the surface of the lake, the motorboat roaring across it.

She thought she'd looked at all this stuff from every angle there was. She knew Celia was saying a nice thing, but she hadn't realized a vote was being held.

Celia was up. "I'm hot," she said. "Let's do the rope swing."

She didn't answer, just followed her friend into the water without even gasping at the shock of the cold.

She didn't have to pass the rope swing test this time because Donna called from the house that there was a phone call.

"Right back," Mattie said to Celia. "Don't go without me." She didn't know why she said that. The best thing would be for Celia to go like fifty times and get it all out of her system.

It was her father. Georgia had opened her eyes. Georgia had said his name.

"Really?" she said. She was thinking about the last time she'd been at the hospital. Georgia hadn't looked like she was going to wake up.

"Really," he said. He sounded like he'd already celebrated as much as he knew how.

"I mean, she's not all better. The doctors say that we have to figure out how much damage there was. But her eyes are open, and she recognizes me. Her parents are flying in tonight. I think you better come on home. Put Donna or Tommy on, and I'll work it out with them."

"Home?" she repeated, feeling like an idiot. "Why do I have to come home?"

There was silence on the other end. She could hear hospital sounds. Someone was saying, "Georgia, can you feel this?" He was in Georgia's room.

"Where's Sam?" she asked.

"He's here. Want me to put him on?" he said sarcastically. "She's your family," he added sadly.

"I know," Mattie said.

"Hold on a minute," he said.

He covered the phone, and she heard muffled conversation. Donna was at the other end of the kitchen, pretending not to listen. Mattie remembered a party once before the divorce. Her father had been standing by the fireplace, telling a long story that everyone was laughing at. Donna was sitting on the couch, her feet up, and as she listened, she'd started taking off her jewelry. Her silver bangles, her earrings, then a beaded Indian belt. She laid everything on the coffee table by her feet. Then her overshirt, her shoes, her socks. Mattie had always wondered what would've happened if his story hadn't come to an end.

Donna caught her eye. They smiled, and Donna were back to chopping her vegetables.

Her father was back on the phone. "Listen," he said. "I've got to call you back."

"Okay," she said.

"When I call back," he said, "I'm talking to the grown-ups. You're coming home," he said.

"It's just two more days," she said.

"I'm calling back," he said.

"Okay," she said. She heard Sam in the background. Someone moaned. What difference would two days make?

"I'm having a really good time," she said.

"I'll tell Georgia," he said, and then he was gone.

She didn't tell anyone. That night, she and Celia camped out. Tommy showed them how to set up the tent and build a campfire, and then he told them a story he thought was scary. They ate marshmallows by the fistful.

He crawled into the two-man tent with them to tuck them in. "See you in the morning, camper girls," he said, patting them each on the head, and backing out of the tent on all fours. They could hear his knees crack as he stood. Years of cutting horse and rodeo riding had made Tommy move like an old Lab. The only place he looked pain free was on a horse's back.

They played shadow games with their flashlights until the batteries dimmed and then died. They talked about fifth grade and about how it wouldn't be too bad since they were in the same class.

They agreed that Julia Roberts wasn't gorgeous gorgeous; she was pretty because she didn't *act* pretty.

They were quiet. There were sounds from houses across the lake. There were frogs. Every now and then something splashed. Mattie could smell the lake, muddy and wet.

"What would you do if you were me?" she said.

"About what?" Celia asked.

Through the screen flap of the tent, she could see the downstairs lights in the house going out one by one.

"You know," she said.

Tommy was standing by the back door peering out in their direction. He turned the outside lights off, then turned them back on. He opened the door a little ways, then closed it again.

"Oh, that," Celia said, as if she'd thought she had meant something more interesting. She sighed, sounding just like her mother. "I don't know," she said. Then she said, "It doesn't matter. Nothing you do is gonna make a difference."

She thumped her pillow into shape and turned on her side. She said it like it was not something to get all worked up about.

"Yeah," Mattie said.

She tried to make out the back of Celia's head in the darkness. She tried one of the flashlights. Nothing. "What're you doing?" Celia asked sleepily.

"Nothing," she said. "G'night."

"Yeah," Celia said.

The next morning, she locked herself in the bathroom. She used the downstairs one in the back, the one with no windows behind the laundry room that no one ever used, so it took them time just to figure out where she was.

She'd brought two books with her, and she sat on the closed toilet and read while they all called for her. She could hear them going up and down the stairs, back and forth through the rooms. Once, Celia stood outside the bathroom door and said her name. Mattie held her breath until she went away.

She could hear them in the kitchen. "Her stuff is still here," Donna said. "So?" Tommy said. "She's not wearing her bathing suit," Celia said. "Did you look in the basement?" Donna asked. Footsteps hurried down to the basement and back up again.

They went outside. Mattie read two chapters while they were out there. They came in through the back door. As Donna passed the bathroom door, Mattie heard, "Who do we call, Hannah or Cole?"

She marked her place in her book and held it on her lap. "I'm here," she called loud enough. "In the back bathroom."

Their footsteps were like kids getting out of school. Someone tried the knob. "Honey?" Donna said. "Are you all right?"

"I'm locked in," she said. She was still on the toilet. One book was in her lap, the other was on the floor. She looked up at the ceiling. Mold was growing over the shower.

"Why didn't you answer us, sweetie?" Donna asked.

Mattie recognized the pitch of her voice. Donna could get a little hysterical. "I didn't hear you," she said.

"I was right outside the door," Celia said in a low voice.

Her parents shushed her.

She was thinking she should've brought something to eat. "I'm hungry," she said.

"Okay, then," Tommy said, his voice getting closer. "Let's see about getting you outta there."

"Don't say anything," Donna whispered.

"What'm I gonna say?" he whispered back.

The knob jiggled again.

"It doesn't work," Mattie said. "I tried that."

"Can you turn the lock for me?" Tommy asked.

"I'm sitting down," Celia said.

"I turned the little handle," Mattie said. "But the lock doesn't move."

The lock was a tarnished brass thing that looked like it belonged on a ship. The knob was cut glass that looked like it should be sharp, but turned out not to be. The keyhole was for one of those old-fashioned keys, the kind evil housekeepers wore on chains around their necks. She remembered the housekeeper in *Rebecca.*

"Goose?" Tommy said.

"Yes," she said.

"I'm gonna go get my tools and take this lock off, and then we'll be all set, okay?"

"Okay," she said.

"You hanging in there?" he asked.

"I'm still hungry," she said.

"I know it," he said. "But I don't think I can get anything in to you right now."

"That's okay," she said.

Celia said she could slide food under the crack in the door. Donna told her to hush. Celia said lots of stuff could fit. She ran off to the kitchen. Tommy went to get his tools. That left Donna.

"Honey?" Donna said. It sounded like her mouth was by the keyhole.

"Yes?" Mattie said.

"Are you okay in there?"

"Yes," she said.

"You know, there's water in there if you need it," Donna said. She looked at the sink. "Okay," she said.

Donna was quiet for a minute. Mattie could hear the fridge and cupboards opening and closing.

"What are you doing in there?" Donna asked.

"Reading," she said.

"You took a book in there with you?" Donna asked.

"I guess," she said. "I always do," she added.

"Oh," Donna said.

There was quiet again.

"Do you want a magazine?" Donna asked. "I could probably get it under the door."

"No, thanks," she said. "The book's good."

Celia was back.

"Oh, for goodness' sake," Donna said. "Put that stuff back."

"She's hungry," Celia said. "Okay," she called. "Coming through."

A slice of salami appeared under the door. Next to it, a slice of American cheese.

"They're going to be filthy," Donna said.

"She can rinse them in the sink," Celia said. "Didya hear that?" she asked. "You can rinse them off in the sink."

"I'm not stupid," Mattie said, getting up to pull the salami and cheese all the way through.

Celia snorted. "Well, you're locked in the bathroom."

Tommy was whistling. His walk sounded like he was carrying something heavy.

"Outta the way," he said to Celia.

"Wait," Celia said, and an unrolled Fruit Roll-Up came under the door.

There was the sound of bodies shifting position, and Tommy lowering himself to the floor by the door, and the toolbox opening, and tools being moved around.

Mattie rinsed the salami and cheese off and shook them dry. She rolled them up together and ate them.

He was still whistling. The knob moved a little with whatever he was doing to it.

She sat on the floor with her back against the wall and opened her book. She rolled the Roll-Up back up and unrolled it bite by bite, eating while she read, enjoying the sounds of someone taking care of everything on the other side of the closed door.

He got the knob off, and peered in at her. "Hey, girl," he said.

"Hey," she said.

She marked her place in her book and stood up. She was ready to get out of here. She didn't know why she'd done this. The early morning seemed like a long time ago.

She stood there, watching him try to get at the lock through the space left by the absent knob. She watched the lock handle move all the way in the right direction, but the bolt didn't follow. It moved a little, but not enough.

"Damn," Tommy said. "Goddamn."

"What?" Donna fluttered behind him. "What?"

"I am bored," Celia announced.

Mattie tried the lock handle herself. She moved it back to the locked position, then to unlocked. It moved freely; the bolt stayed put.

"Just relax," Tommy said to everyone.

As soon as he said that, she felt the asthma starting. Someone was pressing on her chest with two flat hands. She had the urge to cough. She took a breath, but couldn't get it lower than her throat. Her doctor had once told her that during an asthma attack, you were really having trouble breathing out, not breathing in. She hadn't believed that. She still didn't.

She willed herself to speak. "Could someone get my inhaler?"

she said. She was surprised at how normal she sounded. "It's under my pillow in the tent," she said.

"I will," Celia called, and the back door opened and slammed shut.

She sat on the toilet and leaned over her legs. Sometimes that helped. Her throat was tightening from the bottom up. A tube of toothpaste squeezed flat. She tried leaning her head against the wall. Her fingers were tingling. The fingernails were a gray-blue. Breathing through her nose helped for a minute or two, and then didn't. She tried not to imagine the inhaler. Thinking about relief before it got there always made things worse.

The inhaler didn't fit through the hole in the lock.

"I'm calling nine-one-one," Donna said.

Her heart seemed to be pumping blood that had nowhere to go. She lifted up her shirt and looked at her torso. The skin around her ribs felt and looked like it was being sucked inside out.

Tommy was going at the door with something. Big sounds that seemed far away.

Her head filled with heavy air. She laid her forehead against the cool tile floor. The grout swayed. Her skin went numb. She was swollen, a giant bee sting. She pressed her fingertips to her lips and felt nothing, like Novocaine.

She felt scared and stupid. It had never been like this before. Her heart veered left and right. Somewhere she heard a phone.

She woke up with a paramedic next to her. There was a mask over her face. She registered the gurgle of the liquid albuteral before she registered the mask. She was sitting up. She was still in the bathroom. Splinters of the door were around them. An IV tube snaked from her arm.

They were all peering at her from where the door used to be.

"Hey, there," the paramedic said. "Just breathe normally, okay?"

She nodded. There was a plastic clip on the end of her index finger. A red light glowed at its tip. Phone home, she thought.

"Have you done this before?" he said. He tapped the syringe in his hand and rubbed a spot on her arm with a wet cotton ball. The smell of alcohol ballooned up her nose.

She thought he was talking about locking herself in the bathroom, but he gestured at the nebulizing treatment.

She nodded.

"Okay, then," he said. "Ever fainted before?"

She shook her head.

"Tiny pinch," he said, poking her with the short needle. "Just some epinephrine to get you back on track."

She wondered if he knew the paramedics who'd worked on Sam.

He checked her blood pressure. He listened to her chest. It was still tight, but not too bad. The skin across her upper back felt too small for the muscles and bones. Her shoulder blades ached with each breath. After an attack it was like someone had thrown you against a wall a few times.

She heard Tommy say he was going to take the locks off every door in the house. She started to speak, but the paramedic put a hand on her shoulder and said, "No talking. Just a few more minutes."

A second paramedic arrived from somewhere wheeling in a stretcher, and Tommy and Donna took a few steps back to talk to him. She couldn't hear what they were saying.

Celia stayed in the doorway, regarding her. She started to ask something, and then changed her mind.

Mattie pointed the red finger light at her.

"*You're* an alien," Celia said.

Mattie smiled, trying to keep the mask from shifting too much. After they'd seen *Return of the Jedi,* they'd given up E.T. in favor of Yoda. "Oh, Jedi knight you are."

She took a breath and felt her lungs fill and empty.

The paramedic took the mask off. "How're you doing?" he asked.

"Good," she said.

He reached into his bag and pulled out a peak-flow meter. She was supposed to do these at home every night. He asked her if she knew what her normal peak flows were. She tried to remember the last time she'd taken them. "Three hundred is my personal best, I think," she said, using allergy doctor language.

"Okay," he said, handing her the L-shaped plastic thing. "Give this a try. Deep breath in, mouth completely around the mouthpiece, blow out as hard and as long as you can."

She did it. Her breath had felt like a big one, but the red needle barely got to fifty.

"Two more," he said.

The second and third were worse.

"Good job," he said. He glanced at the other paramedic and told Tommy and Donna that they were going to take her in. She needed to be checked out, and the doctors would probably want to put her on a longer, slower dose of albuteral, just to get her airways at normal levels.

"Her father wants her at Norton's Hospital," Donna said.

The other paramedic was angling the stretcher as close to the doorway as he could. Celia moved aside, but kept her head inside the door until her mother pulled her out of the way.

"We're only authorized to take her to the closest hospital," he said. "You can follow and try to work out a transfer from there."

He lifted Mattie onto the stretcher and strapped her in.

"You look kinda pale," Celia said.

"So do you," she said.

Tommy laughed a little and winked at her.

The other paramedic said it would easier for immediate family to arrange a transfer.

"Her mother's on the way," Donna said.

They lifted the stretcher down the back stairs and wheeled her across the lawn. She could smell the lake and the grass and the remnants of the campfire. She closed her eyes and listened. It was like when her parents used to have parties, and she'd sneak to the top of the stairs. Listening to the rise and fall of party voices finally meant more as sound than it did as individual words and she'd fall asleep sitting up, her head against the banister.

"You know, I locked myself in," she said quietly.

If the paramedics heard her, they didn't say anything.

She thought she heard Tommy say they'd be right behind her. She thought she heard Celia saying something about not getting to ride in the ambulance. She opened her eyes as they slid her into the back, telling herself to pay attention to the details for Celia, but it felt too good to be lying down between clean white sheets and have two guys in uniforms wheel her to wherever she needed to be. She felt better than she'd felt in weeks. She'd make something up, she thought, closing her eyes again. Something good.

From her bed that moved up and down in different places, she watched her parents talk to each other in the hospital hallway. She couldn't hear what they were saying, but she could guess.

The words were different in all their arguments, but her father was really always saying *I don't love you anymore,* and her mother was answering *Why? Why? Why?*

They were standing in her doorway as if they were putting on a show. It was getting dark outside; the only light on in her room was the small bedside one. The hallway was lit the way hospital hallways are.

When they looked her way, she pretended to still be asleep. They didn't look like they were fighting. She wished she had a remote to close the door.

A guy pushing an empty stretcher needed to get by. Her parents moved. "I'm so glad for you," her mother was saying.

"Yeah," her father said. "Thanks."

He looked better. He was shaved. He was wearing a fresh polo shirt.

They were coming in. She kept her eyes closed and did her best sleep breathing.

They stood by the bed. "She's sleeping," her mother said.

"She's faking," her father said.

The trick was not to smile.

"You think?" her mother said. "How do you know?"

"She does this all the time at our place," her father said.

"She does?" her mother said. She wasn't upset, just interested. "Is she spying?" she asked.

She resisted the urge to defend herself.

"I guess that could be part of it, but mostly, it's her way of checking out in the middle of the world," he said.

"Oh," her mother said. "Wonder where she gets that," she said.

Cole laughed a little. "Yeah, I know."

They were quiet for a minute. She could feel them watching. It was hardest not to smile when there were people watching you.

"At my place," her mother said, "sometimes she lies."

Mattie felt like her face was giving her away.

"She lies?" he said.

"Silly things," her mother said. "She'll tell me her purple shirt is dirty when it isn't. She ate an orange when she ate a banana. She hasn't fed Potpie when she has."

"Well, what're we gonna do, right?" her father said. "Her life's a little more complicated than most ten-year-olds, I guess."

Her mother smoothed the hair back from Mattie's forehead. "I guess you're right," she said. "But there's things we could do," she added.

Cole was quiet. "I know," he said. "You're right."

He's right? She's right? Mattie thought. Who were these people?

She opened her eyes, not even pretending to be coming out of a deep sleep.

"Hey there," her father said.

"Oh, Goose," her mother said.

She looked at them both, standing there together by her bed. "I locked myself in," she said. "I did it on purpose."

They didn't seem surprised. "Whydya do that?" her father said.

She wished one of them would leave, but there they both were, like a couple boarding Noah's Ark, like anyone's parents.

She looked at him. Her breathing was okay now, but she took a deep breath and heard herself wheeze. "Why did you leave?" she asked.

She'd never gotten this expression from him before. Her mother pinched the bridge of her nose with a finger and a thumb.

"Celia says Donna says that you can be a good parent without being a good husband or wife," Mattie said.

She was saying things without believing them. She was saying things without knowing what she would say next.

They weren't answering. She didn't know what she wished they would say.

She was genuinely hurting them. She could see that on their faces. They weren't looking at each other.

She was crying now.

"What's the matter with you?" she said. It wasn't what she'd meant to say. She didn't like this room. She didn't like any of the people in it.

A guy nurse came in and took in the scene. Her parents tried to smile at him. He acted as if he walked in on things like this all the time. He had long hair in a ponytail and a long moustache that went around his mouth like an upside-down horseshoe.

What kind of hospital was this? Mattie thought.

The nurse had a peak-flow meter with him, which he handed to Mattie. "Let's see whether we can get you out of this place," he said.

Mattie took a big breath in, wrapped her lips around the plastic, and blew out, pinching her breath on purpose. She did the same thing twice more. Her numbers were lower than they'd been in the bathroom with the paramedics.

The nurse jotted down each of the readings on the chart at the end of the bed, and then came around to the head of the bed. He put a pink stethoscope to Mattie's chest. "Big breath in," he said.

Mattie knew how to fake wheezing. All the kids with asthma did.

"Looks like you're here for the night," the nurse said. "Sorry, kiddo," he added, patting her through the covers.

"I'm glad," she said when the nurse was gone.

Her parents still hadn't said anything. Then her father said, "We love you, Goose. You know we do."

And he was right; she did, but she closed her eyes and turned on her side and started to cry some more. She hadn't wanted to

do any of those things, but she'd done them, and that made her
cry harder.

Two weeks later, back at her mother's house, she continued to tell
her father she wasn't ready to see Georgia. She told Lois she
needed another ride. She told her mother Lois was taking her for
ice cream.

"Sounds good," her mother said, busy preparing something
fancy for dinner that night. Jackson was coming over and, if it was
okay, he was going to spend the night.

She shrugged. "I don't care," she said. "Where's he gonna
sleep?" she asked.

"On the cot," her mother said, her hands deep into something doughy in a big mixing bowl.

Mattie said she was going to wait outside for Lois.

"Don't forget your inhaler," her mother said.

"Got your inhaler?" Lois asked as Mattie climbed into the car.

Her car was so old Mattie could sit in the front seat. Mattie
patted her backpack wedged between her feet.

Lois pulled onto the main road and turned towards town.
"Summer around here's not so good for folks with respiratory
problems," she said. "My sister's asthma was a real problem till my
dad scared it outta her."

"You have a sister?" Mattie asked.

Lois's glasses were slipping down her nose. She liked two
hands on the wheel at all times. "Dad took her out to the bridge,
held on to her ankles, and hung her upside down over the railing.
Said he was getting all the bad air out. It worked," Lois said.

Georgia didn't believe Lois's stories. Mattie didn't know what to believe. She liked them.

Air came through the vents in hot little gusts. The car didn't have air-conditioning, and Lois didn't like the noise of the windows open. It was like being inside a dog's mouth. Outside it was an August Tuesday. Hazy and damp. Damp and hazy.

"So," Lois said. "Three more days."

"Three more days what?" Mattie asked.

"Till you've got your meeting," Lois said.

"I know," Mattie said.

Lois accelerated, then slowed. "Thought about what you're gonna say to the lady?"

"The judge is a lady?" Mattie said.

"That's what I hear," Lois said.

"But the judge plays golf with Grandpa."

"Ladies play golf," Lois said.

They were quiet. They were coming into the city the back way. Lois didn't like highways. They stopped at a light. Mattie watched a woman watering her flower boxes. She was using one of those coiled hoses that attached right to your sink tap. Her mother made fun of them when she came across them in her gardening catalogues.

"I locked myself in," Mattie said.

"That's what I hear," Lois said.

"Is everyone talking about me?" she asked.

"Who's talking about you?" Lois asked.

The hose thing was stuck on something. The woman flung it around, trying to free it. The light turned green.

"No one," Mattie said. "It's green."

Lois pulled ahead. They were five minutes from the hospital.

"Mom and Dad," Mattie said. "They were standing there in the hospital, just talking about me."

"What should they have been talking about?" Lois asked.

"I don't know," she said, leaning her head back on the seat.

"I figured you locked yourself in the bathroom to get folks to talk about you," Lois said.

They pulled into the hospital driveway. A car was ahead of them. An old man was being helped out by a hospital volunteer who looked older than the old man.

"I don't know," Mattie said.

The car pulled away and Lois pulled up to the sliding doors. "If you ask me," she said, "it's about time those two started talking about you."

"I don't know," Mattie said, opening her door and grabbing her backpack.

"Well, I do," Lois said. "It might make deciding what you're gonna say to that lady judge a whole lot easier."

Mattie closed the car door behind her. "Thanks," she said. "See you soon."

"I'll be here," Lois said, pushing her glasses up on her nose before pulling away and heading to the short-term parking spaces.

She didn't know whether she was supposed to touch Georgia or not. Most of the tubes and wires were gone, but still. One side of her face was droopy. Georgia didn't indicate what she wanted either way. She said, "Hey," and was genuinely glad to see Mattie, but she didn't hold out her arms or pat the bed or anything. Mattie sat in the vinyl chair she always sat in. She wondered if when Georgia looked at her, she thought of Hannah.

Georgia's braid looked normal again. There was no ribbon. "Your hair looks good," Mattie said.

"Thanks," Georgia said, touching the end of it. "When I woke up, there was a ribbon in it."

Her voice sounded like she'd been at a party for a long time. She talked out of the good side of her mouth.

"I know," Mattie said.

"You do?" Georgia said.

"What was waking up like?" Mattie asked. "Was it like just waking up in the morning, or what?"

"It was like being wheeled down a long hallway with your eyes closed, and then your eyes are open, and you're at the end of the hallway," Georgia said.

Mattie nodded. She didn't know why she kept coming here. All different kinds of rings and bells kept going off at the nurses' station outside.

"It's noisy here," Mattie said.

Georgia smoothed her blanket over her with a hand Mattie wished she hadn't seen. "I like it," she said.

"Are you afraid to go to sleep?" Mattie asked.

Georgia shook her head. She always shook her head like a horse ridding herself of flies. The familiarity of the gesture made it even stranger to see it after so long.

"I came to see you when you were sleeping," Mattie said.

Georgia was quiet. Mattie wished she would say something. There was something strange about her. It was like that time Celia went to Europe for the summer and came back just a little different.

"I wet the bed four times in two weeks," Mattie said. "I locked myself in Celia's bathroom last weekend. If I eat all my food at dinner, I throw up. I lie without meaning to." She took a breath. "I don't know why I do any of these things," she said. "I have to talk to the judge in three days."

Georgia was listening hard, but Mattie couldn't be sure anything was getting through. Georgia looked tired, but she looked
tired like someone else, not like Georgia.

"Do you know about anything that's happened?" Mattie asked.

Georgia rested her head against the pillows and closed her
eyes. "I had an accident," she said. "I had an accident, and I was in
a sort of coma, and I woke up." She took a breath. "I had an accident," she said again. "I was in a sort of coma, and then I woke
up."

She stopped saying the words, but her mouth was still making
them. Her eyes were still closed.

Mattie sat in the chair until Georgia fell asleep. Georgia asleep
was familiar. She sat there watching her, being calmed by her, and
then she started from the beginning. She told Georgia about Sam
and the nail polish and the Benadryl, and Hannah and the barn,
and how Cole had just stayed and stayed at the hospital.

She told her what Sam had felt like when she'd tried to wake
him that morning. She told about the whirlpool day in the pool
with Celia.

She told about Cole and the teenager. She told her that without her, he was angrier. She told her that Jackson was spending
the night at her house tonight. She told her that Hannah and
Cole were both acting different. That she didn't know how to
explain it.

She asked what to say to the judge. She asked what she should
expect of her mother and father. She asked what she should expect
of herself. She asked what was the best she could hope for.

⊃ TEN ⊂

November 1978

"DON'T LET THIS ONE GET AWAY," TOMMY SAID. "SHE'S AN angel," his mother said. "She's a keeper," his sister said. "I don't know what she's doing with you, but you better get her John Hancock before she comes to her senses," his father said.

Cole was at his six-month cut-off point. Instead of breaking up with her, he asked her to marry him. It wasn't just what everyone else thought of her; it was the safety of the familiar and the risk of the new at the same time. Like riding an unbroken horse for the first time.

He asked over the phone. She was in the middle of her senior year at Sweet Briar; he was working horses for a guy in Kissimmee, Florida. She was taking art history and all sorts of other things. His boss was teaching him how to snap grapefruits off a tree with a bullwhip. His boss wore camo gear and called his substantial belly his "toolshed." She was twenty. He was twenty-three.

"I miss you," she said.

"Yup," he said. "There's a similar missing story going on down here."

He knew which pay phone she was at. The one at the end of her hall. He was in his trailer on the edge of the farm. There were orange trees being picked by black guys out his back window. School buses dropped them off in the morning and picked them up at the end of the day.

"So, listen," he began.

"Are you breaking up with me?" she asked.

"Why?" he said. "Should I?"

"It's six months," she said. "I've been waiting for the call."

He could hear college girls moving around in the hallway behind her. He could hear those college girl voices.

"Is this the call?" she asked.

She didn't sound like she was going to be that broken up if it was.

"No," he said. "I was thinking something else."

"Oh," she said.

He couldn't tell whether she was glad or not. Someone's laugh was so loud it seemed like it was on their line. "Who's that?" he said.

"Violet," she answered. "She's always laughing," she said.

He couldn't remember who Violet was. Hannah was in a sorority. When he visited, he stayed in the sorority house. The other sisters kept quiet about it. In exchange, he flirted with them all equally. A couple of girls, he remembered. A couple of girls, he said their names to himself while he mucked out stalls, tightened up girths, lay in bed at night.

"So?" she said.

"So," he said.

"Hold on," she said. "I'll be there in a minute," she called to someone.

Her life there was like a forest to him, impossible to get through even on horseback.

"I was thinking we might get hitched," he said.

There was the sound of doors opening and closing, voices receding down the hallway.

"I love you," he added.

It seemed like his announcement had cleared the hallway. He couldn't hear a thing except her quiet breathing. When she was frightened or anxious, she got very still.

"Well," she said. "Well, jeez. Jeezo."

"Is that a yes?" he asked. Out his window, he could see his boss letting his pit bull out of the stall he kept him penned in during the day. The boss's three-year-old son walked behind him. They were dressed in matching camo. The boss was poking at the boy with a lunge whip.

"What happened to 'Monogamy never happens in the animal world; it isn't a natural state'?" Hannah said.

"Are you answering me?" Cole asked. "Is that an answer?"

"I'm going to have to think about this," she said.

The boss and his son got into the pickup and drove away. The dog chased them for a while, then circled back to the barn and Cole's trailer. Cole realized he was in for the night.

"What's to think about?" he said. "Do you love me or not? I love you," he said again.

"I guess I love you," she said.

"You guess?" he said.

"I do," she said. "I love you. But that's not the only thing to think about here."

"It's not?" he asked.

The dog was sniffing at the trailer door. He took a few tentative tries at it. Cole heard dog nail against metal.

"There are other factors," she said.

"You're sounding like a college student," he said.

"It's *good* to be a college student," she said. "It's *good* to go to college."

"What other factors?" he asked.

He got up and hit the inside of the door with his boot. The flimsy metal twanged. There was silence from the other side.

"What're you doing?" she asked.

"Nothing," he said. "Drinking a beer." He went to the fridge and got one. He flicked the bottle cap down the hall and through the open bedroom door at the end of it. It landed on the bed. There were three others already there.

"There's Jackson?" Hannah said slowly, like she was trying to decide which wire to cut on a bomb.

"Who's Jackson," he asked. This wasn't going the way he'd expected. It made him want her to say yes even more. His desire for her was a solid giant thing inside of him.

"Jackson Ellis," she said. "You know."

Her hometown honey. The guy she'd grown up with. Her childhood whatever.

"I thought he was out of the picture starting last summer," he said. He and Hannah had started dating last summer. She was supposed to have taken care of Jackson Ellis. They'd joked about letting him down easy.

"He is, mostly," she said.

"Mostly?" he said.

A door opened on her end of things. "I know," she called. "One more minute," she said. "I've got to go," she said. "Field trip," she said.

"Have you been screwing Jackson Ellis?" he asked. He looked

out his window. The pit bull was curled up on the grass outside
the trailer. He had his eye on the door.

"You told me you didn't date for longer than six months," she
said.

"I didn't," he said. "Till I met you."

"Well, how was I supposed to know that was going to happen?"
she said.

"Well it's happening now," he said. "I want to marry you. Do
you want to marry me?"

"I don't know," she said.

Someone called her.

"I've got to go," she said. "I'll call you later. I'll think about it."

"Yeah," he said. "You think about it. Think about it on your
field trip."

"Don't be mad with me," she said. "LMNW," she said.

It was their thing: Love you, Miss you, Need you, Want you.
He took a swig of beer and made sure she could hear him swallow.
"Say hi to the girls," he said, and hung up.

He peered out the window. The pit bull was gone, but he realized he was still too chicken to go out.

Over the next few weeks, his desire was a generator. He called her
every day. When he understood that was hurting his cause more
than helping it, he wrote letters. He started the first one with,
"You know I never write letters."

In one he wrote five pages of song lyrics.

In another, he drew a sketch of the house he liked to imagine
them in. It had lots of porches and windows and was set in the
middle of the front paddock, horses munching hay and peering

in their windows all around them. In another, he made a list of his qualities and Jackson's, a kind of compare-and-contrast thing. He tried to remember argument techniques from the writing class he'd taken at the community college. He was fair about Jackson's good qualities. He made a lot more money than Cole would probably ever make. He could offer her stability, reliability, predictability. He was the kind of guy her parents would pick for her. He was the kind of guy some of her sorority sisters were after.

But they weren't the girlfriends Hannah took seriously. The ones she listened to hung out a little too often in her room when he was visiting, laughed too hard at his jokes, kept a conversational hand on his shoulder a little too long. He couldn't believe that Jackson was really the kind of guy Hannah would pick for herself. Maybe he was wrong, but he'd always thought she was more like him, more interested in risk and speed. More an outdoor-sport kind of girl. Remember how much she loved galloping two-year-olds?

When his letters went unanswered, he arranged two days off and an advance on his pay, and got a flight from Orlando. He was at his best in person.

He called Delphine, one of her sorority sisters, to help him work out the surprise. He'd had some time with Delphine in an almost empty hallway during one of his last visits. It was an anniversary, he told her. He'd pegged her as the kind of romantic that would fall for this kind of thing. She was skeptical, but said she'd help.

The flight seemed longer than it was. He went over good moments from the last six months. How, once they'd started dating, he'd race to finish afternoon barn chores. She'd help, and when they were done, he'd check his watch and do end zone dances at the end of the breezeway. Watching her get out of his bed and slip into her jeans. The way, when they kissed, she liked to sniff into his nostrils; the way he liked to return the sniff. The way her body was put together like a good horse. If he divided her in thirds, from point of shoulder to withers, from withers to point of hip, from hip to buttocks, each part was in balance, like a puzzle that couldn't fit together any other way. Telling her when they first met that he was someone with a big sexual appetite that just had to be satisfied. The way she'd laughed and laughed.

That time last summer when he'd been down on himself about one thing or another, and she wouldn't stop asking what was wrong until he told her. There were holes inside of himself that she filled. Her faith in him made him think he wasn't just all about spin. She made him believe he might have substance.

The first time she'd said yes after weeks of saying no. How he'd told her it would be better with her on top, and she'd believed him. The way his hands had felt around her hips; the way she'd responded to his signals to move this way or that, speed up or slow down. How he'd wanted to imagine her like a horse, their lovemaking a training session. How he hadn't been able to. How the whole thing had felt like equal opponents on a level field.

When he came, he'd felt like he'd only felt on certain horses in certain polo games. The hindquarters sank into a stop and the field under him seemed to rise up like the sky on a roller-coaster ride, and suddenly he was going the other way. "You make love like a horse," she'd said, and he'd thought he was as close to flying as he'd get.

Delphine picked him up at the airport and delivered him to Hannah's room. Hannah was in class, she said. She'd be back in half an hour.

He wound a strand of her hair around his finger. "I owe you big," he said.

"Uh-huh," Delphine said, closing the door behind her.

He arranged the things he'd brought on her desk: flowers, a bottle of Maker's Mark, and a bracelet in the shape of a curved polo mallet. When she arrived, half an hour later, she seemed unsurprised, though pleased, by both the gifts and his presence in her room. She seemed more surprised that her sorority sisters had pitched in and gotten them a bottle of Champagne.

"What are we celebrating?" she asked, lifting the Champagne from the plastic bucket filled with ice the girls had left it in.

Just looking at the ice made him cold. He didn't have winter clothes with him in Florida; he'd come without a jacket or a sweater.

"Come 'ere," he said, patting the bed next to him. He was stretched out on his side.

"Take your boots off," she said, coming to sit next to him.

He pushed them off with his heels; they fell to the floor in two even thuds. She was wearing a turtleneck and a cardigan sweater. Her brown hair was long and straight, parted in the middle and held back with a red headband. He pulled the turtleneck out from her skirt's waistband and rubbed her back in small, slow circles. She leaned into his hand. He took his hand out and rubbed the spot between her eyes with his thumb. "Some horsemen believe this is the most effective place to touch a horse," he said.

"To get them to do what?" she said.

She smoothed her long corduroy skirt. Under that, he knew, she'd be wearing knee socks. She hated stockings. She had on her clogs. She wore her clogs all year round except when she was on a horse.

He reached under her skirt and stroked her bare thighs. She flinched a little at first. "Your hands are cold," she said.

He stroked a little harder until they both warmed up.

"When you think about us, what do you think about?" he asked.

"What do you mean?" she said.

He brushed her underwear with his fingers and moved back down to her knee. "What do you think about?"

She closed her eyes. "Gosh," she said. "I don't know." She moved her legs and kicked off her clogs. "Why?"

He moved his hand back to her back and resumed his circles. "*I'm* interested in us," he said.

She smiled. "I remember you reaching up to weight a roll of fly paper with a penny," she said.

She seemed about to say something else, and then changed her mind.

"What?" he asked.

She shook her head. "Nothing," she said.

He snapped her bra. "How's Jackson?" he said.

"Fine," she said.

"Been to see him recently?" he asked. He massaged the small of her back with his thumb. "Training a horse is all about muscle memory," he said.

"Are you quoting somebody?" she said.

"How's your muscle memory?" he asked.

"How's yours?" she asked.

Something in her tone got his attention. He didn't know what she was getting at. Sometimes this happened with her. Her end of the conversation was a deeper ocean than his. He knew she was attracted to his desire for her. No one, he liked to tell her, has wanted you as much as I want you. But moments like this made him worry that someday soon she'd smarten up.

"Are you still fucking him?" he asked.

"None of your business," she said. She pushed him over onto his back and straddled him. "Are you still fucking Delphine?"

Women, he thought. Always talking. "I didn't fuck Delphine," he said.

She closed her eyes.

He wished they were naked. "Take your clothes off," he said.

She pulled her turtleneck and sweater off in one motion. She undid her bra and threw it on the floor. She pulled her knee socks and underwear off. While she was doing that, he pulled down his jeans and underwear, kicking them off his feet. He left his shirt and socks on. She sat back down on him, her skirt arranged like a costume around them.

The lights were all on. The door was unlocked. He could hear those college girls in the hall. "I want to be inside you," he said.

"I know you do," she said. And then she told him that she wasn't going to be sleeping with Jackson or him until she made her decision. Jackson, she said, had understood completely.

"I bet he did," Cole said. He could feel her wetness. "What's Jackson do to you?" he asked quietly.

She sat there, staring at him.

"A lot of things you don't mind missing, I guess," he said.

"You guess all you want," she said. Her hips were moving in tiny ways.

"Do you remember when you told me I made love like a horse?" he asked.

She shook her head. "I said you didn't make love like a horse, you made love like a horseman."

He took her by the hips and pushed her down a little. "Same thing," he said.

She snorted.

He hated when she snorted.

"Other girls talk about a horseman's smooth easiness. The way their hands are all about soothe and calm," she said. Her hands were folded in her lap like she was in church.

"You're all about switchbacks and fakes," she said. "You make love like a horse," she said again. This time there was none of what he remembered about the description. This time there was something like mockery, something like pity.

He took her wrists in one hand and flipped their positions. He held her hands above her head. It was a position she liked to sleep in. He pulled her skirt up with his other hand. She was twisting beneath him. "Quit it," she said quietly. "Quit it," she said again.

He pushed her legs open with his knees. He thought about Jackson. He leaned down and sniffed her the way they liked. He put his mouth near her ear. "We're made for each other," he said.

Her eyes were closed. She'd stopped twisting. Her legs were open for him. She wasn't saying yes, but she wasn't saying no, which he took as a good sign. He would show her he was right. He was sure of it. Horses could be taught almost anything, but sometimes the teaching had to go on in layer after layer, like a good varnish.

She came down to Florida for the abortion. When they arrived at the clinic the first time, the nurse at the front desk greeted him by name. Hannah said, "Perfect," and started crying. He should've known then not to try and make her go through with it.

The second time, she didn't cry at all. They'd discussed it; they'd agreed.

He'd planned to wait for her. He'd told her he'd be there. But there were other people in the waiting room. Other men and other women, and he couldn't stand it. He got up for a drink of water at the water fountain, and slipped out the front door into the bright Florida sunshine.

Back in Kissimmee, he worked to avoid the teasing and insinuations of his boss. "Well, something musta gone wrong," the balding man said. "'Cause I ain't seen you work this hard all winter."

Cole was tending to a pregnant mare who'd gotten tied up in one of the barbed-wire fences. Her cannon was stripped to the bone. His boss didn't have unreasonable expectations. He just wanted to get the foal out safe and sound. Cole thought he might be able to save the mare too. An Argie he'd worked with in Texas had shown him how they did things down in Argentina. A thick poultice changed often, long soaks. The poultice was supposed to be a mixture of *quebracho,* the hardwood Argies used for fencing. Cole had tracked some down at an Argie-owned farm nearby. No wraps. The whole process went against everything he had been taught in America, but he figured there was nothing to lose.

His boss was standing by the stall they had her in, watching him mix the poultice in a large bucket. The mare was patient, her damaged leg cocked at the pastern like a debutante offering her hand.

"Do you know the Texas cure for choking?" his boss asked.

"Can't say I do," Cole said.

"Two cowboys are having a beer at the bar. Suddenly a woman down the bar begins to cough. The cowboys turn and look at her.

'Kin ya swaller?' asks the first one. The woman shakes her head. 'Kin ya breathe?' asks the other one. The woman's beginning to turn blue. She shakes her head again. The first cowboy walks up to her, lifts the back of her skirt. He yanks down her panties and runs his tongue from the back of her thigh up to the small of her back. With a violent cough, the obstruction flies out of the woman's mouth and she begins to breathe normal again." The boss looked down at Cole. "Sure I ain't told you this before?"

"No, sir," Cole said.

"Well, then. The cowboy walks back to the bar and takes a pull on his beer. His partner says, 'Ya know, I'd heard of that there hind lick maneuver, but I ain't never seen anybody do it.'"

The boss laughed, taking his hat off and wiping his forehead with the back of his hand. "Damn," he said. "That's a good one."

Cole laughed politely. "Yes, sir, it is," he said.

Usually, his boss's jokes were about the only thing he really did like about the guy. He'd told a good one last week about foreplay. He didn't know why he wasn't laughing harder now. Maybe it was kneeling down beside this sad leg.

He rinsed the old poultice off by filling a big sponge with clean water and squeezing it out against her knee. She flinched a little at the water running down her cannon. Her teats had filled out last week, and there'd been wax buildup on them for two days. She could foal any time now.

He couldn't get over the heat. He missed watching horses pick precisely through the snow with their soft mouths for the pellets and grains. He missed sweeping dry a horse dusted with snow, warming the bit in his hands.

The boss's son appeared in the stall doorway. He was dressed in his camo gear and was carrying his BB gun. "I'm ready," he said to his father.

Cole's boss worked the night security shift in the orange groves. He carried a .357 Magnum. Some nights, he took his son with him. He called it training exercises. Some nights, they painted their faces.

The boss put his hand on his son's shoulder. "Everything under control here?" he asked.

"Yes, sir," Cole said. "Good luck in the groves."

"Yup," his boss said. "Maybe tonight we'll get lucky. Right, Scotty?"

"Right, sir," the boy answered.

They headed out of the barn, and Cole heard the boss say, "Scotty, what do you call foreplay in Alabama?"

"I don't know, sir," the boy said.

"Honey, tell your brother turn his back," Cole said to the quiet mare. The good thing about this joke, the boss had said last week, was it worked for any state you wanted.

Cole had told Hannah some of his boss's jokes. She'd giggled and blushed, which he thought was better than the joke itself. He'd thought about calling her a million times in the last ten days, but he didn't know how to put what he was feeling into words. Every time he tried a sentence out, whispering to himself while he fed and watered, and mucked out stalls, he reminded himself of a sappy movie, and ended up feeling embarrassed and discouraged.

He smoothed the new poultice on the mare's leg, trying to be gentle. Every now and then, she lifted her leg and held it away from him for a moment before returning it with a sigh. He liked the feel of her breath on the top of his head. He liked her smell mixed with the smell of the clean straw bedding. The barn hand who'd gotten this foaling stall ready had filled it with shavings. Cole had been all over him. "Don't you know anything?" he'd said, meaner than he'd had to. "Shavings can stick to a foal's wet nostrils and suffocate it. Straw. Clean straw. Try to get that through your tiny brain."

He looked over his shoulder at the empty aisle. If the boy had been there, he would've apologized. If there was one thing he prided himself on, it was knowing when he'd fucked up, knowing when it was time to say he was sorry.

The mare foaled that night. The boss wasn't back from the groves yet. Cole heard her pacing and low whinnying from his trailer. He knew to leave her alone for this part of things. He checked his watch and went to the tack room and gathered some things. He'd never delivered before, but he'd seen other people do it. He'd told the boss he could handle it. Iodine for the navel. A towel for the foal, a blanket for the mare. A small syringe in case the foal was impacted and needed an enema.

He tried to move quietly. She'd try to hold off if there were people around.

He sat in the doorway of the tack room and listened hard. He heard her water break. Even landing on straw, two to five gallons of water made itself heard. He checked his watch again. Expulsion of the foal shouldn't take longer than twenty minutes. Longer than that, and she might need some help.

He picked up the phone and dialed Hannah's number. It was three in the morning. The phone rang and rang. Finally, a voice half sleep, half anger. Delphine.

"Hey, Del," he said. "It's me, Cole."

She didn't say anything.

"Could you get Hannah for me?" he asked.

"I don't think so," Delphine said. She didn't seem sleepy anymore.

"I know it's late, but I've got something I want to tell her," he said.

"I've got lots I want to tell you, but I don't call you up about it," she said.

The mare sounded like she was getting up and down a lot. Rolling. He checked his watch.

"Just tell her the mare's foaling," he said. "Okay? Will you do that?"

"Anything else?" she said.

He thought about it. Yes, he wanted to say, everything else. "No," he said. "Just that. And thanks again, Del."

"Any time," she said dryly, and hung up.

He didn't like to think about what some of those girls had to say about him. He had no idea why he wanted Hannah to know about the mare. She wouldn't even know what mare he was talking about.

He gathered the supplies and headed to the mare's stall. She was standing, her head twisting around to nip at her flank. She was sweaty. Her stall was dirty with manure and urine. She groaned softly and kicked at her belly.

"Hey, girl," he said. "Hey."

The placenta and one foreleg were visible. The mare contracted again. She got up; she got down. She lay on her side, her giant awkward legs moving like pistons. The leg with the poultice had straw stuck to it in haphazard ways.

He looked at his watch. Forty-five minutes. He knew he was supposed to call someone if the foal hadn't been delivered in twenty. The guy who didn't know anything wasn't supposed to try and fix the problem. The guy who didn't know anything was supposed to keep the mare up and moving and wait for the guy who did know something. He also knew this part of things could

take up to an hour. He also knew how much the boss hated vet
bills.

He waited. Ten minutes later another foreleg appeared, but
no head. The head should've been resting on the outstretched
legs. But there were the knees with no tiny nose on top of them.
He knew he should call someone.

With each contraction, the mare grunted softly. She stared at
her side like it was a stranger she was willing to meet.

Ten more minutes, he told himself, and he'd call the vet.

The mare rocked side to side and threw herself to a standing
position. One more contraction, and there was the head. Then
the shoulders, the body, and the outstretched hind legs. And there
was a horse, tiny and wet, half-draped in the placenta, sitting quietly on a bed of straw.

He stood there, staring.

The foal began to thrash, ridding himself of the sac. Cole
stepped into the stall, and helped the little guy out. The mare
joined him, nickering and licking her boy. Cole made sure the foal
was breathing okay; he blew into the foal's mouth and rubbed the
ribs with the towel. He dipped the navel stump in the iodine. He
stepped out of the stall and watched the foal make his way to his
mother's udder. The mare kept the weight off her bad leg, her
head hanging sleepily.

He lost track of how long he stood there watching them. He
inhaled. He'd had nothing to do with this, and still, he felt like a
hero.

Two weeks later, she called him from that same pay phone in the
hall.

"Hey," she said.

"Hey," he said. "I'm sorry," he said.

"I know," she said. She offered a variety of explanations for his behavior, none of which he'd thought of.

"It was probably all of those things mixed together," he said.

She acted like that was the right thing to say.

"So I was thinking we could just call the past a wash," she said. "Start from here."

"Sounds good," he said.

She was quiet for a minute. "I remember that camping trip to Maryland," she said. "When I think about us," she added. "I remember that storm. How it seemed like there would be nothing but thunder and lightning. Like the rain wasn't going to show up at all."

"I remember that," he said.

"I remember the herd of wild horses. I felt them before I heard them, and I woke you up, and we both went to stand outside."

"The ground was trembling," he said.

"The horses were making those sounds we'd never heard horses make," she said.

"It was so dark, they were around us before we could really make them out," he said.

"Remember what that felt like?" she asked.

He nodded and then realized she couldn't see that.

"Like getting hit by lightning without getting hurt," she said. "That's what you do to me."

He was quiet. His whole life had been hopping from island to island. She was his mainland.

"You still want to get hitched?" she asked.

He did. More than he had before. He felt like she was someone who could've lived next to him when they were five-year-olds.

They set the date for the following October. He didn't know how she'd made her decision. He didn't ask.

"LMNW," she said.

"Ditto," he said.

It was October. Two days before the wedding, she found a quiet moment away from negotiating between their two families, and presented him with a small scrapbook. In it, she'd pasted photographs of their life so far, small sketches, ticket stubs, restaurant receipts, motel keys, racetrack bets, notes they'd left each other.

The letters he'd written her were there. And in the last few pages, their wedding invitation, the announcement from *The Courier-Journal,* and a page of excerpts from her diary.

> *He's humming and singing and making me smile.*
> *The advice of my mother and Seventeen magazine: Find out what he likes and learn to like it too.*

One was from a trip they'd taken to the Cataloochee Lodge in the Smoky Mountains the previous fall. They'd played a word association game. It had been her idea. She'd copied down her questions and his answers in calligraphic lettering.

> *Best Friend—Dog*
> *Marriage—Scary*
> *Hannah and Cole—Together*
> *Hannah—Friend*

The first time he told her he loved her.

Lying on the bed this afternoon. He says, "I'm a-feeling, a-touching you." I say, "A-liking." Him: "No, a-loving." This from the guy who said he never tells anyone he loves them.

Don't expect Cole to be later what he isn't now.

She watched him read.

"I didn't know we were supposed to get each other something," he said.

"It's kind of a tradition," she said. "But it doesn't matter."

Every single part of the wedding planning had made Cole feel like he was at a party he'd crashed. Everyone, even his parents, knew things he didn't know.

He spent much of the next day putting together his own present for Hannah. He got some nice paper from the paper store in town she liked. He got it in pale orange, her favorite color. He started by writing down a list of how she made him feel, but he couldn't get the words right. Instead, he snuck the *Bartlett's* off her parents' shelf and spent a few hours going through it in the basement play-room. When people called him, he pretended not to hear.

He looked up topic words like Marriage and Wedding, like Love, and copied down the quotes he liked the best.

Napoleon sent a letter to Josephine: "I will be arriving in Paris tomorrow evening. Don't wash."

Given that Hannah had insisted on not sleeping with him for the week before the wedding, he thought this was particularly appropriate.

"Whatever it is we want to hear, we get to hear it when we're newly in love." Anonymous.

Stendahl said about taking walks with his sweetheart, "Whenever I gave my arm to Leonore, I always felt I was about to fall, and I had to think how to walk."

He didn't know what it was about that one, but it said something he felt sure he felt and had been trying for some time to say.

He folded the pale orange sheets in half, put them carefully in their matching envelope, and snuck upstairs to stick them between the precisely folded clothes in Hannah's already-packed honeymoon bag.

And then he sat on the end of her pink bed, staring out the window at her childhood view, imagining their first kiss as husband and wife. Below him, the bustle of the planning sent movement he could feel through the floor, up his legs, into his heart.

And the next night, at 6:35 on an unusually warm October evening in the small stone church where Hannah had been baptized, the kiss was what he'd imagined it would be. It was hard and sure, safety and salvation. They kissed and kissed as if kissing could save them from themselves.

∞ ELEVEN ∞

August 2000

THE JUDGE HAD A NICE OFFICE. THERE WAS COOL AIR coming from somewhere Mattie couldn't see.

Lois was waiting in the front office by the secretary. It had been Mattie's idea that Lois drive her. Hannah and Cole had agreed it was a good idea.

She uncapped and capped the inhaler she was carrying. She'd been up in the night twice from asthma and twice with a dry mouth. On her way to the bathroom the second time, she'd thought of a few years ago when she'd get up to pee or get a drink half-asleep. For a six-month stretch, she'd had a series of bumps on her forehead.

The secretary had told her to make herself comfortable; the judge would be in shortly. There were two other doors besides the one Mattie had come through. She bet herself which one would open.

The office was what she'd expected. Red leather furniture. Lights with green glass shades. Books on bookshelves.

There was a photo on the desk of four smiling children. A bulletin board on one of the shelves with snapshots of kids and parents. It reminded her of her pediatrician's office, and photos of all the children the doctor had taken care of.

She'd tried to think about this visit over the last few days, but believed what Celia had said: nothing she said was going to matter very much. These decisions came out of the forest of what grown-ups did and why.

The judge came through the door Mattie'd thought she'd come through. She wasn't wearing a black robe.

"Where's your robe?" Mattie asked.

The judge laughed. "Would you wear that when you didn't have to?" she said.

Mattie decided to forgive her for answering a question with another question.

Even without it, the judge seemed to sweep around the room with something long and regal swishing around behind her. She gathered some file folders from a table behind her desk, and came around to sit in the chair that matched Mattie's.

"Thanks for coming," she said.

Her hair was light brown and piled in a loose bun at the back of her head. Whatever she'd used to hold it there wasn't doing so well. She had blue eyes and unfreckled skin. Mattie imagined it would feel like a horse's muzzle without the whiskers.

She waited for the questions.

"Call me Jude," the judge said.

It sounded like a name from the Bible. Someone wise who should be a judge. She couldn't imagine Jude playing golf with her grandfather.

Jude was looking at her. She wondered if she was supposed to ask the first question.

"Is it fun playing golf with my grandfather?" she asked.

"When I win," she said. "When he wins, he's impossible."

Mattie nodded. She'd seen that side of him.

"Do you spend a lot of time with your grandma and grandpa?" Jude asked.

"I guess," Mattie said. "I'm not so good with time."

"I'm not either," the judge said. "What kinds of stuff do you do with them?"

She didn't see what this had to do with anything, but she was happy to talk about it. "I watch videos with them. Grandma and I bake. Grandpa gives me Hershey kisses."

"I bet he does," Jude said. She leaned forward. "You know, he keeps a dish of them in his desk drawer. He thinks no one knows about it, but we all do. There are little balled-up foil wrappers all over his office."

"Dad says Grandpa's idea of baby-sitting is throwing fistfuls of candy at me," Mattie said. She watched the judge's face. "He's joking," she added.

"Your dad seems to have a good sense of humor. Does he make you laugh?"

"Sometimes," she said. "Sometimes he's just embarrassing."

"Most dads are," Jude said. "What makes him laugh?"

Mattie thought. Her dad laughed easily, but rarely hard. Getting him to laugh hard was like winning a prize. "Some movies," she said. "He likes *Raising Arizona* and *The In-Laws*." She couldn't tell if the judge knew what she was talking about.

"His best friend, Tommy." She thought of them on either side of her in the front of the truck, laughing hard at things she didn't understand.

"Do you make him laugh?" Jude asked.

"Sometimes," she said. "By accident."

"When's the last time you made him laugh?" Jude asked.

Two days ago someone had given her dad a book called *Bizarre Books,* a list of funny real-life book titles and authors. They'd spent some time after they'd put Sam down reading together on her father's bed. He'd been laughing so hard, he'd been crying. She'd gotten up to brush her teeth, and had stood in the doorway, so he could keep reading. One title had made her laugh so hard, she'd fallen in a heap and toothpaste had come out her nose. He'd laughed at her laughing.

She smiled thinking about it.

"What?" the judge said.

She brought herself back to the office. Some of the titles were kind of rude. She wasn't sure the judge would understand. "I can't remember," she said, trying to quit smiling.

"What about your mom?" the judge asked. "What does she think is funny?"

A buzzer on the desk lit up. The judge reached across and pressed something. "No interruptions," she said before whoever was on the other end had a chance to speak. She used a different tone than she'd been using with Mattie. She sat back and sighed. "Sorry," she said. "Go ahead."

Mattie understood what lay beneath everything they were talking about. She thought of it as a sleeping dragon in a castle dungeon.

And she understood that Celia might have been wrong.

She folded her hands around her inhaler. "If I tell you who I'd rather live with, are you going to listen to me?" she asked.

"It would be one of the things I'd listen to," Jude said.

Mattie considered her.

"I don't much like having to meet with children in custody cases," she said. "I only do it when there's no other way."

Mattie felt embarrassed and proud that their case had come to this.

"I'm just asking for information. Information that it's turned out I can't get any other way. I'm not asking you to choose between your parents," Jude said. "That isn't the kind of thing a kid should have to do."

She sounded like Lois.

Mattie said, "Whenever people have a choice, they choose Cole." She didn't know what had made her say it.

"Why do you think that is?" Jude asked quietly.

She shrugged.

"What about your mom?" Jude asked, again.

Mattie thought about her. She knew her mother needed her more than her father did. Her father had Georgia and Sam. Her mother had no one. Jackson didn't count.

What she'd planned to tell the judge was what she'd been telling herself since that night in July. That all she wanted was to be left alone. She wanted to get through fifth grade and the rest of her life.

But maybe she'd known even before being here that what she really wanted was the opposite: the kind of attention she'd seen them paying each other ever since the divorce. The kind of attention that seemed dangerous, like something on a high shelf, out of the children's reach.

She couldn't figure out how to make what she was feeling come out in words that would be clear to anyone.

The judge was waiting.

"My mom needs me," she said.

"What do you need?" the judge asked.

It was like she was that little red dragon Georgia had given her. She opened her mouth to try and make things clear, but all she

felt was the dragon's hot breath coming out her mouth in sense-
less clouds of steam.

Two to three days for her decision, the judge had said. A week at
the most.

Two days came and went. So did three. Her mother took her
back-to-school shopping and didn't veto anything. Mattie spent
her time rearranging the outfits on hangers in her closet. She
finished up the school story. She ignored calls from Celia. She
didn't call Lois for rides to the hospital. She listened to conversations between her mother and father. There seemed to be more
of them than usual. They were hushed and conspiratorial. They
made them sound close to each other.

A few years ago, when they all still lived together, she'd come
out of the bathroom after brushing her teeth before bed. She
passed her parents' room. They were lying on their bed next to
each other, talking. She'd stood by the door for a minute watching. They hadn't been touching, but she remembered feeling like
she was watching a whole other world, a place where things happened with feelings she had no clue about. It made her feel taken
care of.

Friday ended and she realized there'd be no news until Monday at the earliest. On Sunday, her mother drove her over to her
father's, but instead of leaving, she settled herself in the living
room, and patted the seat next to her.

Mattie looked around like her mother was gesturing to someone else. Her father appeared from upstairs and roughed up her
hair. "Hey, girl," he said.

"Where's Sam?" she asked.

"With Riona," he said.

"Hmm," she said.

He sat in the chair opposite. They all looked at each other for a minute. She remembered her mother sitting in here with Officer Tanya. She couldn't remember the last time all three of them had sat together like this. She thought what she'd thought the first day of kindergarten: *This could be fun, if I survive.*

"So," her father began. "Your mom and I've got something to tell you."

Of course, she thought. They would know first. She realized she'd been waiting for the judge to call her. But of course that wouldn't be the way it worked.

She closed her eyes.

"Well, to talk to you about," her mother added.

Now Mattie was the sleeping princess, waiting for what came next. Some kind of happy ending, or more deep sleep.

"We called the judge," her father said, "and told her to forget about it."

She opened her eyes. "Forget about it?"

"We decided on our own," her father explained.

"We called off the hearing," her mother added.

"You decided on your own?" she said.

It seemed a bad idea to have eliminated Jude, but her parents had it all worked out. They'd decided that being divorced from each other didn't mean being divorced from Mattie. They'd realized that they were going to be parents the rest of their lives and they had to start thinking like parents. They were going to keep the living arrangements the way they were, and they were all—Mattie included—going to try and make things work. It was the least they could do for each other.

They were sorry for having taken so long to realize what needed to be done.

They said it like they weren't quite sure they believed it. She could tell they'd tried to collapse lots of talk into a few easy-to-understand sentences. She could tell they were trying to do a lot of hard things.

She felt like the princess who's been kissed but wakes up to find everything the way it was when she went to sleep.

"What do you think?" her father asked.

He was genuinely nervous.

"I don't know," she said. "What am I supposed to think?"

Her mother touched her on the knee. "You're not supposed to think anything," she said.

"Okay, then," she said.

Her parents waited, like she was supposed to offer something else.

"I wrote something," she said. "For school."

Neither of them seemed to know what to say to that. "Good for you," her father finally said.

"D'you want to hear it?" she asked.

There was a flurry of nods, yeses, of-courses, and you-bets.

She dug around in her backpack and came out with the neatly copied final draft. She took the paper clip off the corner and clipped it to the edge of her shorts. She glanced up at her audience. "The assignment was Family," she said.

Her parents exchanged looks. She pretended not to see them. She put the pages facedown in her lap.

"You know, I told the judge who I wanted to live with," she said.

Her mother seemed to want to reach forward and touch her. "Do you want to tell us what you said?" she asked.

"If you want," Mattie said.

Her father gave her mother a look. They turned their eyes from each other to her.

It was like everyone had decided to take responsibility for themselves. She was surprised and not surprised at the same time.

"Why don't you read?" her father said.

"Hang on to the other information for another time," her mother said.

Mattie shrugged. "If that's what you want," she said, and started reading.

"My father loved watching my mother talk to the horses. When my father went on trips, my mother asked him to send dirty clothing back home for her to have until he got back. She said cowboys love rope and knots almost as much as sailors do.

"But how did this all begin?

"My parents met in Alabama. My mother is from Anchorage, Kentucky; my father is from Newton, Massachusetts. My mother's name is Hannah Baker Thompson. My father's name is Cole Thompson.

"In Alabama, my dad was training racehorses for a guy with a big horse operation. My father ran away from home three times before it stuck. My mother never ran away.

"She was working at a farm in Virginia, near where she went to college. She was training hunter/jumpers. Her instructor said it was time to learn to gallop a horse. She made a phone call right there and then and got her a job down in Alabama at this big horse operation.

"She was perfect for galloping racehorses. Everyone said she was small, but ropy.

"My father first saw her on the practice track, waiting to gallop her first two-year-old.

"My mother says the tiny galloping saddle and the short stirrups felt too tiny and too short. She grabbed mane, and then let go. You're not supposed to grab mane.

"My father teased her about the mane. It took her a while to learn when my father was teasing and when he wasn't.

"He liked the way my mother held her reins. He liked the way her hair was pulled back. He liked the way she fluffed the ends of it when she thought no one was looking.

"She liked that he wasn't like anyone she'd ever met. She liked that he kept steering his horse to bump into hers. She liked that he chewed tobacco and smoked a cigarette at the same time. She liked that when he rubbed his eyes, he rubbed his whole face.

"She told me that she didn't understand why someone like him would be with someone like her.

"My father told me the same thing.

"Then they got engaged. My father gave my mother a ring that used to belong to his grandmother. My mother still has it.

"They got married in October. In his toast to her at the wedding, my father said the two of them together were better than he was alone. He said my mother made him a better person. My mother cried, and couldn't see the cake while she was cutting it.

"They had me in 1990. My name is Mathilda Baker Thompson. I am ten.

"That is how my parents met."

She didn't read the part that said, *The End*. She tried to see her parents without raising her eyes. Her mother was crying. Her father was quiet, and then cleared his throat.

All three of them sat as still as animals in a drought.

She kept her eyes on her paper. It felt like the thing to do. She thought of how her parents said things were going to be from now on. She didn't know if what she was feeling meant she'd gotten what she wanted or what she hadn't. What was possible opened up in front of her, simple and big.

She decided to pretend to keep reading. She made things up as she went.

She said, "My father says that my mother was the treasure he didn't know he was looking for. My mother says my father was her runaway horse." Her voice was strong and even. Her parents acted as if they had nothing to do but listen.

She had one more sentence, and then she would stop. She didn't know if it was true. "My parents," she said, "say that if they had it to do all over again, they wouldn't change a thing."

ACKNOWLEDGMENTS

I couldn't have written this book without the help of many people who know so much more than I do. For their time and expertise, thanks to Abigail Allen, Detective Laura Calamita, Jude Chenail, Dr. Thomas Edwards, Sherron Knopp, Lynn Lyons, Dr. Marian Madden, Dr. Debra Miller, Dawson Tanner, and Terry Tolk.

For their rigorous reading eyes, thanks to Cathleen Bell, Cassandra Cleghorn, Sandra Leong, Marsha Recknagel, Shawn Rosenheim, Geoff Sanborn, Eric Simonoff, Jennifer Weis, and Gary Zebrun.

And, again and always, to my husband, Jim Shepard.